Cowboys, Cops, Killers, and Ghosts: Legends and Lore in Texas

Cowboys, Cops, Killers, and Ghosts: Legends and Lore in Texas

Edited by Kenneth L. Untiedt

Publications of the Texas Folklore Society LXIX

University of North Texas Press

Denton, Texas

10 9 8 7 6 5 4 3 2 1

Permissions:
University of North Texas Press
1155 Union Circle #311336
Denton, TX 76203-5017

The paper used in this book meets the minimum requirements of the American National
Standard for Permanence of Paper for Printed Library Materials, z39.48.1984.
Binding materials have been chosen for durability.

Library of Congress Cataloging-in-Publication Data

Cowboys, cops, killers, and ghosts: legends and lore in Texas / edited by
Kenneth L. Untiedt. -- First edition.
pages cm. -- (Publications of the Texas Folklore Society ; LXIX)
Includes bibliographical references and index.
ISBN 978-1-57441-532-2 (cloth : alk. paper) -- ISBN 978-1-57441-544-5
(ebook)
1. Legends--Texas. 2. Legends--Mexican-American Border Region. 3.
Texas--Biography--Anecdotes. 4. Texas--History--Anecdotes. 5.
Texas--Social life and customs. I. Untiedt, Kenneth L., 1966- editor of
compilation. II. Young, Jerry (Storyteller) Recalling a Texas legend.
III. Series: Publications of the Texas Folklore Society ; no. 69.
GR110.T5C68 2013
398.209764--dc23
2013033576

Cowboys, Cops, Killers, and Ghosts: Legends and Lore in Texas is Number LXIX in the
Publications of the Texas Folklore Society

Part I opening photo (pages x–1) courtesy of Len Ainsworth; Part III opening photo
(pages 150–151) courtesy of Lee Haile; Part IV opening photo (pages 226–227)
courtesy of L. Patrick Hughes.

The electronic edition of this book was make possible by the support of the
Vick Family Foundation.

CONTENTS

PREFACE

I've always said that the backbone of the Publications of the Texas Folklore Society series is miscellanies, collections of articles on a wide variety of topics—or at least four or five that can be arranged in chapters. This volume is just such a miscellany, and it has something for everyone. The first paper I ever presented at a TFS meeting was on lore in the law enforcement field, and Chapter 1 of this book features a good bit of occupational lore, including a unique, personal look at a famous outlaw, followed by two articles on some of the people who stand on the other side of the law, cops and attorneys. You'll also find a few papers on cowboys—both legendary ones and the relatively unknown, forgotten men who worked their trade day by day wherever they could. Articles in other chapters cover many of the customs, rituals, legends, ghost stories, and treasure hunting tales that make up the lore of Texas and the Southwest. You'll learn about a teacher's passion for encouraging her students to discover their own family culture, country churches and unusual weddings, bikers and their customs, somewhat questionable ways to fish, and one woman's love affair with a bull.

This is the 69th full-length book in our regular PTFS series. These books offer a glimpse of what goes on at our annual meetings, as the best of the papers presented are frequently selected for our publications. Of course, the presentations are only a part of what the Society does at the meetings; the tours of local attractions in the different cities where we meet are also an integral part of the annual get-together, along with the Hootenannies, the banquet, and, perhaps most importantly, the fellowship among members. Reading these publications—especially the miscellanies—offers readers insight into our members' interests in everything from rodeo cowboys and pioneers of Tejana music to serial killers and simple folk from small-town Texas. These works also suggest the importance of the "telling of the tale," with an emphasis on oral tradition, as well as some of the customs we share. All of these things together— the focus on tradition at our meetings, the familial bond amongst our members, the diversity of our research, and our continuing effort to preserve this lore and make it accessible to others through our publications—are what sustain the Texas Folklore Society and make it one of the most unique organizations of its kind.

As always, I thank the many contributors whose works appear in this book. Some of them are, once again, "first-timers"; in other words, these papers were the first ones the authors ever presented at a meeting, or that they've ever had published. Their efforts are commendable. I also want to share my appreciation of some other key people who help make these publications possible. First, I thank Karen DeVinney and all the staff members at the UNT Press who help us put these books together each year. I want to show special gratitude to a couple of people at Stephen F. Austin State University who continue to generously support the Society, including Mark Sanders, the Chair of the English Department, and Brian Murphy, the Dean of the College of Liberal and Applied Arts. In addition to these individuals, I thank all the other administrators and my colleagues who make us glad to call SFA and Nacogdoches home.

Finally, I gave special recognition to Janet Simonds in the preface of last year's book, noting how much she did to contribute to the process of publishing these books. I said that I knew I could do a book without her, but that it wouldn't be easy. Well, I suppose I jinxed myself, as she announced her retirement shortly thereafter, and she left at the end of August 2012, before I got too far into selecting and editing any of the submissions. She did stay on as our Treasurer through the 2013 meeting, held in Corpus Christi. (The location for that meeting had been her idea, by the way.) During the annual Business Meeting I presented her with a plaque acknowledging her time as Office Secretary and TFS Treasurer, although that comes nowhere near showing my appreciation for all that she had done to make my job possible. Mary Margaret Gonzales is our new Office Secretary (and Treasurer), and she has worked with me to put this volume together; it's definitely a complex job, but the system that Janet and I established together makes the entire process much easier.

I dedicate this book to Janet, and I thank her for her dedication and service to the Texas Folklore Society.

Kenneth L. Untiedt
Stephen F. Austin State University
Nacogdoches, Texas
May 22, 2013

On the Job:

Legends and Language in Occupational Lore

The Booger Red Wild West Show (date unknown): Booger Red Privett is the third rider on the left; the boys to Booger's right are two of Booger and Mollie's sons, and the black cowboy on horseback is probably Bill Pickett. Courtesy, West Texas Collection, Angelo State University, San Angelo, Texas

RECALLING A TEXAS LEGEND: SAMUEL THOMAS "BOOGER RED" PRIVETT

by Jerry Young

INTRODUCTION

Thomas "Booger Red" Privett is a Texas legend who doesn't fit the mold of the hard- drinking, hard-fisted, fast-on-the-draw, womanizing Texas cowboy of Hollywood and pulp westerns. Thomas Privett was a teetotaler and a devoted family man. He was a gentleman with a horribly scarred faced. His work clothes were ducking jeans and a chambray shirt. Booger didn't measure tall by some standards, but his five feet, five inches dominated the world of bronc riding during the first quarter of the 20th Century.

In 1915, *The San Francisco Chronicle* identified Booger Red as ". . . the famous Texas cowboy known from the Atlantic to the Pacific."[1] Foghorn Clancy, a chronicler of early rodeos, assessed Booger Red this way: "For more than a quarter century, Booger Red was regarded as the greatest bronc rider in the world."[2] Booger Red's home town paper, the *San Angelo Morning Times*, extolled him as "the Paul Bunyan of Outlaw Horse Riders."[3] Reality and legend often become indistinguishable in the Booger Red saga, but the legend tips closer towards reality by his championship record. "He took firsts in bronc-riding contests in San Angelo and Fort Worth. At the 1904 World's Fair in St. Louis, he was recognized as the best all-around cowboy after winning 23 awards in the six-week contest. In 1915, at the age of 53, Booger Red was named world's champion bronc rider at the San Francisco World's Fair."[4] The man's extraordinary horsemanship, his showbiz savvy, his moral character, and his devotion to his family shaped the legend that is Booger Red Privett.

After his death in 1925, the legend slowly faded from community memory. Occasionally, a newspaper column or a magazine article reprised Booger Red's feats. In 1975, Thomas "Booger

Red" Privett was inducted into the Cowboy Hall of Fame. But for the most part, Booger Red lay forgotten in an unmarked grave in the Miami, Oklahoma Cemetery. The purpose of this paper, then, is to present a retrospective of the legendary Booger Red Privett.

Samuel Thomas Privett was born December 29, 1858, in Williamson County, Texas. He had woodpecker red hair. Little Red, as his parents called him, was the runt of a string of siblings. When he was six, his family resettled on a ranch south of Dublin in Erath County. Like most ranch and farm boys, Lil' Red rode calves to entertain himself. By the time he turned twelve, he had graduated to mustangs, and his skill as a bronc buster earned him the honorific title "The Redheaded Kid Bronc Rider."[5]

Life altering tragedies struck Red Privett in his teen years. The Christmas that he was thirteen, he and a friend decided to produce their own fireworks show. The boys packed gunpowder into a hollow tree stump. When they set fire to the gun powder, the explosion killed his friend and critically burned Red's face and hands. His parents loaded him in a buckboard and started for the hospital. Before the wagon left the yard, one of Red's buddies looked in at the injured boy and quipped, "Gee! Red is sure a booger now, ain't he?"[6] And the name Booger Red stuck to him for life.

The next year his dad died of Bright's disease. The following year his mother died, and Booger was on his own at fifteen years of age. He hired out as a bronc buster for ranches in Tom Green, Coke, and Runnels counties. His services were in high demand, as the ranchers regularly needed additional working horses. In 1900, Booger established the Texas Wagon Yard in San Angelo. (The wagon yard was located where the Tom Green County Library is now located.)

Booger met Mary Francis Webb one evening while playing his harmonica at a church social in Winters. Better known as Mollie, Mary Francis was an experienced horsewoman. In those years, churches and schools sponsored "pie suppers" to raise cash for various needs. The young ladies presented their pies in fancy, decorated boxes or baskets. The young men bid on the pies for the honor of eating pie with the lady of their eyes. Booger Red began to eagerly attend the pie suppers around Winters and Bronte so that, as Booger explained, "the ugliest man living or dead" might have the privilege of eating pie with the "prettiest little girl I ever saw."[7]

The couple's courtship consisted of moonlight buggy rides and Sunday afternoon horseback rides. Booger felt that Mollie wouldn't marry him because of his horribly burn-scarred face. One Sunday, Booger and Mollie rode to visit the ruins at Fort Chadbourne. On the way home, Booger timidly asked Mollie "if she would like to ride with him for life." She flippantly replied, "Well, what took you so long to ask?" "Look at me," he said. "Can you stand these scars?" "What scars?" she returned. "I don't see any." Then she patted his faced and kissed his lips. Mollie and Booger married December 29, 1895. Mollie was fifteen, and Booger was thirty-seven.[8]

BOOGER RED'S HORSEMANSHIP

It is near impossible to separate fact, fiction, reality, or legend when assessing Booger Red's horsemanship. The *San Angelo Standard Times* observed that Booger Red knew what a horse was thinking.[9] Foghorn Clancy notes: "[Booger Red] just seemed to get in time with the bronc, so that no move the animal made was a surprise to him."[10] The Booger Red legend becomes more like a Texas tall tale when people attempt to tally the number of horses Booger rode in his lifetime. It is suggested that Booger Red rode as many as 25,000 broncs in his lifetime without being thrown. According to Mollie Privett, he regularly rode five to fifteen horses a day during the Wild West Show season.[11]

One year the military outpost at Fort Concho hired Booger Red to break about 200 head of just-off-the-range mustangs. The government offered Booger an option of pay: $1.00 for each horse he broke, or a salary. Booger opted for the $1.00 per horse. The first day Booger broke eighty-three horses. The military people promptly revised the contract to a monthly salary.[12]

Booger made his first ride at the Fort Worth Stock Show in 1898, the third year that the Stock Show was opened. The rodeo arena was just an area of open prairie north of Fort Worth. People watched the action from horseback, buggies, and wagons. One afternoon, a grey outlaw pitched a rider from the saddle. As the rider stood up, the horse killed the young man with a kick to his chest. The crowd clamored for someone to ride down the grey to avenge the cowboy's life. Booger's riding prowess was well known at the time, so the crowd cheered for Booger to ride the man-killer. Booger agreed to ride the grey if a purse was put up. A hat was passed, and Booger threw his leg over the grey's saddle. The mustang did its best to unseat Booger, but regardless of how viciously the grey fish-tailed or zigzagged, Booger rode the outlaw to a standstill.[13]

Mollie Privett related one story about Booger's horsemanship that illustrates the folklore that surrounded the man:

> In a rodeo contest in Fort Worth once [Booger] won $500.00 and a fine saddle. When he went to the hotel with the rest of the crowd he took both his old and new saddle with him and hastily checked the new saddle as his buddies were rushing him to come on and eat. He pitched the old one in as he rushed after the boys. "Come back," yelled the clerk, "you haven't checked your other saddle." "That's all right," Booger shouted back, "if any one uglier than I comes along just give it to him."[14]

Foghorn Clancy places this event in the Maverick Saloon in Fort Worth.[15] Vernon Payne, an acquaintance of the Privett family, sets the story at a hotel in St. Louis during the Columbian Exposition.[16] Wherever it occurred, it is a good story.

THE BOOGER RED WILD WEST SHOW

After he opened the Texas Wagon Yard in San Angelo, Booger invited people to bring their wildest horses to the wagon yard on Sunday afternoons for pickup contests. A hat was passed among the spectators, and the competitors received a share of the "pot." Generally, the "pot" was pretty lean. As the contests became increasing popular, Booger moved the event to a canvas arena on the outskirts of town.[17]

One year a cowboy from Montana brought in a horse that he claimed had never been ridden. He bet Booger $1,500 that he couldn't ride the outlaw. Booger Red mounted it, and horse and rider pitched and bucked around the arena. At one point, they broke through the fence into a bunch of horses tied up on the outside. One of those horses reared up, fell over backwards, and broke its neck. Booger and the outlaw rode out on the prairie. The horse tried every trick it had to unseat Booger before it bucked itself out. As Booger rode the more docile outlaw by the grandstand, he called out, "Ladies and Gentlemen. I knew I was ugly, but didn't know I was ugly enough to scare a horse to death."[18]

Booger not only won the $1,500, but he bought the horse, which he named Montana Gyp. Booger and Montana Gyp were the star performers in Booger Red's Wild West Show. Booger and Montana Gyp established a cantankerous relationship that extended over twenty

Booger Red Aboard Montana Gyp; Booger and Montana Gyp were the star performers in Booger Red's Wild West Show. *Courtesy, West Texas Collection, Angelo State University, San Angelo, Texas*

years. In all that time, Montana Gyp never threw Booger from his back, but neither did Booger Red break Montana Gyp's outlaw spirit.

Booger began selling tickets to the Sunday rodeos. To draw spectators, he added calf roping and horse racing. When ticket sales continued to lag, he and Mollie put together the Booger Red Wild West Show in 1904.[19] From the start, the Wild West Show was "a mom and pop" operation. They started out with a covered wagon, a couple of buggies, and a few bucking horses. The *San Angelo Morning Times* reported: "The wagon show at its peak had 32 wagons, 22 broncos, 12 head of steers, 12 saddle horses, and 15 cowboys and cowgirls."[20]

Charlsie Poe self-published a book titled *Booger Red: World Champion Cowboy*. Mrs. Poe records the names of several of the cowboys who rode with the Booger Red Wild West Show. If their exploits were as colorful as their names, the Privett shows were total entertainment. One bronc rider was named Panhandle Slim. There was a one-legged bronc rider named "Hackberry Slim" Johnson. (And yes, he wore a wooden leg made of a hackberry limb.) Then there were Bob "Rear Around" Johnson and Oklahoma Curley Roberts. And finally, there was the rodeo announcer Foghorn Clancy, who trailed with the Privett's show for two or three years.[21]

According to Poe and Kent Biffle, Bill Pickett performed in the Booger Red Wild West Show. Dean Chenoweth, editor of the *San Angelo Standard Times*, suggests that Pickett's first public demonstration of his "bite-em-down style of bulldogging" took place with Booger's show.[22] Pickett and Booger both worked for the 101 Ranch Wild West Show. (Curiously, there are no references in Pickett's biographical items to connect him with Booger Red or the BRWWS.)

Booger Red's Wild West Show opened and closed each season in San Angelo. Trailing wagons, buggies, and livestock, the company made its way to small towns in Texas, Oklahoma, Louisiana, and Arkansas from April to October.[23] The company set up in school stadiums, on fair grounds, city parks, or lots on the outskirts of a town. The cowboys riding with the show manned posthole diggers to dig the holes to set the posts that held the canvas side walls.[24] When the Wild West Show trailed into town, Booger nailed up placards that proclaimed, "Come see him ride! Booger Red! Ugliest man dead or alive!"[25]

Mollie Privett was an equal partner with the Show. Except for times when she was pregnant or caring for an infant child, she rode in the shows as a fancy rider. Once Mollie and Booger's six kids learned to ride, they became part of the show, also.

Road life was sparse for the performers and crew. They lived in tents set up near the show grounds. Mollie recounted that she loved the life on the road. She looked after the performers, stitching up cuts, setting broken bones, and bandaging sprains and bruises. She also did the cooking for the crew. She related in an interview that:

> The boys all called me Mother and they took a notion of hot biscuits one day. I cooked their biscuits in a Dutch oven over an open camp fire. "Why, I can't cook biscuits today, boys," I said. "It is raining and will put out the fire." "Make 'em Mother, make 'em," they all shouted, "we'll get out there and hold our slickers over you and the fire while you cook them." That was too much and I made up the dough while they built the fire under the canopy of slickers and we cooked and ate biscuits like that until everyone was filled.[26]

BOOGER RED, THE SHOWMAN

The Booger Red Wild West Show became "known as the best Wild West Show on the road," according to Mrs. Privett.[27] The show drew crowds wherever it opened. Much of the show's popularity is attributed to Booger Red's instinctive showmanship. Prior to Booger Red's time, it was the custom for bronc riders to keep their eyes on their mount in order to anticipate the horse's next move. Booger "originated the act of riding with his thumbs hooked in this suspenders and looking back" while talking to the crowd.[28]

One year at the San Angelo rodeo, the riders were challenged to ride a white steer billed as "un-ridable." There were no shoots to crimp the steer, so the riders dropped onto the steer's back from a bar over the gate as the steer ran into the arena. When it came Booger's time, somehow he dropped onto the steer's back facing the steer's rear end. Not missing a beat, Booger grabbed onto the steer's tail and rode all the way around the arena, fanning his Stetson over the steer's rump.[29]

At a show in Midlothian, Booger doubled for Mollie when she became ill and couldn't ride. Booger put on Mollie's dress and tucked a wig under her bonnet. He had the barker announce Mollie's substitute as "the ugliest woman rider from the San Angelo country," and he rode into the arena in bustles, wig, long skirt, and bonnet.[30] However, the showman hadn't adequately fastened on his costume, and as he rode around the arena the disguise started to peel off. Once people realized that it was Booger, they went wild with laughter and applause.[31]

The Booger Red Wild West Show was just one of several such shows that trailed the back roads of the country during the early years of the 20th Century. The shows created a venue for out-of-work cowboys to show off their ranching skills of riding, calf roping, bulldogging, and bronc busting. Some of the larger shows like Buffalo Bill's show created a romantic image of buffalo hunts, stagecoach robberies, and attacks by wild Indians. Regardless of size and showmanship, those popular shows had one thing in common, a shortage of cash. Some wild west shows lasted only a season or two. The Booger Red Wild West Show entertained crowds from 1904 to 1910. The small wild west shows were on their way out when Booger sold his show stock to the 101 Ranch Wild West Show, and the Privetts moved to Caddo, Oklahoma.[32]

BOOGER RED'S LAST RIDE

After moving to Oklahoma, Booger worked with several big name shows. He was the livestock wrangler for the 101 Ranch Show at the San Francisco Exposition in 1915. When the A. G. Barnes Circus offered Booger an opportunity to produce a wild west show, Booger took the job.[33] Booger Red and Mollie traveled with the Ringling Brothers and the Hagenbeck-Wallace circuses. The Privett family worked together with Buffalo Bill's Wild West Show, an engagement that left them with less than fond memories of the old showman.[34] Booger Red suffered with Bright's disease, the same illness that caused his father's death. As the disease progressed, Booger retired from show business.

In 1925, he attended the Fort Worth Fat Stock Show rodeo. Not wanting to be recognized, Booger left off his boots and wore a ball cap. He slipped through the crowd and made his way to the top row of the grandstand. The spectators watched breathlessly as an outlaw horse viciously threw the rider. The young man lay motionless on the ground until handlers removed him to the first aid station.

The announcer called out, "Who'll ride this outlaw?" A lady sitting near Booger Red recognized him, and shouted, "Here's Booger Red! Booger Red will ride him." The crowd wildly chanted "Booger Red. Booger Red." The old man resisted at first, but as the crowd's chant persisted, Booger walked down and climbed on the outlaw. It was a jarring, gut-wrenching ride, but Booger rode the outlaw to a standstill. The crowd cheered and applauded Booger's feat. Spectators climbed into the arena to shake Booger's hand, but the old man had slipped away unnoticed.[35] Two weeks later, newspapers carried a dispatch from Miami, Oklahoma—Samuel Thomas "Booger Red" Privett was dead at age sixty-seven.

The man who was regarded as the greatest bronc buster in the world during the first quarter of the 20th Century[36] lay buried in an unmarked grave in the Miami, Oklahoma, GAR Cemetery for eighty-five years. In December 2010, a grave marker was placed on Booger Red's grave through the efforts of Jerry Bullock of the *San Marcos Daily Record*, Jim Lanning, and folks at the *Miami (OK) News Record*.[37] Jim and Judy Lanning included an account of Booger and Mollie Privett in their book *Texas Cowboys: Memories of the Early Days*.[38]

Finally, the legendary bronc rider is remembered with a grave marker and with this paper, demonstrating that Booger Red Privett's life, his legendary horsemanship, and his uncanny showmanship have a place among the annals of Texas folklore.

Endnotes

1. "Young Girl Thrills by her Daring Riding." *San Francisco Chronicle.* (Unknown date, 1915.)
2. Foghorn Clancy. "Memory Trail." *Hoofs and Horns* Vol. II. No. 4. October 1937. 8.
3. "Booger Red, the Paul Bunyan of Outlaw Horse Riders." *Frontier Times.* 10.9.333-398 [A reprint from the *San Angelo Morning Times.* April 25, 1933.]
4. Kent Biffle. "Red Looked Good Only on a Horse." *The Dallas Morning News: Texas & Southwest Section.* May 5, 1996. 47.
5. Charlsie Poe. *Booger Red: World Champion Cowboy.* Winters, Texas, 1991. 1.
6. Ibid. 2.
7. Ibid. 15.
8. Ibid. 16, 17.
9. Marydawn Webber. "Rodeo Hero Left a Legend in West Texas." *San Angelo Standard Times.* "Out Yonder." March 7, 1983.
10. Foghorn Clancy. *My 50 Years in Rodeo.* San Antonio, Texas: Naylor Co. 1952. 6.
11. Elizabeth Doyle. "Interview with Mrs. Mollie Privett, February 8, 1938." American Life Histories: Federal Writers' Project, 1936–1940. Manuscript Division, Library of Congress. 2.
12. Biffle. 47.
13. Poe. 7–9.
14. Doyle. 5.
15. Clancy. *My 50 Years in Rodeo.* 6.
16. Vernon Payne. "The Singing Prairies." *Avalon Dispatch.* September, 1984. 15.
17. Poe. 20.
18. Ibid.
19. Ibid.
20. "Booger Red, the Paul Bunyan of Outlaw Horse Riders." 393.
21. Poe. 51, 52.
22. Dean Chenoweth. "'Booger Red' Was King of Texas Bronc Riders." *San Angelo Standard Times.* February 19, 1963. 7A.
23. "Booger Red, the Paul Bunyan of Outlaw Horse Riders." 393.

24. Poe. 32.
25. Doyle. 3.
26. Poe. 26
27. Doyle. 5.
28. Ibid. 3.
29. Poe. 26.
30. Tom Mulvany. "Booger Red's Last Ride. *The Southwest Review*. 30:1. Autumn 1944. 33.
31. Poe. 24.
32. Ibid. 61.
33. Ibid.
34. Payne. 13.
35. Mulvany. 30.
36. Clancy. *My 50 Years in Rodeo*. 7.
37. Jerry Bullock. "Life's Like That." *San Marcos Record*, January 23, 2011.
38. Jim Lanning, and Judy Lanning eds. *Texas Cowboy: Memories of the Early Days*. College Station, Texas: Texas A&M Press, 1984. 218–229.

WORKS CONSULTED

Bean, Stew. "Red Sublett, Cowboy Clown." *Hoofs and Horns*. 23.10 (1954). www.phillip.1.sublett.1.sublett.com/family/RedSublett.htm.

"Cowboys: There's a Myth for Each of Them." *San Angelo Standard Times*. May 6. 1984.

Cox, Nellie B. "An old timer tells of Booger Red." c. 1938. American Life Histories. Federal Writers Project, 1936–1940. Manuscript division, Library of Congress.

Dobie, J. Frank. *Cow People*. Austin: University of Texas Press, 1964.

Fairly, Bill. "Booger Red: A Rider's Rider." Special to: *The Fort Worth Star Telegram*. January 14, 1999.

Jones, Cindy. "Privett, Samuel Thomas, Jr. [Booger Red]. *Handbook of Texas Online*. (http://www.tshaonline.org/handbook/online/articles/fpr29), accessed July 10, 2011. Published by the Texas State Historical Association.

Payne, Vernon. *EVANESCENT*. November, 1978. 2–4.

Phipps, Woody. "Interview with Elbert Croslin, c. 1938." American Life Histories: Federal Writers' Project, 1936-1940. Manuscript division, Library of Congress.

Porter, Willard. (NCHF Rodeo Historical Society). *Who's Who in Rodeo*. Oklahoma City, Oklahoma. 1982.

"Ridin'est Family in the Nation." *San Angelo Standard-Times*. January 7, 1945.

Courtney Elliott

THE LEGACY OF BILL PICKETT, THE DUSKY DEMON

by Courtney Elliott

For what reason would a cowboy run his horse full-blast after a calf, bail off sideways onto its head, then pull the animal to a halt? One explanation for such eye-catching behavior could be attributed to either the cowboy's real life experiences, or to the sport of rodeo in which he vigorously competes. Both of these motives were true for Bill Pickett at one point or another. He fought an uphill battle while participating in a pastime that was dominated by white men. It surely was not easy for him to gain respect from his fellow competitors when his ethnicity was discovered to be that of an African American. Coming from the most humble of beginnings, he persevered through it all to develop a rodeo event so that generations to come would remember and cherish the cowboy way. Steer wrestling has become one of the most unique of the rodeo events, stemming directly from an incident that happened not in an arena, but on the range. Bill Pickett, a native Texan and the first African American to make it big in rodeo, left a remarkable legacy by founding the steer wrestling event, which is still vigorously competed in today, worldwide.

William Pickett, known as "Bill" to nearly everyone, was born around 1870 in Texas.[1] His mother was a "Native American of the Choctaw Tribe," and his father was a "mixture of African, Native American, and Caucasian."[2] Both of his parents were former slaves (Johnson x).[3] During this time opportunities for African Americans were scarce.[4] The result of the Civil War was still sore to most southerners. Any job found for an African American was usually a labor filled and low paying one. When Pickett was about ten years old, he began hiring himself out on ranches where he learned to rope, ride, and break horses. By working on many different ranches, Pickett had the chance to learn the many techniques a cowboy uses on a working ranch.

Around the year 1877, the time of the American cowboy was reaching its peak. The demand for beef on the Eastern coast of the United States caused cattle drives and ranches to spring up and flourish in the frontier. To earn a living, some men offered services that would greatly help the many ranches. In the 1890s, Pickett (with his brothers) started the "Pickett Bros. Broncho Busters and Rough Riders Ass'n"; they claimed to break wild horses with care and declared that catching and taming wild cattle was their specialty.[5]

One might ask how a man would come up with a way to wrestle an enormous cow. Only standing five-feet, seven-inches tall, and weighing 145 pounds, he was not the muscle man that one would expect to see pulling a steer to the ground that had an average weight of 1,000 pounds (Johnson xi).[6] One day, Pickett watched an English bulldog go into the brush where a rope could not be thrown, to bring a steer out; the dog bit the cow's lip to overpower it. He dwelled on this some, then kept the technique in the back of his head, perhaps to use it one day.[7] Then when a rogue steer broke from the herd and came straight for Pickett's horse with its horns, he reached down and grabbed the steer; "In that moment the thrilling sport of steer wrestling was born."[8] Perhaps, how this rodeo event came to be called bulldogging arose from where Pickett got his inspiration, a bulldog. He used his new skill to "recapture animals that broke away from the herd."[9]

Pickett's bulldogging soon caught the eye of his boss, Lee Moore. Moore saw how marketable such an act could be and took Pickett to county fairs and gatherings to display his skill for admission fees.[10] When Pickett was first starting out he "bulldogged at various events in Houston, Fort Worth, Taylor, San Angelo, and most of the other cow towns in Texas."[11] Around the turn of the century, he became widely known for perfecting the technique of bulldogging.[12] In his act he would ride his horse along the left side of the steer, and then when he caught up to his target he would lean out towards it and grab it by its neck, dismount his horse onto the animal, reach up and grab its horns, dig his heels into the dirt, and then twist the cow's head until he could reach its nose to bite down on it with his teeth (therein copying how a dog overpowers an enormous cow) to bring the beast to the ground (Johnson 2).[13] When humane societies noticed that he bit the steers, they pushed for laws prohibiting such inhumane procedure (Johnson 131).[14] The humane societies' accusations hurt Pickett because he saw his form of bulldogging as a practical matter, not abuse in any way.[15]

In 1903, after signing with a new manager, Dave McClure, Pickett began performing in other states along with the local Texas appearances he had been making.[16] McClure was known for getting larger audiences and being "an expert on crowd psychology" (Johnson 10).[17] At the time, Pickett was known as Will Pickett, but McClure gave him the alias of "The Dusky Demon," which allowed him to advertise the show "without spelling out that he was black"; when the crowd saw that he was black, it "didn't matter because they were so taken by the act" (Johnson 10).[18] Such performances were advertised in *The San Angelo Press.* One ad for an upcoming roping contest declared that the "Dusky Demon" had been "secured to throw steers with his teeth."[19] Had Pickett not been so popular already in his career, the author of the ad would not have used the phrase, "has been secured." On November 4, 1903, *The San Angelo Press* announced that the "Dusky Demon, was laid up for repairs…while doing his steer throwing act" his arm had been broken, but the writer stated that the injury would not "prevent him from making his appearance" there on Christmas.[20] The next month, just as the press announced, the ad came out in the paper with information of the "Grand Christmas Roping Contest," where the Dusky Demon was to "throw two steers each day"; on the ad, his name was printed in the same large size as the main two ropers who were competing that weekend.[21]

Outside of Texas, Pickett was greeted in Cheyenne, Wyoming's famous Frontier Days celebration by twenty thousand spectators (Johnson 10).[22] Even events that had nothing to do with cowboys or rodeo booked him to perform. An invitation was printed in

The San Angelo Press on July 21, 1904, for the United Confederate Veterans of Central West Texas's annual reunion, which would consist of many reputable speakers and as entertainment, "The Dusky Demon was going to perform the 'steer throwing act' with his teeth."[23] Everyone was invited. Surprisingly, even in the era of white supremacy, a black man performed for Confederate veterans. Soon, others gained an interest in getting Pickett in their show because of the huge audiences he drew.

In 1905, he signed on with the Millers' 110,000 acre ranch where he would live with his family as a full-time employee and perform in the Miller Brothers' 101 Ranch Wild West Show.[24] As "one of only three cowboys introduced by name during the grand entrance," he was put in a place of importance uncommon for an African American (Johnson 48).[25] In his act, Pickett was assisted by Will Rogers (later a famous trick roper, comedian, and movie star) and Tom Mix (later a famous movie star), who were his hazers (cowboys who rode alongside the steer to keep the animal running straight).[26] Pickett was given phenomenal opportunities to travel the nation and to other countries displaying his skill and sharing with the world an aspect of the life of an American cowboy. While working with the Miller Brothers' 101 Ranch Wild West Show, he performed in the "Anglo-American Exposition in London before King George V and Queen Mary."[27] He also performed in Mexico City, Mexico, where the fighting bull he faced nearly killed him and his horse, Spradley (Johnson 85–86).[28]

In 1916, after low attendances at many of the big wild west shows, Buffalo Bill and the 101 Ranch teamed up with the Military Pageant Preparedness to put on a competition between the rodeo performers. Called the "Chicago Shan-Kive and Round-up," it merged the wild west show and rodeo (Johnson 130).[29] The name came from the merging of an Indian term which meant having a good time, and rodeo. The event featured "rules for every event and competitions for world titles," and humane societies were pleased with the rule that no one could bite any of the livestock (Johnson 131).[30] While a close competition, Bill Pickett won in the end (Johnson 131).[31] Although an important event for rodeo, the show proved to be "a financial disaster" for the wild west shows (Johnson 132).[32]

Pickett, similar to most African-Americans, had to fight against those who believed in white supremacy. "Even the most professional black cowboy from Texas, Bill Pickett, encountered difficulties" when trying to counter the prejudices against him.[33] Although he had achieved great successes and had become a fan favorite he still had to deal with the idea of white supremacy. He did not let racists discourage him, gaining the support of many people. Some other cowboys that worked in the shows were taught how to execute a similar act when Pickett was banned from performing in a city, such as in Gulfport, Mississippi, because of the racial prejudice (Johnson 136).[34] Pickett's second promoter, Dave McClure, did not identify him as a Negro because "during Pickett's life, at most contests, Negroes were automatically barred . . . even if he carried more than one half Indian and white blood in his veins."[35] Even though the Civil War had resulted in the freeing of all slaves, Southerners did not treat African Americans equally. The segregation that was taking place at the time even kept black actors out of movies on the silver screen unless in comedic or minor roles. However, in 1923, a movie called *The Bulldogger* starring Pickett was released for African American audiences.[36]

As Pickett reached retirement from steer wrestling, he taught many men how to carry out his signature trick.[37] In this way he helped to advance the sport and leave his mark on what would become known as a standard rodeo event. According to one historian, "no one represented the potential of rodeos better than Bill Pickett."[38] Wild west shows were performances that were designed to show the people of the world the job of a cowboy for a price. What Bill Pickett brought to these shows was something entirely different—a unique act that had originated on the range from the need to recapture stray cattle. Just as each of the other rodeo events competed in today were founded upon the actions used by cowboys to tend cattle or horses, steer wrestling earned its place in this select group. What sets steer wrestling apart from the other events is that it came about by one man, who made it his own.

Bill Pickett "was a legend in his own time: he invented and popularized . . . bulldogging which led to the introduction of steer wrestling as one of the standard events in today's rodeo."[39] In the Professional Rodeo Cowboy Association, steer wrestling is one of the seven mandatory events at the 560 sanctioned rodeos around North America each year.[40] Steer wrestling is also competed in professional rodeo associations in Australia, in Canada, and in New Zealand. The event has changed some since Bill Pickett first founded it; the "corriente steers shrank in size from their massive longhorn progenitors."[41] Now cattle used for steer wrestling are limited to those between 450 and 600 pounds, which is much smaller than the cattle used when the event was first founded. Another difference in event rules is that if the steer gets away after the cowboy has dismounted his horse, the competitor can only take one step to catch him again.[42] The current world record in the P.R.C.A. is two and four tenths of a second; this extremely quick time is made much easier by the smaller stock.[43]

Steer wrestlers have been given great opportunities because of the huge amounts of prize money available to them. Last year was a record-setting year for Lee Graves, who earned the most money in a single event for that year with an amount over $251,000.[44] The large purse (amount of prize money) that is offered takes a lot of sponsors and entries. The great interest in the sport of rodeo and all the events it entails makes it worth it for the many cowboys who participate. According to Hanes, "were it not for Pickett, the development of steer wrestling in rodeo might have come much later."[45] Lee Graves should be very thankful that Bill Pickett founded and developed the event that he and many other cowboys compete in today.

Rodeo has been essentially changed because of the influence that Bill Pickett had on the sport. Pickett, by his success and demeanor, led the way for African Americans to not only be accepted among white cowboys but also be respected. Pickett was not only the first African American to be inducted into the

National Cowboy Hall of Fame, but a life-size bronze statue of him bulldogging a steer was placed at the front of the Cowtown Coliseum in Fort Worth, Texas, to commemorate his impact on the sport.[46] None of the other rodeo events can "be attributed to one person, but Bill Pickett is solely responsible for inventing bulldogging" (Johnson 166).[47] Because he found his inspiration for this event from an occupational circumstance, it has served as a reminder of the hard and unpredictable life of the American cowboy. Steer wrestling is widely acknowledged among all of the other rodeo events thanks to its creation by this extraordinary cowboy. Pickett is "still the talk . . . in that section of Texas."[48] Bill Pickett's life greatly affected the future of rodeo, as he opened doors for African American participation in the sport and left his mark on it by establishing steer wrestling that is now a widely accepted event.

ENDNOTES

1. "Bill Pickett." *Legends of the West: A Collection of U.S. Commemorative Stamps.* 1st ed. Kansas City: U.S. Postal Service, 1993. 24–28. Print. 26.
2. Marion Barnes. "Bill Pickett." *Black Texans: They Overcame.* Austin: Eakin Press, 1996. Print. 83.
3. Cecil Johnson. Guts: *Legendary Black Rodeo Cowboy Bill Pickett.* Fort Worth: Summit Group, 1994. x.
4. Andrew Clements. *Bill Pickett: An American Original Texas Style.* Boston: Houghton Mifflin Company, 1997. Print. 7.
5. Bailey C. Hanes. *Bill Pickett, Bulldogger: The Biography of a Black Cowboy.* Norman: University of Oklahoma, 1989. Print. 35.
6. Johnson. xi.
7. Clements. 3, 5.
8. *The Afro-American Texans.* San Antonio, TX: Institute of Texan Cultures, 1997. 22. Print. 22.
9. Barnes. 83.
10. Hanes. 38–39.
11. Ibid. 39.
12. Alwyn Barr. *Black Texans: A History of African Americans in Texas, 1528–1995.* 2nd ed. Norman, OK: University of Oklahoma, 1996. Print. 91.
13. Johnson. 2.

14. Johnson. 131.
15. Clements. 3.
16. Hanes. 40.
17. Johnson. 10.
18. Ibid.
19. *The San Angelo Press.* Vol. 7, No. 43, Ed. 1. Wednesday, October 28, 1903. University of North Texas Libraries. The Portal to Texas History. UNT Libraries: Denton, Texas. Web. 19 Nov. 2010. <http://texashistory.unt.edu>.
20. *The San Angelo Press.* (San Angelo, Tex.) Vol. 7, No. 44, Ed. 1. Wednesday, November 4, 1903. University of North Texas Libraries. The Portal to Texas History. UNT Libraries: Denton, Texas. Web. 19 Nov. 2010. <http://texashistory.unt.edu>. 1.
21. *The San Angelo Press.* Vol. 7, No. 49, Ed. 1. Wednesday, December 9, 1903. University of North Texas Libraries. The Portal to Texas History. UNT Libraries: Denton, Texas. Web. 19 Nov. 2010. <http://texashistory.unt.edu>.
22. Johnson. 10.
23. *The San Angelo Press.* Vol. 8, No. 29, Ed. 1. Thursday, July 21, 1904. University of North Texas Libraries. The Portal to Texas History. UNT Libraries: Denton, Texas. Web. 19 Nov. 2010. <http://texashistory.unt.edu>.
24. Clements. 27; "Bill Pickett." *Legends of the West: A Collection of U.S. Commemorative Stamps.* 26.
25. Johnson. 48.
26. Clements. 39.
27. "Bill Pickett." *Legends of the West: A Collection of U.S. Commemorative Stamps.* 1st ed. Kansas City: U.S. Postal Service, 1993. 24–28. Print. 27.
28. Johnson. 85–86.
29. Johnson. 130.
30. Johnson. 131.
31. Ibid.
32. Johnson. 132.
33. Sara R. Massey. *Black Cowboys of Texas.* College Station: Texas A & M University Press, 2000. Print. 291.
34. Johnson. 136.
35. Hanes. 40.
36. Massey. 14.
37. Clements. 42.
38. Massey. 14.
39. Hanes. xiii.
40. PRCA Communications Department, and Kendra Santos. PRCA Media Guide 2010. 2010. Professional Rodeo Cowboys Association. Web. 19 Nov. 2010. <http://prorodeo.com>. 259.

41. Larry Pointer. *Rodeo Champions: Eight Memorable Moments of Riding, Wrestling, and Roping.* Albuquerque: University of New Mexico, 1985. Print. 13.
42. PRCA. 205, 231.
43. Ibid. 257.
44. Ibid. 256.
45. Hanes. 14.
46. Clements. 45.
47. Johnson. 166.
48. Sherman W. Savage. "Blacks in Principal Western Industries." *Blacks in the West.* Westport, CT: Greenwood, 1976. 89–90. Print. 90.

WORKS CONSULTED

CPRA. "Rodeo Events." Rodeo Canada—Official Home of the Canadian Professional Rodeo Association. Web. 19 Nov. 2010. <http://www.rodeocanada.com>.

Davis, Alvin G. "Black Cowboys and Ranchers in Texas." *HeritageI*, Winter 1994: 10-11. The Portal to Texas History. Web. 12 Oct. 2010. <http://texashistory.unt.edu>.

Dingus, Anne. "Bill Pickett." *Texas Monthly: the National Magazine of Texas.* Feb. 1997. Web. 12 Oct. 2010. <http://www.texasmonthly.com>.

"Event Descriptions." Australian Professional Rodeo Association. Web. 19 Nov. 2010. <http://www.prorodeo.asn.au/>.

Hancock, Sibyl. *Bill Pickett First Black Rodeo Star.* 1st ed. New York: Harcourt Brace Jovanovich, 1977. Print.

Miller, Zachary. "In Response to Bill Pickett's Death." Address. Bill Pickett. 1st ed. Kansas City: U.S. Postal Service, 1993. 24. Print.

"New Zealand Rodeo Cowboys Association—Events—STEER WRESTLING." New Zealand Rodeo Cowboys Association—Rodeo Information in NZ, Kiwi Rodeos. Web. 19 Nov. 2010. <http://www.rodeonz.co.nz>.

Stone, Ron. "APRIL 2, 1932." 56. Eakin Press (a.k.a. Sunbelt Media), 1984. *Texas Reference Center.* EBSCO. Web. 12 Oct. 2010.

Texas Historical Commission Bill Pickett Marker. 1991. Photograph. Williamson County Historical Commission, Heritage Square in Taylor, TX. *Williamson County Historical Commission.* Wayne Ware. Web. 12 Oct. 2010. <http://www.williamson-county-historical-commission.org >.

Tyler, Ronnie C., Douglas E. Barnett, and Roy R. Barkley. "Pickett, William." *The New Handbook of Texas.* Austin: Texas State Historical Association, 1996. Texas State Historical Association. Web. 12 Oct. 2010. <http://www.tshaonline.org>.

Branding and dehorning calves: Still roping and throwing them, 1941

DAY WORK COWBOYS IN THE DEPRESSION ERA

by Len Ainsworth

Dust from the trail herds had long since settled, and the open range was also gone. But "day work" cowboys were needed for ranches large and small during the years between the last two world wars. They were needed for riding pasture fences, doctoring sheep and cattle in the screwworm season, moving livestock, and sometimes for running pumps when the windmills stopped turning as summer winds forgot to blow. They were needed in even larger numbers for roundups.

Roundups were holdovers of the earlier days before fenced pastures, when men from various ranches gathered cattle and sorted them out according to brand and owner. Even after cattle were held in smaller enclosures numbers of cowboys were still necessary for gathering, branding and marking stock, and sorting out animals to be sold, separated, and moved. Some ranches still drove cattle to nearby markets or shipping facilities, and needed part-time help for the drives. Many ranches still had large pastures that required several riders to gather the livestock. But those ranches couldn't afford to maintain a large crew at all times, so temporary help was needed. Hence, the "day work" cowboy was a fixture for several years throughout the west.

This paper will focus on those itinerant workers, almost always men—sometimes as young as early teenagers—who worked for daily wages to perform those duties that were commonplace on the range. Many of the medium- to large-size ranches employed "steady men," paid by the month, on call at most any time, and who worked year 'round. The first such employee was usually the "foreman," who, in addition to his own work, directed the activities of all the other cowboys, whether "steady" or "day work" hands. Depending on the size of the ranch and the type of operation (cow/calf and feeder steer are two examples), additional steady men could be on monthly salaries as well. Some ranches were large enough for a full-time cook, but the foreman's wife (more rarely the owner's spouse) often performed that duty, even when the crew was swelled by day work hands.

Before and during the Great Depression there were men who had often worked as cowboys as regular hands, but who no longer had steady jobs. The day of the "grub line" of the drifting cowboy on horseback was gone. Elmer Kelton aptly described those changing times of just a few years earlier in his novel about Hewey Callaway called *The Good Old Boys.* Many of the cowboys who earlier drifted from job to job on horseback could no longer do so easily, because of the fenced ranges. Many of those single men gravitated to small towns across the west where living was relatively cheap and part-time work was sometimes available. Married cowboys, often

Elmer Kelton signing copies of *The Good Old Boys*

approaching middle age, also chose to live in smaller towns in ranch country. The families chose the towns for schools, churches, and a bit more social life, as well as for job possibilities.

This essay will focus on one of those small towns as being typical, and because I grew up there, lived there, and knew its people and many of the surrounding ranches. That community that still exists largely but not entirely on the ranching industry is Water Valley in Tom Green County, Texas. Twenty-some miles north and a little west of San Angelo, the community lies just east of the North Concho River. As "birds of a feather flock together," so had a number of cowboys, former cowboys, and would be cow boys gathered in that small town by the early 1930s. My dad was a common example: having quit a steady job after losing the privilege of running some stock on his own, he moved to the small village. Water Valley was a typical early 1900s West Texas village in which everyone knew everyone else, and there were various community and communal activities. Most men of working age were involved in supplying services to the surrounding ranches, whether as a storekeeper, windmill repairman, farmer raising feedstock, or a cowboy.

The little town became well known across a broad swath of West Texas as a source of ranch hands, men who were "sure 'nuff cowboys." The men who worked out of Water Valley had cowboyed far and wide, and former employers came for them again and again when temporary help was needed. The owners and foremen represented ranches in a large part of the Edwards Plateau and the Permian Basin regions of the state. In the 1920s and '30s with only sparsely improved roads to the southwest, past Reagan County, to Rankin, Crane and beyond, the employers came from more than a hundred miles away. And from the north to Big Spring and the higher plains, northwest past the 7Ds to ranches in Midland County, cowboys from "the Valley" were periodically called. They worked the roundups on the Spade in Mitchell County to the northeast, and their reach to the east included Tom Green, Coke, Runnels and Concho counties.

Saddled horse by store, trained and ground tied

The work was seasonal and sporadic. So, small groups of men gathered daily at "the store," a local Red and White grocery that also housed the Post Office. They sat on the porch, hunkered down on their boot heels, or leaned back against the front wall to swap tales of horses, roundups, and ranches, and waited for much-needed work. Some had years of experience as cowboys. Others had none or little, but came for the likelihood of work during peak periods. Some of each category drifted away or into other occupations, even picking cotton or shocking feed when cowboy jobs were less likely to be found. A few "got on" with the county road crew for brief stints. They were a diverse group, bound temporarily by their occupation and need for work. Recall that these were days before welfare or unemployment pay, or government work except for county or state road crews.

There were older single men, such as John Gillespie, called Juan Colara'o by those who spoke Spanish and Johnny Red by others.

The red-head had been a cowboy in his youth, a top hand by all accounts, and then he married, tried farming, lost his wife to another local resident, and took to drinking and existing on occasional day work, as a cowboy again. Len Mayes (my eponym) was the son of a trail-driver that had taken herds from the Concho country to the railheads of Kansas. Len had cowboyed to New Mexico and Arizona and back again. Never married, Len and John liked to try to "see the elephant" on Saturday nights. These two were examples of real, albeit hard living, cowboys who had rolled their beds in many bunkhouses and roundup camps across the Southwest.

There were family men, including my dad, Gid Ainsworth, and our neighbor Lewis Young, each of whom owned houses and small acreages with barns, windmills, tanks, corrals, hog pens, and garden plots. Others, including Otho Bannister and Henry Vandevanter, had larger places with a few head of stock but depended on day work as well. A generation of small ranchers in the area, and some sons of ranch owners, supplemented their income with some day work, although they often simply "traded work" with others in similar circumstances. An older resident, "Pop" Smith, had followed a common pattern from cowboy to chuck wagon cook to his garden in the small town, but he could still make it to the store porch and tell of how it used to be when there were "real cowboys." Pop, like my grandfathers, had ridden the Concho ranges and roundups before there were even drift fences, much less small pastures.

Several Smith sons and one son-in-law walked separately to the "store" at various times of the day, ensuring one of the family was around if a job were to become available. Almost everyone walked while in town from the 1920s and into the '40s. Except Johnny Red, whose slowly moving Model A Ford was a common sight. And my dad, who usually had a young horse or two in training, rarely walked when he could ride. Leaving a saddled bronc tied near the store got the pony accustomed to traffic and was a sure conversation starter. Since there were few telephones in the community during those decades, a rancher would drive into town and ask about men he knew or had heard of. For longer jobs, the men chosen would usually be given a few days to get their gear together before the rancher came to collect his crew.

Only two Hispanic cowboys worked in the area during that period. One was Polo Estrada; his English was a source of amusement, but his skill with horse and rope a source of respect. Family man Jim Luna made a ranch hand for years until age and aches caused him to move to San Angelo for inside work. Patriarch Manuel Juarez operated a contract shearing crew out of Water Valley for many years. Members of the crew were truly itinerants who moved on as the work ended in late spring. Manuel, as other contractors have been known to do, sometimes overcommitted to ranchers as to the day his crew would arrive. His work was essential to the ranches, but earned him some harsh words as well as praise for that particular part-time work. Delay in the shearing crew's arrival could mean a difference in day work cowboys' income, and possibly the rancher's as well.

A younger generation of cowboys was well represented in the 1930s decade. Laverne Baker and Roy Walraven had cut their teeth as cowboys on the 66 Ranch further east, but called Water Valley home for a time. Buddy Clark drifted in and on out to the JAs in the panhandle. Tom Vandevanter and his older brother Henry worked out of Water Valley, as did Tommy Spurgin and Tommy Newton, into the early 1940s. These were some, a good cross section, of the men who rolled their beds and saddles and loaded them into pickups to go for a day or two, or even months of work on ranches throughout West Texas in those earlier times. This chronicle could have been told without naming the individuals, but they were important to their families, to the community, and to the major industry of that time and place. To those of us whom they helped to survive and to enjoy the fruits of their labor, they are certainly deserving of recognition, even though it is belated.

The day work cowboy was expected to supply his own gear, including bridle and saddle with blanket or pad and a catch rope (although if one broke a rope the ranch would sometimes provide a replacement). Chaps and spurs were optional, but expected and

Gid Ainsworth ready for work, 1930s

usually necessary. Most also carried a pair of leather work gloves since the true nature of the work might include building fence or barb-wire-fence repair. If the work was to be for more than a day the cowboy was expected to bring his own bedroll (as this was before fancy sleeping bags) and clothing for the duration. If the man smoked or chewed, which was common then when one could afford it, he had to take enough tobacco for the expected length of the job. Some of the roundup jobs could be for a month or more, with rare chances for resupply.

One of my early 1930s memories is of my dad putting folded heavy quilts together, with spare clothing laid between them, packing sacks of Bull Durham tobacco from a carton into his pillow case, and rolling it all inside a long bed tarp for a month-long roundup on the Bar S ranch out of Big Lake, Texas. The long tarp was needed to cover one's head when rains came while sleeping out in the open. My dad also carried a small valise with other clothing and essentials, including a bar of soap and a straight razor (but no mirror, because if broken bad luck might follow). A later recollection was that he slept in a bed two days on that roundup, the night that he arrived and once two weeks later when he was sent back to the ranch to bring a wagon with more supplies back to camp. He laughed that the chuck wagon cook, an older man, berated the men for bringing even a small bag or suitcase, grousing about the new "thirty-six model cowboys." He grumbled that in his day of "real cowboys" all that extra gear wasn't needed or allowed. That particular roundup was made with a crew of about fifteen men, a sizeable remuda with a wrangler, and a camp with chuck wagon and hoodlum wagon for the beds and other gear, that moved every couple of days. The stories of each day's work, from horses pitching on frosty mornings to breakaway critters to foibles of the individual cowboys, became grist for story telling for months and years after. Stories were related on the "store porch" and in other venues, as the folklore of that lifestyle was passed around. The wagon boss on that roundup, Tom White, became larger than life to me as tales of his dealing with individual cowboys, accidents, and bosses were told, as did stories by other men of other cowboys and other roundups.

Much of the day work was for shorter periods and decidedly less than glamorous. A couple of days of "drenching" sheep were welcome for the pay, but as dirty and nasty a job as could be found. It might consist of a short, early morning rounding up of a flock and penning them, but then the dirty work began. Each sheep, mostly large ewes, had to be held, clamped between one's legs with their snotty nose yanked up, while another man inserted a large metal syringe with a blunt nozzle into the sheep's mouth and pushed the plunger so a purple liquid (permanganated potash) went into the throat, deep enough that swallowing occurred. That was repeated until all in the flock were served those preventive doses.

As a youngster I caught a few of those days, and can attest that it was both hot and vile work. The grease from the wool permeated one's clothes, and the dirty mucus and spilled drench added another layer by day's end. This was day work, but could barely be called cowboy work. In the Depression era the day workers could hardly pick and choose their duties. If a man accepted work, he was expected to do whatever came along without asking what it might entail. There were other jobs for which additional help for the "steady" men was required. "Fixing" water gaps after the rare deluge, or work in the shearing pens, or more to any cowboy's desire, roping and treating stock (again, usually sheep) for screw worms was common.

"Wormy" cattle were more often penned and treated in chutes by the time I was old enough to be involved, but part of the folklore of earlier days of the Concho country remained. The story of a young bull roped in a downhill chase took on epic proportions; the roped animal "forked a tree," that is, went on one side of a tree while horse and rider went on the other and caused the horse to be jerked down in a major wreck. A tale of a cowboy who unwisely roped a turkey buzzard had comedic overtones. With rope tied firmly to the saddle horn, the young rider charged and roped a buzzard that was feeding on a dead animal. When the big bird suddenly took flight, the horse bucked and the rider was in the middle. Not wanting to cut and lose his rope, he finally maneuvered the flopping bird into some brush, whereupon the cowboy was able to cut only a couple of feet off his "twine," but suffered the ignominy of scratches and a splash of the peculiar vomit that those birds can eject. The odor was probably gone long before his gleeful colleagues quit reminding him of the incident.

The little community's day work cowboys of the Depression days had largely disappeared by the end of WWII, having gone to other work, retired or passed away. Several went into military service early in the war and didn't go into ranch work after returning. After that war there were generally more fences, smaller pastures, more corrals, better pickup trucks and trailers, and the screw worms were becoming controlled. As pastures became smaller the numbers of cowboys, particularly of the day work variety, became fewer. The work on ranches was done with fewer hands, if not less effort, by those involved. Technology keeps improving equipment and work practices. Increase in productivity has been a feature of American life in many aspects, and ranching is a real example. Accordingly, the Bureau of Statistics in 2012 postulated that there will be continued reducing of need for farm and ranch hands, estimating another eight percent decline by 2018.1 There are only a few large ranches today that hire large crews for their roundups, and some of those they employ are individuals (including a few women) who take time away from their regular jobs to participate as a cowboy in that aspect of western life.

Similar stories of counterpart cowboys could be found in other communities across the American Southwest during those earlier times of changing ranching practices. Some of those day work cowboys of the Depression era were men who had a hard time leaving the work they grew up with, and some even had a hard time believing or accepting the changes that were occurring about them. They were, however, part of the continuing notion of the cowboy as an icon of the west. The day work cowboys were important to the economy, as are workers everywhere. But they also filled a unique place at a particular period in the industry and way of life that is ranching.

There is a western adage that "it takes about eighty years to become a cowman." I might have made it, as both my grandfathers and my father were cowboys for a combined period of most of a century, except for a couple of factors. One was the industry changes mentioned above. The other is personal and yet poignant to me. In high school, since my dad was a respected cowboy, a few local ranchers came to me when I was barely a teenager, for some sporadic part-time help with small roundups, riding pastures, and looking after their ranch while they went on vacation. I enjoyed the work and the pay that it provided. During my senior year my dad gave his chaps and his pair of spurs to a young man just back from military service. I had secretly coveted those spurs; they were a Crockett 1930 model, iron working cowboy spurs, with raised shanks and a large silver sombrero mounted on the outside bands. When I asked my dad why he had given his spurs away, he answered simply that he didn't want me to follow the cowboy trade. He said that he had enjoyed his life, but didn't see any future in it for those who worked for wages, and that education held a better promise. And thus, the days of day work cowboy ended for me as well as it had for many others. They do still live in memory, and occasionally I wish for that pair of spurs.

ENDNOTES

Occupational Outlook Handbook, Bureau of Labor Statistics, July 18, 2012. Summary, assessed online via: www.bis.gov/ooh/management-farmers-ranchers-and-other-agricultural-managers-htm .

Ebra John Red Overton, on left. Courtesy, Joan Echols Taylor &
Joe Don Echols

RED OVERTON, SOMERVELL COUNTY CEDAR-CHOPPER

by Robert J. (Jack) Duncan

If they made a film about Red Overton, I don't know who they could get to play him—now that John Wayne and Robert Mitchum are permanently unavailable. Maybe there's a stuntman out there who could pull it off, but I really doubt it.

Red Overton was a larger-than-life backwoodsman who lived in Somervell County, Texas. He was a big, raw-boned man with big hands. Some called him "Bear Track" Overton because of the size of his feet. Red stood six-foot-two. And he was as tough and gnarled as the cedar (actually juniper) growing on those rocky Somervell County hills.

Red was a quiet man. He didn't have much formal education, but he was wise in the ways of the woods. In the 1920s and 1930s, Overton was a post cutter: he cut cedar posts for barbed wire fencing and sold them for a few cents apiece at a nearby crossroads store. Sometimes he traded them for cans of Prince Albert pipe tobacco, from which he rolled his own cigarettes.

Red Overton's full name was Ebra John Hardy Overton. He was born on January 12, 1893, in Randolph, Alabama. He moved to Texas as a very young child with his family. He died on October 7, 1962, at the age of 69, in Glen Rose, and he is buried in the Nancy Smith Cemetery several miles west of Glen Rose. Overton's tombstone even has his nickname, "Red," written in stone. Overton had light blue eyes, red hair, and a ruddy complexion. He was married to Lydia Wade, who was also known as Lottie. They had at least eight children.

During the Depression, Red took a Works Progress Administration (WPA) job to feed his family. They poured a lot of concrete, and the cement worked into the pores and wrinkles in Red's hands. It made them so rough that he could strike kitchen matches on them—the outer part of his thumbs—for the purpose of lighting his hand-rolled cigarettes. If he had an audience, he would strike the matches on his face.

Several months ago, I got a Red Overton story second-hand by way of email. Joe Don Echols told his cousin, Joan Echols Taylor, a vignette about Red, and Joan relayed it to me. Joan said:

> Joe told me a new story about "Red." He said he was a "mighty" man, both in stature and in strength. . . . He said that a traveling western show came to Glen Rose that had a wrestling event. The locals anted up and got Red to sign up. When the opponent came into the ring, Red looked him square in the eye, reached for his tobacco, and rolled a cigarette. Then he struck the match on the side of his cheek. The opponent eyed him, they stood for a long minute, and the fellow said "no go." He returned the money, and that was the end of the match. The locals went wild.

Joan Taylor told me that her informant, Joe Echols, was born and raised in Somervell County, as was his father. She said that Joe is "86 years young" and that his mind is clear and his hearing is good. Joe loaned Joan a snapshot of Red Overton to scan and send to me. It shows Red working on a rock crusher when they were building a road between Glen Rose and Cleburne. Joe said that he never heard Red Overton called anything but Red.

Once upon a time, Red got into a fistfight with Scott Fretwell out in the cedar brakes. Jess Hopson was the only witness. Scott wasn't as big as Red, but he was rugged and tough, and he was a good fighter. Jess later reported that the two men fought for about an hour. Whenever they both got exhausted, they would sit down and rest for a while, like boxers between rounds. Then after a couple of minutes, they would go at it again. Every few minutes, they stopped to rest.

In the hills around Glen Rose, where the term "hard-scrabble farm" is no exaggeration, the making of moonshine whiskey was a way of life, a learned art, and an honorable profession, even during Prohibition. They say that Red operated stills for several different distillers.

"Uncle" Joe Dodson was the Somervell County Sheriff from 1923 to 1928. He used to tell about the Texas Ranger who took Red Overton into custody and was going to transport him to the town of Ranger. The dirt roads were muddy, and the lawman was afraid that if his car got stuck, Red might get away. The Texas Ranger hated to do it, but he decided that he had better render Red unconscious for the trip. Uncle Joe Dodson said that the Ranger pulled his big long Colt revolver out of its holster and hit Red on the head with it as hard as he thought his gun could stand.

I collected almost all of these vignettes about Red Overton when Elizabeth and I spent a week in Glen Rose in the summer of 1979. I was doing some research on Ernest Tolbert (Bull) Adams, another highly unusual Somervell County resident who was contemporary with Red Overton. As I interviewed people around Glen Rose about Bull Adams, two or three of them also recounted a story or two about Red Overton, and I wrote them down, too. It made a nice little bonus.

One of my informants was the late Temple Summers, the father of the famous Texas artist Robert Summers. Temple spent his later years as Bob's business manager. Earlier he had served as Somervell County's county judge for fifteen years, and he was as reliable a source as any writer ever had.

Temple told me that around 1922, his father, J. C. Summers, was driving a horse and buggy near the community of Hill City, in the vicinity of Comanche Peak. J. C. came upon Red Overton, who was walking home from Glen Rose, many miles away, after

buying groceries and supplies. Red was afoot. If it had been anybody but Red Overton, J. C. probably wouldn't have believed his
eyes. He said that Red was carrying a 100-pound bag of sugar on
one shoulder and a 48-pound bag of flour on the other. In one
hand he had a five-gallon can of coal oil and in the other a tow sack
full of groceries. Red's trips like that were legendary in the county.
Folks said he usually made the whole trip without once setting
down his load to rest.

One time Red was making one of these trips when he came
upon two men from the telephone company who were trying to
set a pole for the new phone line. Red stood there holding his load
for a few minutes, watching the two men. They were having a lot
of trouble getting the telephone pole into the hole they had dug.
Finally, Red set down his groceries, walked over and offered to put
the pole into the hole for them. The telephone men later swore
that he set the pole by using just one of his huge hands!

Another of my informants in 1979 was Fort Worth Attorney
Richard Moore. He owned a ranch in Somervell County, and also
Barnard's Mill, the oldest and most historic building in Glen Rose.
For many years, Dick Moore divided his time between Somervell
County and Fort Worth.

Dick told me that Red Overton was in the penitentiary in
Huntsville at one time. The captain at the prison had some bloodhounds that he was mighty proud of, and one morning he got to
bragging about how smart they were. It irritated Red, so he said:
"There ain't a dog alive that's as smart as Red Overton."

The captain took exception to Red's brag, and he offered him a
challenge. Dick Moore told me that the captain said: "Listen here,
you cedar chopper. I'll prove to you how smart my dad-gum dogs
are. I'll let you out of here at noon today. I'll give you an hour's
head start. If my dogs ain't caught you by sundown, you can just
go on home. You've only got three or four months left to serve
anyhow. If you can outsmart my hounds, you can go free."

Red said he knew dern well that he was smarter than any damn dog. Said he believed he'd just take the captain up on that little deal. So at noon, Red took off. He pulled every trick he knew. He walked in creeks, he climbed from tree to tree, but he still heard the dogs on his trail. Before Red had left the mess hall that day, he had put some red pepper in a napkin and stuck it in his pocket. As a last resort, he took off his denim jacket, tromped all over it to make sure it had his scent, and sprinkled it liberally with that red pepper. Then he left it on the ground. The dogs had a sneezing fit and lost his track. Red watched from a distant treetop. The captain was thoroughly disgusted; the tracking party returned to Huntsville.

That evening there was a loud knock upon the massive wooden gate of the prison.

"Who's there?" demanded the guard.

"Red Overton," came the reply.

"What in the world are you doing back here?" asked the guard, who could hardly believe his ears. "Didn't you hear the captain say that if you got away from them dogs you could go on back home?"

"Yep, I heared him all right," Red replied, "but I ain't et my supper yet. Open up and let me in." Red came in and ate his supper, and then he set off for home, a free man. Maybe he spent the night first, but I don't know that. It makes sense; however, the story didn't say. If he did, I'll bet he demanded his breakfast, too.

Attorney Dick Moore told me that in later years, Overton worked for him on two days a year: March 15 and September 15, shearing days for Moore's Angora goats. Red would gather up the sheared goat hair, put it in bags, and tromp it down. One day one of Moore's neighbors asked Red if he could help him build a fence. "Nope, I can't do'er," Red allowed. "I'd be right proud to help you out if I could, but I can't take on any more responsibility right now. I've already got a steady job with Dick Moore, workin' regular. Much obliged, though."

The neighbor was a good friend of Dick's, and the neighbor drove over to see him. "I didn't know Red Overton was working for you all the time now," the neighbor said.

Dick said, "He's not. Why did you think that? He just works for me two days a year—March 15 and September 15—when we shear the goats."

"Good Lord!" the neighbor exclaimed. "He told me he had a steady job with you out here."

Dick laughed. "Well, it's steady, all right, but it's still just two days a year." The neighbor had a laughing fit.

My late friend Lloyd Shipman was a good storyteller. He grew up around Glen Rose and knew the town and the people well. Lloyd gave me another Red Overton story. The county line between Somervell and Erath counties bisects a long curve of Highway 67. Lloyd told me that Ed Lynch, a deputy constable, lived on Highway 67 just inside the Somervell County line.

One day during the Depression, Red Overton was walking down the highway toward Erath County. As Overton approached Ed's house, he tried to hide a gallon jug under his ragged and faded denim jacket. Lloyd said, "Deputy Lynch, a great hulking, three-hundred-pound mountain of blubber, came waddling hurriedly out of his yard, having spied the protrusion."

"Hold up there, Red," Ed commanded. "Whata ye got under yer jumper, there?"

"A jug of `syrup.' What's it to ya?" sneered Red as he hurried on, looking back over his shoulder.

"Like fun, it is!" hollered the deputy, breaking into a run. Red, unwilling to surrender his dignity yet, allowed Ed Lynch to overtake him. "I'm puttin' you under arrest, Red!" Deputy Lynch wheezed.

"What fer?" demanded Red. "Is it again the law fer a feller to walk down a state highway nowadays?"

"You know dern well what fer; I'm arrestin' you fer transportin' bootleg liquor!"

"You can't prove I got liquor!" Red challenged.

"I'll prove it or bust!" Ed panted, grabbing Red around the waist, trying to bodily restrain him.

"Bust, then!" shouted Red. He whirled around and gave Ed a mighty jab with his elbow, sending the deputy into the bar ditch, where he rolled over and over from the tremendous momentum generated by the thrust. By the time Ed Lynch had heaved himself back upon his feet, Red had waltzed on down the highway a few steps—just far enough to be across the county line, out of Ed's jurisdiction. Red marched on down the road, whistling a little tune, a free man on his way to deliver the jug of moonshine to a customer in Erath County.

As I was preparing this article, it occurred to me that I needed to document that Red Overton had, indeed, been in the Huntsville, Texas, State Penitentiary. It crossed my mind that if I couldn't determine that historical fact, a disgruntled descendant of Red Overton might come out of the woodwork to accuse me of besmirching his forefather's name. So, I got ahold of a microfilm copy of the convict records from the Texas State Archives. This is precisely where history—or biography—intersects folklore.

Sure enough, I learned that E. J. Overton ("Red"), convict number 56758, served time in the Huntsville prison in 1926 and 1927. The records are quite detailed. In fact, I found in them something that perhaps even corroborates the bloodhounds story: the scheduled date for Red's official release was May 7, 1928—but the records also show that he actually left a little over four months earlier, on December 29, 1927.

The specific details that can be found in these records are really somewhat mind-boggling. I found that Red was convicted of "possessing equipment for making liquor" after pleading "not guilty." I also read in those records that, although he had attended just two years of public school, he was literate—could read and write. And I learned that he wore a size 12 shoe. Probably the most personal detail was that he had an "outie" belly button—or what the prison records more officially and properly referred to as a "protruding navel." Now, for my money, that's getting pretty personal!

Somervell is the third smallest county in Texas. The courthouse is built on a smaller scale than most county courthouses, so as you approach it, it seems farther off than it is. You could almost bump into it before you know it. The county may be small, and the courthouse may be small, but the rule doesn't apply to a lot of the people. Case in point: Red Overton, a mighty man—and a mighty unusual one.

Jack Duncan

John Wesley Hardin, from a tintype made in Abilene, Kansas in 1871.
Courtesy, The Robert G. McCubbin Collection

FOLKLORE OF GUNFIGHTER JOHN WESLEY HARDIN: MYTHS, TRUTHS, AND HALF-TRUTHS

by Chuck Parsons

John Wesley Hardin was born in Fannin County, Texas, in May of 1853. He was too young to fight in the Civil War, but was the right age to mature as one of the *Unreconstructable Rebels*. The study of that period makes Texas post Civil War history so fascinating. In spite of being the son of a circuit riding preacher, he ignored the sixth commandment, the one that says: "Thou Shalt Not Kill." He killed his first man in 1868 in Polk County; he killed many more all over Texas, Indian Territory and Kansas, before being finally captured in Florida in 1877. He was tried and convicted of second degree murder and sentenced to twenty-five years in Huntsville Penitentiary, and was then pardoned in 1894 by Governor Hogg. After some time spent in Gonzales where he passed the bar exam and became a full-fledged attorney-at-law, he drifted west to Junction, then on to Pecos and then on to El Paso.

At the time El Paso was wild and wooly, just what he liked. He could not avoid trouble, and John Wesley Hardin was shot to death in the Acme Saloon in August 1895. Contrary to what many of the Old West gunfighters left behind—nothing—among Hardin's many personal effects was a manuscript justifying every act of his life. Every killing, or so he claimed, was justifiable homicide.

Also in those personal effects were three weapons: one .41 caliber Colt revolver, serial number 68837; one .38 caliber Colt revolver, serial number 84304; and one .45 caliber Colt revolver, serial number 126–680. Two other weapons were also listed in his effects: one .44 caliber Smith & Wesson revolver, serial number #352, then in possession of the District Court; and one .45 caliber

Colt revolver, serial number 73728, then in possession of the El
Paso County Sheriff.[1] These are the authentic weapons of gunfighter John Wesley Hardin; we know they belonged to him
because court records say so, giving the proof of possession and the
serial numbers. This is excellent provenance.

In the Buckhorn Saloon in San Antonio is a double-barrel
shotgun, which according to the available provenance, was used by
Hardin to kill one-time State Police captain and one-time DeWitt
County sheriff, Jack Helm. The evidence of this is not as excellent
as a court record, but it has been handed down from a Gonzales
County sheriff to the present owner. The origin of this weapon is
acceptable by historians as being an authentic Hardin weapon.[2]

But what about the guns which current owners claim belonged
to John Wesley Hardin? If we could possess all the guns the owners
claim had belonged to him, we would have a small arsenal. In
Nixon, Texas, down near Gonzales, there is a gentleman who
claims to own the gun Hardin used to kill his first man.[3] That
would be in 1868, when Hardin killed a former slave. I have seen
this small pistol, and have held it. It could be, of course, what the
owner claims. But there is absolutely no proof. Like so many
aspects of gunfighter Hardin's life, it could be . . . but perhaps not,
as there is no way to prove what the owner claims.

Is this a myth? Folklore? Or simply a falsehood? The word
provenance can become a fighting word in this situation. It is similar to the situation of interviewing someone about a historical person or incident. If you are interviewing, say, a Mr. Jones, and Mr.
Jones tells you that his great-grandmother fixed a meal for John
Wesley Hardin and she told her son about it, and he told it to his
son—are you going to question the source? If he says: "My great-
grandmother was an honest woman and would not lie or make up
a story," would you challenge him? No, you would probably thank
him for the story and forget about provenance in this situation.

Which brings us to a revolver I have in my possession. It is
what remains of a pistol owned by John Wesley Hardin. It is rusted

and worn. The serial number is obliterated, so we cannot check factory records to see who it was shipped to or when or where. I know actually very little about guns, but my guess is that it is an old Colt revolver. I assure you it is a pistol owned by John Wesley Hardin. No doubt about it.

How do I know? What is the provenance? Here is the provenance. After my father-in-law, Wendel Marshall Baker, passed away a few years ago, his children examined his effects. Among other things there was an old shed which contained his tools, license plates, batteries, and other various things which were a mystery to me. I did not even recognize what many of them were, but among them was found this old pistol. Then someone said:

"Remember when Daddy told us about that outlaw going through the pasture?"

"Yes, and that outlaw was Wes Hardin running from the State Police."

"Yes, and Daddy said he must have lost that gun galloping away from them through the pasture."

So here was this old pistol which "Pete" Baker, as he was known to all, had picked up, and it was talked about in the family down through the years. Did somehow the person who lost it become John Wesley Hardin? Perhaps so. Maybe Hardin did lose it, or maybe a State Policeman lost it while he was chasing Hardin through that pasture . . . and one day someone was plowing the field and picked it up and put it on a shelf, and later it managed to find its way to the shed which now held old tools and things that meant little to most people. Somehow the family thought it had been a pistol of Hardin's. Who would be so discourteous to contradict? To ask for the evidence?

A genuine Hardin pistol, if placed on the auction block, would go for many thousands of dollars—if it had confirmation of authenticity. A genuine Hardin pistol might go for $500,000; or it might sell for twice that amount. This pistol, which is rusty and bent out of shape, has absolutely no provenance acceptable to a collector. It would bring nothing on the auction block. Strangely enough, I showed it to a friend who has a deep interest in John Wesley Hardin and anything connected to him, and I was offered $100 for it—not because it is a Hardin pistol, but because it is "cool." Or maybe the person said it was "neat." To me, it is only an interesting old pistol with an unverifiable story, but nothing more.

A pistol, which may or may not have belonged to John Wesley Hardin, is only one aspect of the gunfighter's life. There are tales about the man as well. There is a John Wesley Hardin tale which many of you are familiar with, and some people accept it as the gospel truth. I will attempt to show you it is part of the folklore about the gunfighter; maybe it is simply a half-truth. At least it is an interesting story which includes some actual facts.

Many of you recall back in 1974, when Time-Life Books brought out a series of handsomely designed and heavily illustrated volumes entitled "The Old West" containing color and black and white photographs. One of the twenty or so books in the series was entitled *The Gunfighters*.[4] The book reads well and the illustrations are authentic and numerous. As you know, Time-Life Books had an excellent advertising campaign, and it seems that every library—public or private—has a set of these books. In promoting *The Gunfighters*, which seemed to focus on John Wesley Hardin, the advertisement ran something like this: "John Wesley Hardin was so mean he once killed a man for snoring."

He killed a man just because he snored? He must have been a really mean man to kill a man for snoring.

We have the book in our collection, and find that on page 176 there is a photograph of Hardin, reproduced from a tintype made in Abilene, Kansas, in 1871. Why was Hardin in Abilene, Kansas? He was there because at the time he was a cowboy, and had helped drive longhorns up the trail from Texas. Some cowboys had their photographs taken while still in their work clothes, and these are prized images for collectors. Hardin is not dressed like he was out on the trail, but in what in 1871 passed for a three-piece suit: he is wearing a black vest, black coat, black trousers, boots, a white shirt, and a *white hat*. There is no weapon in sight, but he may have had one stuck in his waistband hidden from the eye of the camera. The caption reads: "Wild Bill Hickok briefly befriended him—until Hardin shot a snoring hotel guest for disturbing his rest and had to leave town."[5]

That episode in Hardin's life remains controversial. Was it an actual case of Hardin shooting a man just because he snored, a case certainly of premeditated murder . . . or was this an example of Time-Life Books creating a story in order to hopefully sell more copies of the book? The advertisement was so effective that today many people consider it true, that Hardin did indeed shoot a man just for snoring.

As mentioned, Hardin wrote his autobiography, entitled *The Life of John Wesley Hardin, As Written by Himself*. It was published shortly after his death and today a copy in good condition might bring $400 or more.[6] Hardin apparently began writing it while still in prison, or perhaps shortly after his release. It ends rather abruptly, suggesting he was about through writing his life story but then was killed; it remained unfinished. The manuscript was among his personal effects, and fortunately his children won custody of it and had it published by a printing firm in Seguin, Texas, a little ways east of San Antonio. The question you may be asking is, does Hardin tell about shooting a man just for snoring?

Actually, no, but that is where the controversy comes in, and that is where Time-Life Books managed to work in the terrific statement that he did exactly that. Hardin did write of his experiences while in Abilene, Kansas, in 1871. Wild Bill Hickok indeed was the City Marshal at that time. Hardin did write that one night in the American House, an Abilene hotel, a thief attempted to break into the room where he and cousin John Gibson "Gyp" Clements were sleeping. Hardin woke up in time and shot the intruder to death, his corpse cluttering the hallway. Afraid City

Marshal Hickok would not understand why he had killed this man, Hardin and Clements jumped out the window as Hickok and deputies came to investigate the shooting. The pair skipped out of town and headed for relative safety back in Texas. Hardin wrote about this incident with such a flair that it seems authentic, and many people believe that is the way it happened.[7]

Did this nineteenth-century serial killer actually kill a man for breaking into his hotel room? Or is there more to it than that? One might say Hardin here is creating the legend which he wished to be accepted. As we all know, people who write their life story present their actions only in the best light. Hardin was no exception.

Accepting that Hardin was creating his own folklore, what did the local newspaper have to say about this incident? Fortunately, the *Abilene Chronicle* did report the killing; it wrote that a shooting occurred and a body was found in the local hotel. In the issue of August 10 the Chronicle reported the following:

> The most fiendish murder was perpetrated in the American House, in this place, on the night of the 6th inst. The murdered man's name was Charles Couger, and that of the murderer Wesley Clements. . . . Couger was a boss cattle herder, and said to be a gentleman; Clements [Hardin] is from Mississippi [*sic*, Texas]. Couger was in his room sitting upon the bed reading the newspaper. Four shots were fired at him through a board partition, one of which struck him in the fleshy part of the left arm, passing through the third rib and entering the heart, cutting a piece of it entirely off, and killing Couger almost immediately. The murderer escaped. . . .[8]

Hardin not only killed people, he also used aliases, such as the surname of his first cousin, John Gibson Clements. Apparently, he was known in Abilene as Wesley Clements. Here the contemporary press, within days of the happening, reports the man was sitting on his bed reading a newspaper—certainly not asleep snoring!

Another newspaper, the *Topeka Daily Commonwealth*, reported: "A man was shot in Abilene last Saturday night. Two men in disguise entered his room . . . and fired two shots into his breast. The assassins escaped. . . . They are supposed to have been former partners of the murdered man and took this method of ridding themselves of pecuniary obligations."[9] Pecuniary obligations? In other words, they owed him money and in order not to pay him they shot him. Snoring does not enter into the picture at all.

If we accept the contemporary newspaper accounts, and we have no reason not to accept them as accurate, Hardin and cousin Gyp Clements shot a fellow herder to avoid paying him for his work. Writing years later, Hardin chose to make this killing an act of self-defense, of self-preservation.

Gyp Clements told his nephew Joe Clements about his adventures in Kansas in 1871. Later, historian and folklorist C. L. Sonnichsen interviewed nephew Joe in El Paso. Apparently, Gyp told more details to nephew Joe, who then later related the following to Doc Sonnichsen:

> [Hardin and Clements] went to bed. In the middle
> of the night, they heard someone trying the door.
> Then there was a knock and they were told to open
> up [by] officers. The [young men] did not want to
> be arrested, so they went out the window [and left
> Abilene for Texas.][10]

What Gyp failed to tell his nephew was that Hardin had earlier killed a man in that very hotel. In Hardin's memoir he would have us believe it was a justifiable killing done in order to protect his property. The contemporary press, not caring for folklore or how history perceived Hardin, instead reported it as what it was: a "most fiendish murder."

But for the sake of the record let's give Hardin the benefit of the doubt in this instance. Maybe the editor of the *Abilene Chronicle* had had a run-in with Hardin and wanted to give him all the bad press he could. Whether this killing was justifiable or not, let's take a look at the number of men he killed. He had to have killed more than his fair share for a gunfighter, for in 1874, after the killing of a Brown County deputy sheriff, Governor Coke raised the reward for his capture—dead or alive—to $4000. Was that a lot of money in 1874? It was indeed; and it would be a lot of money today for those of you who are not among the "filthy rich."

How many men did he kill? If we believe his autobiography, Hardin killed somewhere around forty men. In his mind they were all justified killings, justified because in every instance the man he killed was trying to take away his freedom or kill him.

John Wesley Hardin's Grave, Concordia Cemetery, El Paso, Texas.
Courtesy, Ken Untiedt

Hardin didn't know the term but he may have considered himself a "Freedom Fighter." But the inherent problem with most of those killings was that he did not stick around to see whether the man he shot was dead or only wounded. Many of the killings were from ambush; numerous times he was one of a group. Only a ballistics test could determine if the bullet from Hardin's gun was the fatal one, or if it was a bullet from another person's gun. One significant example, perhaps, remains the killing of Jack Helm, mentioned earlier. Hardin and friend Jim Taylor both shot him down: Hardin used a shotgun and Taylor a six-shooter. One account of the killing mentions Hardin shooting Helm in the shoulder while Taylor emptied his pistol into the head and breast of Helm. Hardin claimed the kill as his own, but perhaps Taylor should receive the credit, or the blame.

Another example is that of the killing of that Brown County deputy sheriff, Charles Webb. It happened in Comanche on Hardin's twenty-first birthday. Hardin claimed in his autobiography that Webb drew his pistol and shot him in the side, while he and Jim Taylor and cousin Bud Dixon fired back, killing Webb. At his trial three years later Hardin claimed self-defense. He also pointed out that Jim Taylor fired the fatal bullet. Of course, by then Taylor was dead and could not defend himself. Bud Dixon was dead as well. What is significant is that if we look at Hardin's life with an objective eye, we find that many of his killings credited to him and by him should perhaps not be credited to him at all. Many of the men he shot may have lived, thus reducing the number of his kills.

But on the other hand, there were probably killings which Hardin conveniently forgot about in writing his autobiography. After Texas Rangers captured him in 1877, the adjutant general wrote to the district clerks of many counties asking if there were outstanding indictments against him which ultimately could be used against him in court. Many district clerks responded, pointing out there were charges against Hardin for killing a man in their county, or two men in some cases. For example, Hardin wrote of the gunfight with Benjamin B. Bradley taking place in 1870 in Towash, a little community now under the waters of the Whitney Reservoir in Hill County. Of course, it was a case of self-defense, killing this one man. But a Travis County man reported to the adjutant general that Hardin had told him that he had killed two men in Peoria, Hill County.[11] With Bradley's death these two would make the number in Hill County a total of three. Hardin overlooked these two Peoria killings. If we are aware of one example of conveniently overlooking a double homicide, were there not others? These cases of Hardin killing a man, or men, did not get reported in his life story, although Hardin certainly could not have forgotten about them. They were perhaps what Hardin did not want to become part of the folklore about him—the premier gunfighter of Texas.

ENDNOTES

1. Richard C. Marohn. "A Gunfighter's Estate 1895" in *The Last Gunfighter: John Wesley Hardin* (College Station: Creative Publishing Company, 1995), 282–83.
2. Interview with David George of the Buckhorn Saloon during a visit.
3. Interview with a Nixon resident who wishes to remain anonymous.
4. Paul Trachtman. *The Gunfighters.* The Old West series. (New York: Time-Life Books. 1974).
5. Ibid., 176.
6. The autobiography was published in a soft-cover format in 1896 by Smith & Moore of Seguin, Texas. It was reprinted by J. Marvin Hunter in 1926 and later published by the University of Oklahoma Press in 1961, with a new introduction by Robert G. McCubbin. Ramon F. Adams identified it as "scarce" in the revised and enlarged edition of his *Six-Guns and Saddle Leather: A Bibliography of Books and Pamphlets on Western Outlaws and Gunman*, published by the University of Oklahoma Press of Norman in 1964.

7. John Wesley Hardin. *The Life of John Wesley Hardin, as Written by Himself.* Seguin: Smith and Moore Publishers, 1896. Reprint: University of Oklahoma Press, 1961. 58–59.

8. The *Abilene Chronicle*, August 10, 1871.

9. The *Topeka Daily Commonwealth*, August 9, 1871.

10. Undated interview cited in Leon Metz's *John Wesley Hardin: Dark Angel of Texas* (El Paso: Mangan Books, 1996), 71.

11. "Accusations Against Wesley Hardin" in the *Austin Daily Democratic Statesman*, August 30, 1877.

The author as a "wild-eyed cowboy"

HOUSTON COP TALK

by Scott Hill Bumgardner

— ❦ —

Every occupation or walk of life seems to have unique terminology. I plunged into a world that was full of unique slang and terms that have entered the realm of oral tradition. In September of 1976, I became a cadet in the Houston Police Department's academy. My career as a Houston Police Officer and Sergeant spanned more than twenty years, until I retired in 1997. Even in the academy my fellow trainees and I were exposed to a few of the terms, but the real enlightenment began when we were assigned to the department's patrol functions. Some of this jargon is commonly used in other police departments. Several of these terms have been used in police novels and film portrayals. But, I believe many of the terms I include here were born on the streets of Houston, Texas.

The following paragraph is an example of Houston cop talk. It is written in the descriptive vernacular an officer might use to detail what happened during his day of work to another officer. The slang words are underlined.

"We s.o.'ed as unit #15E10 with shop #2420 and immediately received a call about a driver that was acting hinky. We arrived and stopped the described vehicle, thinking that it might be a hijacker or even some local knob knockers. It turned out to be just a rolling G. The driver was known as a fender lizard by one of the old heads who checked by. The actor said she was an officer's chip and that she was watching his x10. She was acting like a real zipperhead and kept saying, 'Who me?' My partner got a little fed up and replied, 'No, the mouse in your pocket!' At this point she looked down and said, 'I ain't got no mouse in my pocket.' This space cadet started getting real froggy and hollering that we were ginning her, so we put her in the back seat and hauled her to the gray bar hotel. On the way there she yelled a lot and we were tempted to give her a screen test or swat her with a slapper but we resisted the urge. On the way back to our district later, we had to wait for a yellow wheel. Thank goodness we were by a Stop and Rob, where we could drag the sack for some coffee. We sure wished a q-man was around during the long wait. Our sergeant accused us of milking the arrest, but was happy with the ducks we listed on our work-card."

Below is a translation of the previous conversation. The officer might have described his shift to a very trusted civilian friend in this manner. Obviously, this is not politically correct and several things mentioned are just plain old wrong. But, even cops can fantasize when under pressure.

"We signed on as unit #15E10 with patrol car #2420 and immediately received a call about a driver that was acting suspicious. We arrived and stopped the described vehicle, thinking that it might be a robber or even some local safe burglars. It turned out to be just a DWI. The driver was known as a car hop by one of the veteran officers who checked by. The suspect said she was an officer's mistress and that she was watching his home. She was acting like a real stupid idiot and kept saying, 'Who me?' My partner got a little fed up and replied, 'No, the mouse in your pocket!' At this point she looked down and said, 'I ain't got no mouse in my pocket.' This clueless suspect started getting real aggressive and hollering that we were falsely charging her, so we put her in the back seat and hauled her to the jail. On the way there she yelled a lot and we were tempted to slam on the brakes so she would hit the cage divider or swat her with a blackjack but we resisted the urge. On the way back to our district later, we had to wait for a spare tire. Thank goodness we were by a convenience store so we could get some free coffee. We sure wished a barbeque man was around during the long wait. Our sergeant accused us of taking an excessively long time during the arrest, but was happy with the arrest we listed on our work-card."

The following definitions and explanations would be useful for the average citizen to translate any Houston P.D. conversations.

HOUSTON POLICE JARGON DICTIONARY
(ABRIDGED VERSION, OF COURSE)

actor: When I hit the streets in 1977, the department had been using the word actor to indicate the suspect or person of interest for a decade or more. I suppose the administration thought this term would be a little less accusatory than "suspect." Lo and behold, we must have upset the actors' guild, and the department embraced the term "suspect" in the 1980s. Actually, it was likely changed to better fit in with national standards.

chicken eye: A few crooks would peer at us, with their head turned sideways, one eye focused and the other squinting. This looks similar to hens or other birds when they are checking out a bug or some other curiosity.

chip: This was a crude term that an officer might use in place of "girlfriend." Unfortunately, the common usage was to refer to an officer's mistress.

dirty leg: This was a common reference to a prostitute. It was also used to refer to a woman who was known to sleep around a lot.

drag the sack: Numerous restaurants would feed cops for half price. If we hit the proverbial donut shop, our money was no good. Upon retiring in 1997, it sure was a shock to pay full price for a cup of coffee. Though we were discouraged by policy from accepting any gratuities, the department gladly sought donations and gifts when it needed local businesses to help supply some special event. Officers would be sent out to beg for cash or goods to be used at the event, and they were literally "dragging the sack."

ducks: Officers turn in a work-card at the end of the shift detailing their activities. In an analogy for going hunting and bagging some ducks, arrests and tickets are an officer's ducks. Once upon a time, it was said that "Two ducks a day, keeps the sergeant away."

fender lizard: Drive-in burger joints were once the kings of the fast-food business. Houston had a number of these restaurants that offered curb service delivery. Prince's was our most successful drive-in, where car hops delivered food to you in your vehicle. The girls were usually attractive and sometimes, attracted to cops. The designation fender lizard was pretty generic to refer to these young ladies, but was probably used more often to refer to those that were attracted to cops. (There was a Prince's that we often frequented in my beat at Main and Old Spanish Trail; when it closed in the 1980s, we lost another link to Houston history.)

froggy: Sometimes, when a citizen was getting very agitated and ready to fight, an officer would say he was acting froggy. An officer might say, "Mister if you are feeling froggy, then jump!" This was like saying, "Bring it on!"

gin, ginned, ginning: This is when someone is framed for a crime or traffic violation. This is a very rare and unfortunate occurrence. It is, however, an often used false accusation. The term is commonly used by officers. "That drunk woman said she is sober and that we are ginning her."

gray bar hotel, or 4594: Gray bar hotel is a common and appropriate description of the jail. However, cops of my era would be more familiar with the number 4594, the jail's phone extension. We would advise the dispatcher that we were taking a prisoner to 4594. The same system was used whenever we had to stop at another division or police office.

hijacker: Before I joined the department, the only time I had ever heard of this term was in relation to the taking of an airliner by armed men. In Houston, officers use this term to indicate all robbers. It is sometimes shortened to "jacker." The shorter version is common in the community when referring to a robber. Sometimes "jack" is used as a verb, to rob, as in, "Man, he would jack you up!" Carjacking is now the common terminology for a robbery of someone to steal their vehicle.

hinky: Well, I had no idea that this word, which means suspicious or acting strangely, was an honest to goodness word that could be found in the dictionary. It is commonly used in the department, but I would bet it is rarely found elsewhere.

knob knockers: This is a term that has faded away with time and technology. Retired Officer Denny Hair, our former police museum curator, told me that this was a common term in the 1930s. It was used when referring to safe burglars that would steal a safe and take it somewhere else to break into it. They would knock the knob off while attempting to gain entry into the box. Someday soon, special words will probably grow out of the similar snatching of ATM machines.

milking: Well, I guess milking cows is a time-consuming job. Officers who waste a bunch of time on a call, report, or arrest are said to be milking the clock. Basically, it would be stealing time from the department.

misdemeanor rape: Prostitutes, on occasion, falsely accused their dates of rape, simply to force them to pay for the services rendered. This kind of theft of services was sometimes jokingly called burglary of a coin operated machine.

N.O.P.: In a time when Houston was suffering through amazingly high crime rates, a new chief decided that we would begin a system known as "Neighborhood Oriented Policing." We had barely enough officers to handle the calls for service, and suddenly we lost officers to new divisions and offices. There were many good ideas in the system, but the manpower was not available to make it work, so most of us called it "nobody on patrol." This chief was trying to make a splash on the national scene, causing him to travel extensively. His frequent trips earned Chief Lee P. Brown the unflattering nickname, "Out of Town Brown."

old heads: Young officers call older, veteran officers "old heads." This term is often used as just a simple, innocent recognition of seniority. The term is relative to the department's hiring rates.

In the '70s, an old head might have had ten or more years of service. Today, an old head probably has at least twenty years on the department. Sometimes, it is used derisively; after all, these young officers are full of vim, vigor, and vast intelligence. But in the blink of an eye, we all turn into the old heads.

q-man: This is the barbeque cook. For many of us late night creatures it was sometimes difficult to find a meal. A few of the nightclubs would have a cook that would set up in the parking lot to feed the hungry club patrons. While working nightshift patrol in Houston's Sunnyside neighborhood, a few of our officers would visit the q-man who set up outside of the LaChat Club on Scott Street. This barbeque man had an old "beater" car that had the trunk lid removed and a fifty gallon drum pit set down in the trunk area. The pit was only inches above the gas tank, but he sure made a mean rib sandwich.

rolling G: In the city jail, the municipal complaint forms were filed in alphabetically designated slots. Probably the most commonly used complaint form that had to be filled out when booking someone was public intoxication. Just by chance the form was kept in slot G for several generations. A simple drunk suspect was sometimes called a G. However, within our agency's common language, virtually all references to Driving While Intoxicated suspects or complaints are called rolling Gs.

scooter scum: The outlaw bikers we dealt with were the scum of the earth. They were dangerous users of women and drugs. The Bandidos that were active in our area were second only to the west coast-based Hell's Angels as a motorcycle club. Both clubs have engaged in organized criminal activities. There was no shortage of members that were suspected of violent crimes. One Bandido that we occasionally arrested, "Big Jim" Richardson, was suspected of killing, dismembering, and disposing of someone in one of our local bayous. In the old days these bikers were filthy and never cleaned their "colors" (motorcycle club vest). There was even a photo I had seen of an initiation of several prospective members being vomited on while wearing their

On the job, with a Bandido

club vest. They have since cleaned up their appearance and
often appear in public clean and shiny, like the professional mid-
dle-age bikers who mimic the appearance of the outlaw bikers.

screen test: Houston patrol cars in the '70s had a steel grid divider
between the front and rear seats. The screen protected the officers from the prisoner. It is reported that some areas of Houston had way too many stray dogs and that officers occasionally
had to slam on the brakes to avoid them. The poor spitting,
screaming, handcuffed—and unseat-belted—prisoner in the
back might wind up getting a screen test. Years later the vehicles were equipped with aluminum and Plexiglas dividers that
helped to isolate the prisoner. Less spit, fewer stray dogs, and
the installation of rear seatbelts have likely made the screen test
a thing of the past.

shop: Most agencies call their patrol cars just that, patrol cars.
Some former Detroit officers who joined the H.P.D. called

their vehicles "scout cars." Prowl car is a term that is common in several other jurisdictions. In Houston our patrol cars are oddly called "shops," which came about because of the identifying number that is usually on the car's rear window or trunk. It originated as a number that the garage assigned when the vehicle was put in the shop for repairs. Eventually, saying that you were assigned shop number "such and such" was used so much that the cars came to be called shops.

slapper: A slapper, or blackjack, is an offensive striking weapon with a flat surface. They are constructed of heavy leather with a core of lead. For decades they were commonly carried in the belt or back pocket of patrol officers until the department began formal training with night sticks. Night sticks or extra-long heavy flashlights are much better defensive weapons. The first time I met and F.B.I. agent was in 1975 when I was in college, riding along with officers in Monroe, Louisiana. During an arrest, I witnessed an officer use his slapper on a suspect. It left him with a big gash on his head, but it definitely stopped his struggle for freedom. The agent was assigned to investigate the brutality complaint. He asked me if the force used was necessary and I responded, "Something needed to be done to calm him down and stop his violent actions." They work, but they are bloody if you hit someone in the head. But, the same goes for nightsticks and flashlights.

s.o.'ed: This means that an officer has signed on for work. Patrol officers inform the dispatcher by radio or computer that they are on duty.

space cadet: This is similar to the term zipperhead, but usually means that someone was *really* out there, acting extremely weird.

stop and rob: The robbery of convenience stores is a daily occurrence. The Stop and Go chain began in Houston, where it dominated the convenience store market. They also dominated the robbery market; thus, the slang term Stop and Rob, which has become a generic defining reference for all convenience stores. If you want some exciting, life-threatening employment, become a clerk at your local Stop and Rob.

turd: It ain't pretty, but this is the all-time favorite term used in Houston to describe a crook or a very uncooperative person. Crime fighters are society's garbage collectors of the flotsam of humanity.

yellow wheel: Our patrol cars were not equipped with spare tires. If you had a flat, a tire shop truck was dispatched. The spare they supplied would have a wheel that was painted yellow. Yellow wheels were for temporary use until you could take the time to go to the tire shop. I have also seen yellow wheels on other fleet vehicles, and I'm sure no one remembers where the use of these yellow wheeled spares began.

x10: An x10 is an officer's home. The dispatcher would occasionally tell an officer to call or go to his x10. It was not too unusual with our divorce rate to hear an officer being told to call his ex-x10.

zipperhead: When dealing with someone who was acting really stupid, an officer might call him a zipperhead. Perhaps you could unzip his head and take his brain out—and see no difference.

INTERESTING PHRASES

The following five little phrases were not all in common usage, but I thought they were interesting. Several of them are somewhat smart aleck replies we used when dealing with difficult people. Others listed here are descriptive of the situation that was at hand. Perhaps they can give you a better perspective of how our officers saw their world.

"No, the mouse in your pocket!"

This was one of my all-time favorite answers to the endless responses of "Who me?" It sometimes seemed that ninety percent of the suspects we talked with face to face, would repeatedly respond to our questions by saying, "Who me?" On occasion our response would be, "No, the mouse in your pocket!" I have actually had a couple of crooks look down and say, "I ain't got no mouse in my pocket." Well, that elusive mouse was hard to catch. Officer George Islieb was the first officer I heard say this fun response. George was a hard worker and several street thugs had trouble with George's name, so we sometimes heard him described as, "That big Frankenstein-looking mother."

"The rotations of the Earth are about to spin him off."

I first heard George Leitner say this phrase when we worked together in 1978. George has moved on to the field of education, but odds are he picked up the term from someone else. It is a great description of the staggering drunk's effort to fight the forces of nature.

"He was clowning and performing without a license."

It may have faded away by now, but this was a popular phrase during my career. We would sometimes say this when someone did something dumb that brought them to our attention. I remember the crook, Phillip Wayne Franklin, passing my partner and me on Main Street—while smoking a joint! We were driving side by side as he took a deep draw of marijuana smoke, and then he looked over and was shocked to see us watching him. Phillip was definitely clowning and performing without a license. Ole Phillip clowned himself right into the grave, when he tried to run over an officer while driving a stolen car.

"We have two DOAs, one bad and one not so bad!"

Well, I guess the manner of one's death could be worse than another fellow's. But, when we heard this comment about a major accident go out over the radio, we just had to shake our heads.

"You can beat the rap, but not the ride."

Though this is the last phrase I'll offer, it is certainly not the least among them. After listening to a suspect protest that he was innocent of the charge, you might use this saying. In other words, tell it to the judge, maybe you will beat the charge and be found innocent, but you're going to jail anyway.

There you have it friends: the good, the bad, and the ugly unvarnished terminology of my Houston Police Department. Many of these terms are fading away to be replaced as time marches on, but some are so ingrained within the culture that they will remain forever. Police work can make the best of us become cynical and shield ourselves with the armor of black humor. Former Chief of Police Harry Caldwell once called our past, "The bad old days." Indeed, my career began as police work was beginning to transition into a more supervised and controlled profession. But, when I hear these police terms I remember "The good old days." The good old days of our youth was a time when brother backed up brother, when we were thrilled by the danger, and when we thrived on locking away predators.

Houston police badge

Grayson County Courthouse. Completed in 1936 and heralded as an example of New Deal architecture, the Grayson County Courthouse included courtrooms for two Texas District Courts (15th and 59th) as well as county offices and a jail

JURY SELECTION THE OLD-FASHIONED WAY

by Jerry B. Lincecum

~~

Anyone who has reported for jury service and made it to the *voir dire* phase may have wondered how attorneys decide whether to strike or accept potential jurors. With the literal meaning "to speak the truth," the French phrase *voir dire* denotes the preliminary examination the court may make of potential jurors to determine competence or bias. Trial lawyers know that jury selection is an art, and today in publicized or important trials, highly trained consultants in jury selection are hired by opposing counsels. These modern day specialists are trained in social psychology, and they make a careful study of every person on the list of potential jurors. The purpose is to ascertain, as far as possible, how the lives of a potential juror might influence that person's decision in a given case.

However, social psychology as a specific field of knowledge applicable to jury selection has been codified for only a few decades. How did "old school" Texas country lawyers handle jury selection back in the pre-WWII and mid-20th century era? This essay will address that question in two ways: (1) by making a case study of several thousand 3 × 5 cards belonging to a Sherman, Texas, law firm, which contain brief but incisive observations and judgments on the traits, behaviors, and characters of persons summoned for jury panels in Grayson County; and (2) by gleaning some insights from the autobiography of the attorney who used those cards and chose to make them available for research.

It used to be commonplace for trial lawyers to maintain files on potential jurors, but they were considered proprietary and kept secret. In most cases the cards were destroyed when the law office closed. A notable exception to this rule occurred when Neilson Rogers, who practiced law in Sherman for more than sixty years and owned a law office started in 1899, decided to keep his juror cards after his retirement. Eventually, he came to the conclusion that they should be archived and made available for research. Rogers loved history, enjoyed doing research, and liked to share his knowledge through talks to local history organizations and in self-published books. Upon retiring (after practicing law for six decades), he not only wrote a very candid memoir but also indicated a strong desire to share some secrets of his profession, designating the author of this essay as his literary executor. He left behind in manuscript numerous short essays as well as several longer pieces.

The neatly alphabetized card file of juror information notes contains an estimated 10,000 cards, with entries for approximately 8,000 persons who had been called for jury service in the various courts that met in Sherman (and sometimes there are multiple cards for a person who was summoned more than once). In his unpublished memoir Rogers describes the role this card file played in the Webb law office, which he joined in 1938 and later inherited:

> To assist them in assessing potential jurors, Spearman [Webb] and his father [Judge G. P. Webb] had close friends and relatives throughout the county, and in the middle of the week before a jury trial the list of prospective jurors (those sent notices to report for service on a given Monday) would be carefully studied and inquiries made. A card file was kept in the office which compiled the names of all Grayson County jurors who had been summoned previously. Notes were made and regularly updated on almost every person's card, regarding such matters as his profession or place of employment, temperament, religious or political tendencies, and how he had voted in earlier trials. As each new jury panel list was received in the office, cards on the potential jurors already in the file would be pulled, studied,

and updated, while fresh cards were created and annotated for newcomers to the list.

One secretary was given the job of continually updating the juror information cards. Over time she typed the information that had previously been handwritten on old cards, and she consulted city directories and other sources to verify or update addresses, listed occupations, etc. It was also her job to check obituaries and write "dead" on the cards of former jurors who had passed away (their cards were kept in the file, since information on a family might be pertinent to any of its members). It was common practice among trial attorneys to keep this type of information on file. However, the Webbs had more human sources to give assessments of people they knew, and their file was more complete than most. Accordingly, on the Monday morning when he first examined the panel for a new trial, Spearman Webb had considerable information about its members. Armed with this kind of intelligence to help him select plantiff-oriented jurors and avoid anyone who had hung a jury or otherwise caused trouble before, he confidently expected to win the case and almost always did.

When Neilson Rogers began working for the firm in 1938, Spearman Webb was the most sought after and successful trial lawyer on the plaintiff's side of the docket in North Texas. Judge G. P. Webb died in 1943, and with the sudden death of Spearman Webb in 1950, the office, its excellent law library, and the card file passed to Rogers. Judging from dates on the cards, the file continued to be updated well into the 1960s.

This card file provides a mid-20th century record of something trial lawyers have been doing for hundreds of years: drawing on outside information to "read" potential jurors in order to choose the ones they believe will side with their client or at least be neutral. In the 1970s and '80s, experts trained in social science began to be hired as consultants to help attorneys assess the members of the jury pool. This practice was highlighted during the jury-selection phase of the O. J. Simpson trial in 1995, which was televised and drew a large audience. In his novel *Runaway Jury* (1995), popular novelist John Grisham, who was an attorney before he turned to writing, gave emphasis to the extensive use of consultants and technology in selecting juries for high-profile and high-dollar damage suits, and a film version of the book was a box-office success in 2003.

One of the best known of these jury consultants is Jo-Ellan Dimitrius, who gained prominence during the Simpson trial. Dimitrius has co-authored a book with Wendy Patrick Mazzarella entitled *Reading People* (2008). While intended for a broader audience, the book discusses a number of points applicable to jury selection. Without giving away too many secrets, it summarizes a few theoretical points. One key principle is "Know what you are looking for."[1] One way of fulfilling this requirement is: "Prepare a juror profile that lists the traits of jurors who will view your case most favorably."[2] Moreover, "to read people effectively, you must gather enough information about them to establish a consistent pattern. The pattern is what reveals the person."[3] Another note states that it is desirable to get information about potential jurors from outsiders: "You can learn an extraordinary amount from third parties."[4] The card file compiled by the Webb law firm was rooted in this principle.

Spearman Webb primarily represented plaintiffs, and a review of selected cards from the firm's juror files will focus on the one criterion identified by Neilson Rogers as most important when choosing jurors favorable to plaintiffs, namely, their attitudes toward money and wealth. He had learned from the Webbs an important lesson: the Great Depression had resulted in a deep chasm of thought and prejudice between those who were "well off" financially and those who were poor. The following notes from juror cards will clarify and expand on this distinction. The individual jurors discussed have been assigned random numbers to protect their privacy.

On any given card, the basic information on a potential juror begins with name and address taken from the official list of jurors summoned, with corrections or additions made by a secretary after consulting a city directory or similar publication. Information on juror 50-0101, for example, appears on two cards stapled together: the one on top has nothing more than his name and address, plus the note: "Jury Panel, 59th DC [District Court], 10/16/50." That note exemplifies one piece of information almost always given, namely a listing of jury panels or court cases each person took part in. The other card on this juror starts with the name and address, followed by: "jury panel 59th DC 4/4/49." Written in pencil is the following: "Runs X&Y Café [name changed, address given]. Used to be used car dealer & real estate. [handwritten note] ? L-- is afraid of him [i.e., has doubts about his being a good plaintiff's juror]." In general the comments reflect the desire to know as much as possible about a potential juror's occupation(s) and to have judgments about his character from trusted individuals who have knowledge of his behavior patterns, family background, past performance on a jury, and other pertinent data.

The card on juror 62-1136 has this note: "On jury chosen in [named case]; tried Feby 14th 1962; Jury hung Feby 15 in 15th Dist. Ct. N.R. [Neilson Rogers] for pltf; David S. Kidder deft [full name of law firm given]. THIS JUROR FOR PLAINTIFF." That note is typical of the information given when a person actually served on a jury, including "inside" and "improper" information as to how this juror voted. Sometimes the official court record number for the case is included, as well as (in rare instances) the name of anyone who might have "hung" the jury or signed an affidavit about jury misconduct in the case. For example, the card on juror 58-1135 has a lengthy note, which names a case and includes the case number for the 15th [Dist.] Court and states this man served as foreman on the jury that was "dismissed hung 10/25/58. [name given], Denison, hung the jury, all others for pltf."

The card for juror 53-1129 reports that he was on a jury in a case where the verdict was returned 14 October 1953 and he "DID NOT sign affidavit for [name of plaintiff] telling of jury misconduct. Told in jury room of men he knew who had lost arm or leg, and what they were able to do." There are cards for others who served on that jury which indicate they did sign an affidavit for the plaintiff telling of jury misconduct. As one studies these cards, it becomes evident that the Rogers firm was able to obtain a great deal of privileged information about jury deliberation and how jurors voted in a given case.

Now to focus on the issue of attitudes toward wealth. Notes on the juror cards indicate that having "too much money" is sufficient reason to avoid a juror. For example, juror 50-1179 was said to be the son of a deceased physician and one informant's assessment of him says: "? to no: too much money now." Juror 49-1115 is said to be connected with a certain business and "may have too much money to be good juror for us." The note for juror 00-1114 (for a federal court) reads, "I think his sympathies would be toward the other side. He is from a moneyed family. I would hesitate to take him." Besides indicating that juror 00-1175 is a farmer of "about 40–45," the notes by two different informants are: "Think ok" from one and "may have too much money" from another. Juror 49-1116, who was said to own a meat packing company and grocery, was summoned in several jury panels and the comments on his card are: "have [sic] a lot of money," "probably works several colored people," "owned [name of a boat] that burned on [Lake] Texoma," and "NO." Juror 49-1120 had said to have retired as owner of a business and the comments included the following: "TOO MUCH MONEY. Inclined to look down on laboring man" and (underscored) "DON'T TAKE." Even more damning was this comment on juror 00-1171: "owns [name given] Bakery and is the type of man who made his money under the new deal [sic] and turned Republican; would not have him under any circumstances."

At the opposite end of the spectrum, perhaps, are those who believe in "share the wealth," indicated as characteristics of jurors 52-1186 and 52-1111. Juror 49-1142, rated as "think OK" is said to be "for underdog," whereas 50-1187 is seen as "for big money." More common are persons considered "close with money," such as 50-1134 (a farmer who owns his land, about 65–70 years old). Juror 49-1167 (another farmer) was in this tightwad category, but he was also seen by another commentator as "argumentative," without a yes or no recommendation given. The owner of a grocery store in Sherman (#50-1130, age 65–70) was said to be "very close with money, otherwise fair minded" and given a "think OK"—however, a later note indicated he was deceased. A retired Austin College bookkeeper (#51-1184, age 60–65) was described as "very religious, fair-minded, close on money" and given two "no" votes. Another farmer (#50-1124, about 70) received these notes: "OK, believe he would be fair and honest; set in his ways; old bachelor; made money hard way—tight; has about $70,000." On the other hand, juror 49-1139 was given a "?" because he "might not want to give much damages [sic]." A Katy (MKT railroad) fireman (#00-1172) was seen as "very penurious; loyal member and advocate of unions; good juror"; nevertheless, he was scratched on a case in which the Rogers firm represented the plaintiff.

Spearman Webb had another advantage when it came to selecting jurors. A curious circumstance made the Hall Sandwich Shop in Sherman play an important role in the trial of civil cases in the local state courts, and Webb knew how to use it as an asset. Located in downtown Sherman on the north side of the square, directly across the street from the main entrance to the county courthouse, this modest restaurant was the last surviving remnant of Sherman's formerly bustling saloon trade. (Before the sale of whiskey was banned at the turn of the century, there were eleven saloons on Travis Street.) In 1938, it sold beer as well as its famous sandwich and also housed a sizable domino parlor. The front portion of the Hall Sandwich Shop contained a long bar with a brass rail extending its full length, with some eight or ten tables, each with four chairs and a set of dominoes. This very popular place was filled with white men most of the time.

An unusual jury selection procedure that existed when Rogers came to Sherman in 1938 and continued well into the 1940s made the Hall Sandwich Shop very important to trial lawyers. Near the middle of the week before trial settings in the state courts, notices were mailed to enough male citizens, selected from a list of registered voters, to fill a panel from which a jury could be selected. From experience the district judges knew that at least thirty prospective jurors would be needed to start the selection process, in order to wind up with twelve jurors.

Over the weekend before the Monday trial date, the judges, being elected to their office by popular vote, usually were rather lenient in granting excuses to prospective jurors who contacted them with a request to be excused. Thus, on Monday morning there often would not be enough prospective jurors for the court to proceed. A sheriff's deputy would be sent around the square to "pick up" enough prospective jurors to bring the panel up to the minimum number. Since the sheriff was also an elected official, his deputy would be hesitant to force a man to leave work against his will. Accordingly, the deputy usually entered the Hall Sandwich Shop, where a considerable number of white men, some of whom were unemployed, would be congregated; in fact, some of these men knew of this practice and were hoping to be "picked up" and selected for a jury, where they could receive payment of $1.00 a day and also enjoy the drama of a trial.

In 1938, the courthouse was not only a justice center but also a place of entertainment, with trials being thought of as similar to soap operas. Radios were readily available then, but it would be more than a decade before television shows were regular entertainment in Sherman. Court trials were well attended by a certain segment of the public, and the Hall Sandwich Shop was the most popular place for white men to eat during the noon recess. Often the entire jury would go there for lunch. All trial lawyers followed them, making sure that no improper evidence was discussed, nor any other objectionable occurrence might sway them. Moreover, lawyers in trial continued the practice of lunching there for many years, even after the practice of "picking up" jurors was discontinued. In this fashion the sandwich shop became a platform or stage for lawyers to use.

Spearman Webb regularly visited the Hall Sandwich Shop. He knew all its regulars, often bought a round of beer for all, and was welcomed and respected by its employees and customers. The shop was also an important information center. Any interesting event occurring in the county was sure to be discussed there. If a jury was hung, there might be a man there who claimed to know which juror was causing the problem or what special issue was the sticking point. This improper information would sometimes prove to be correct and would then enter the files of local law offices. Jurors who hung juries were to be avoided in future selections, especially if they made such statements as "I will stay here for a year before I will vote in favor of defendant X." Rogers observed that any "pick up" jurors from the sandwich shop were likely to be plaintiff-friendly and also partisans of Spearman Webb.

Jury panels for federal court cases were chosen in an entirely different way, and that accounted for a troubling phenomenon which Rogers observed and puzzled over. How could the same set of contested facts be presented to two different juries, who would render opposite verdicts? In 1938, this phenomenon was regularly occurring in Sherman. There were two district court jurisdictions, state and federal. The juries selected for trial in the state district courts were generally plaintiff-oriented, while in the federal district court the juries were usually defendant-oriented. When selecting a court to file a case in, local lawyers representing a plaintiff would try to avoid the federal jurisdiction. At the same time, lawyers representing defendants would make every effort to remove their cases to the federal courts because of the known bias.

Eventually, Spearman Webb gave Rogers an insight that accounted for this difference in a rational manner. There were good reasons why the state court jurors were biased in favor of the plaintiff (usually thought of as the "common man" over against the business interests or the wealthy). In the first place, many prospective jurors were excused by the state court judges and those "picked up" to replace them were often unemployed. Viewing the other side of the coin, lawyers representing plaintiffs believed that federal court juries, selected from a list created by a commission, were prejudiced against them, in favor of defendants. The paradox was that both state court and federal court juries believed themselves free of all prejudices.

The key to success as a plaintiff's attorney has always been knowing as much as possible about the biases of potential jurors and insuring that you seat as many as possible on the jury who are likely to favor your client. In Grayson County during the 1930s and '40s, the state district courts were your best venue, and you needed an extensive network of friends and other informants to provide background information on potential jurors.

To end with a personal jury experience, I became a permanent resident of Grayson County in 1967, upon joining the faculty of Austin College. When I answered my first jury summons three years later, a senior colleague (who had also been summoned) assured me that college faculty were never seated on juries in Grayson County. Thus, I was surprised not only to be placed on a jury but also, when deliberations began after a week of testimony, to be chosen as foreman. Despite being summoned at least a dozen times in the four decades since, never again did I get past the *voir dire* phase. Numerous faculty colleagues have served, so maybe I was written up in some attorneys' files as "juror non grata." However, there is no card for me in the files of the Rogers firm. Given the amount of information about individuals that can be gleaned from the Internet these days, keeping a card file of this type is unnecessary. We are fortunate that Neilson Rogers chose to save his juror files and make them available for study.

Endnotes

1. Jo-Ellan Dimitrius, Wendy Patrick Mazzarella. *Reading People*. Rev. Ed. New York: Random House, 2008. 4.
2. Dimitrius and Mazzarella. 11.
3. Dimitrius and Mazzarella. 25.
4. Dimitrius and Mazzarella. 53.

Sources Consulted

John Grisham. *Runaway Jury*. New York: Doubleday, 1995.
Neilson Rogers. *Country Lawyer*. Unpublished memoir.

A SAMPLING
OF TEXAS
CULTURES:

From Bikers to Knanaya Catholics to Tejana Culture

Prime riding

THE TEXAS BIKER SUB-CULTURE AND THE RIDE OF MY LIFE

by Veronica Pozo

The idea for this paper was inspired by my then-fiancé's newfound interest in joining a bike club in 2012. My initial response was surprise and confusion. Who was this man whom I have been dating for the past four years? In my opinion, he was nothing like the stereotypical bike club member. After all, a bike club was just another name for a gang filled with drug dealers, pimps, and murderers. Right? My future husband definitely does not fall under any of those categories, but I have to admit that he has always had a passion for motorcycles. That man is like a little boy in a candy shop the minute he steps foot into a Cyclegear, and the more miles he puts on his bike, the closer he is to solving his problems. He once said to me, "Whenever I ride, I leave all my stresses and worries of life behind me." I did not understand what exactly he was talking about until he took me for a ride for the first time. After that first experience, I had to agree with him. The adrenaline rush is hard to express in words, but I get the same feeling every time I hear the sound of a motor. Therefore, my increasing passion for riding, along with my intimidations and suspicions of bike clubs, motivated me to do some research of my own. After spending some time with the BikerBoyz-BikerBabez, I realized that my initial thoughts concerning the biker community could not have been more wrong.

The BikerBoyz-BikerBabez motorcycle club (BBMC) was founded in Houston in August 2007. Charlie Wells II, Maricela Pina, and Craig Brown are credited as the founders. Today, the club consists of thirty-seven members. According to the Bikerboyz-Bikerbabez website, the founders "had a vision to bring together bikers of all nationalities and sexes, and created a foundation of TRUE riders."[1] Therefore, the club's diversity sets BikerBoyz apart from the rest. I want to note that throughout this paper I will refer to the group as "the BikerBoyz" for short, but I am still referring to a coed group.

I noticed the diversity the first time that I met the club, which was on a Sunday in April. My fiancé and I were invited to meet with them at Joe's Crab Shack to learn about the club and discuss his possible membership. As we arrived at the restaurant I saw African Americans, Caucasians, Hispanics, and Asians all sitting at a table located in the outdoor patio. Both men and women were wearing black vests with the initials "BB" in yellow. The Biker-Boyz' president introduced himself as "Kaoz" and introduced us to the other members by their nicknames also. I was shocked when I noticed children at the table sitting on their parents' laps. Isy, the club's secretary, must have seen the surprise on my face because she then explained to me that the club members bring their families to their monthly meetings. After observing how family-oriented the BikerBoyz were, I let my guard down and just let myself enjoy their company. I have to admit that I had a good time.

BikerBoyz claim "to be a national bond to all people who have the LOVE of owning or riding a motorcycle."[2] At a bike show, I witnessed a strong bond between members such as Zero and Six-0, where the love of bikes transformed two enemies into close friends. Before they owned bikes, Zero and Six-0 admitted they actually hated each other, but they soon discovered they were more alike than they realized. They now share the same passion for riding, which was able to outweigh their differences.

On the one hand, my first impression of Zero was that he was a smart, intelligent, young man. After a few minutes into an interview, I found this to be fact. He is a good student who is great with technology, and he currently works for a Yamaha dealership. Before being introduced to a bike, Zero was a racecar driver, so he has always had a need for speed. Zero is known for his daring stunts. He is also called the "Corner Carver" because he specializes in turning and drifting on his bike. He explained to me how he learned to perfect quick turns such as the "Jay Turn" and the "Hook Slide." BikerBoyz call his 2002 Suzuki GSXR 1000 "The Revolver."

Although Zero has developed impressive control over his bike, he was once involved in an accident that was far beyond his control. "It was my first real experience on a bike," he admitted. He was on his way to a local pool party, feeling good, and ready to show off his new ride. Unfortunately, he was only about a block from his house when a car ran a stop sign and crashed into him. The car was traveling about sixty miles per hour, so it sent him flying off his bike until his helmet smashed onto the curb. Zero landed on his arm and skidded forty feet down the concrete. As he lay there unconscious, the car did not even stop to see if he were alive. In fact, twenty minutes passed before a neighbor spotted him and called for an ambulance. During the interview, I witnessed the road burn scars throughout his body, along with the scars from his reconstructive hand surgery. The first question that came to my mind was, "Did you ever consider giving up riding after your accident?" His response to me was: "My arm was still healing when I started riding again." Today, Zero's bike has 52,000 miles on it, the most out of any other bike in the club. Although his first real experience on a motorcycle almost cost him his life, he claims, "Motorcycles have shown me a *new* meaning to life."[3]

On the other hand, Six-0 seemed like a laid back, nice guy. He says his nickname was given to him back in high school. His classmates called him Six-0 because his football jersey number was 60, and he has been six feet tall since he can remember. Six-0 currently works as a manager at Walmart and describes himself as "just your average Joe." In his spare time, he just likes to hang out with the guys. BikerBoyz events such as long runs (road trips) to Austin and Texas relays give him an escape from the ordinary workday. Six-0 described himself at these events as being in "Hooligan mode." In other words, "Hooligan mode" is a time where he can be out of character and just have fun. During an interview, he shared one of his favorite pastimes since becoming a member about a year ago. "We were at the #1 Stunna party in Houston," he recalled. He explained that the #1 Stunna party is a huge hotel party that invites bike club members in the Houston area. He then laughed as he said, "About fifty people tried to fit into one elevator. Then the elevator broke down and we were stuck there for a good twenty minutes before they got it working again."

As the interview progressed, I soon learned that Six-0 has lived through an experience similar to Zero's. As he was pulling up to a stop light, Six-0 claimed, "It was raining, and a hoopty [an old, beat-up car] hit me from behind!" Unfortunately, Six-0's accident was just another case of a hit and run. I could not help but ask, "Wasn't there anything you could do about it?" His response was: "Yeah . . . I got up . . . went home and took a shower . . . then went to work."[4] Six-0's scars on his elbows, forearms, and legs, constantly remind him to stay aware of his surroundings, but they will never stop him from riding.

Testimonies such as those of Zero and Six-0 are just living proof of the passion that BikerBoyz share for riding. After their individual experiences, they both confessed that they find safety in numbers. For this reason, one of the BikerBoyz' main priorities is to look out for one another on the road. "Slow buggie," which means "Take it easy on the highway," is a term that every member is familiar with. Therefore, one of the top qualities they look for in a prospect is a safe and experienced rider.

In April of 2012, my fiancé, a.k.a. "Prime," was the newest prospect of the BikerBoyz. Whether he is delivering a pipe-load on his eighteen wheeler Freightliner, or riding around town on his Kawasaki Ninja, he has always enjoyed the open road. His nickname, Prime, is inspired from his favorite TV show as a child. Long before *Transformers* came out on the big screen, he watched characters such as Optimus Prime every afternoon in his living room. My fiancé is transformed from Mauricio Pozo to Prime every time he hops on his motorcycle. He even made an Optimus Prime helmet that turns heads everywhere we go, especially at the lights. He loves to see the smiles on little kids' faces when they roll down their window to wave at him. He had been looking for some people to ride with, but none of his friends or coworkers knew how to ride a motorcycle. After all, going from eighteen wheels down to two is a big transition. One day, he met a member of the BikerBoyz in a mall parking lot. After spending about an hour with him talking about motorcycles, he decided to check them out. So, the prospect period began.

According to the current club president, although the club does not discriminate against anyone, there are several steps involved before someone can become a fully vested member. The entire process can take anywhere from three months to a year, depending on how serious and committed someone is about joining. The minimum requirements consist of the payment of fees, along with participation in the club's activities. A total of two hundred dollars will cover all basic costs, including the application fee, the vest, and the patches. In addition, all members are expected to pay their "monthly dues," which are forty dollars each month to cover extras such as T-shirts and upcoming events. Even if all fees are paid, BikerBoyz will not consider prospects until after they have attended at least two monthly meetings and participated in at least three events.

Throughout the Biker community, becoming a vested member of a club is considered a great honor. BikerBoyz take their full membership very seriously. For example, BikerBoyz consider it an offense if a member lets anyone else even try on his or her vest. In order to make this message clear, Kaoz picked his son up into his arms and said, "This is my baby. I love him to death. I would do anything in the world for him, but I would never let him wear my vest."[5] Also, BikerBoyz do not consider themselves as a threat to society, but rather as citizens who contribute to their society. For example, members hold charity events such as dinners for the homeless. If the BikerBoyz find out that one of their members broke the law while wearing a BikerBoyz vest, serious repercussions will follow. On the contrary, outlaw biker gangs such as the Banditos have given biker clubs like the BikerBoyz a bad name.

The Banditos were founded in Texas by Marine veteran Donald Chambers in 1966. The club started with a small group of stock workers in the fishing village of San Leon. When the war ended, veterans were attracted to the "brotherhood" that the Banditos offered them. Young men were also attracted to the respect that came along with being a Bandito. Membership numbers grew in at an impressive rate. Within just a few years, new chapters were established throughout the state of Texas. For example, "in San Antonio, Banditos are like tortillas and tacos; they're part of the landscape."[6] Today, the banditos are one of the largest outlaw motorcycle clubs in the world.

Texas Banditos take pride in their organized crime and ruthless behavior. In fact, members who have committed crimes such as murder earn patches on their vests that read "Expect No Mercy." According to the American Biker Association, 99% of motorcyclists are law-abiding citizens. They have distinguished the other 1% as "One Per-centers" or "antisocial barbarians who'd be scum riding horse or surfboards too."[7] Outlaw biker gangs like the Banditos have taken the AMA's insult and transformed it into a One-Percenter Creed. In their creed, they make it clear that "A 1%er is the 1% of 100 of us who have given up on society and the politician's one-way law."[8] Although outlaw gangs make up such a small percent of the entire biker community, their rebellious lifestyle receives the most attention and publicity, especially from law enforcement. Since their founding, members have been charged with "murder, assault, kidnapping, prostitution, money laundering, weapons trafficking, etc. . . ."[9] According to FBI agent Alex Caine, "These men are drawn by the promise of power, wealth, and camaraderie and are willing to get themselves in a whole world of trouble just to feel accepted."[10]

In the Bandito family, brotherhood is more important than life itself. Journalist Julian Sher, who has spent years covering motorcycle gangs, knows that if someone cuts one, they all bleed. She reports that "the blood has never stopped flowing."[11] In other words, if anyone messes with *one* Bandito, they mess with *all* of them, and they better be ready to face the consequences. By now, everyone should know what happens to a "citizen" who disrespects a Bandito. The founder of the gang set the prime example. Chambers' daughter Donna described him as a "hell-raiser." She once said, "Daddy was famous for the way he could throw a punch. And if that didn't work, he'd pull out his knife and start swinging that around too."[12] Chambers was eventually sentenced to two consecutive life terms in prison in 1972 for the murder of two drug dealers. After a drug deal went bad, Chambers and two other Bandito members forced the dealers to dig their own graves. They then shot them and burned their bodies.[13]

Richard Merla, a.k.a. Scarface, was another Bandito who earned the "Expect No Mercy" patch. Merla is currently serving forty years behind bars because he murdered a friend who, he claimed, "disrespected" him in front of another brother. His story can be heard on an episode of *Gangland*. Catholic parents raised Richard, but he always considered himself the "black sheep of the family."[14] As a kid, he idolized outlaw gangs such as the Banditos. One of the Bandito mottos is "We are the people our parents warned us about."[15] Though most people he knew feared the Banditos, Merla dreamed of becoming one of them since the first time he saw them in his hometown. He finally became a member in 1977. At last, the "black sheep" found a family that he fit into. Although no longer a Bandito today, Merla claims he does not regret murdering boxing champion Robert Quiroga at all. He admitted, "I don't have no remorse. I don't feel sorry for him and his family. I don't and I mean that."[16]

Reading about specific murder cases led me to wonder, "How do Banditos deal with the death of one of their own members?" According to Judd McIlvain, "A Bandito will never identify a dead member of their gang."[17] Because Banditos refuse to enter the morgue, the Harris County Coroner's office asked Judd to come and identify the bodies several times. Once a body is identified as a

Bandito, unless the cause of death was a suicide, the members will hold a Bandito funeral for their beloved brother.

More than four hundred bikes, coming from "as far northwest as Washington and as far southeast as Alabama," came to San Antonio to pay their last respects to Luis Bonilla, a.k.a. Bandito Chuco. An early member, Chuco devoted the majority of his life to the gang up until liver cancer claimed him at sixty-five. According to an issue of *Texas Monthly*, his casket was "surrounded by bouquets of flowers, along with photos of him in his younger days standing beside his motorcycle or next to topless biker chicks."[18] Bandito Chuco was buried in his "favorite black T-shirt, black jeans, and his Banditos Vest."[19] The newest members and retired members alike were present at the funeral. With the exception of Merla, Banditos are brothers until the day they die, but the transition from a "citizen" to a brother of the gang is only achieved by a certain few.

First of all, unlike the Bikerboyz-Bikerbabez, women can never become a vested member of the Banditos. Women are not only banned from membership, they are considered as "property." Banditos don't even refer to women by their names, but rather as "Old Ladies." Although they are allowed to ride behind their Bandito, they will never own a bike of their own, or even drive one if the Banditos can help it. Most of these women become "Old Ladies" at a young age—if not in their late teens, then in their early twenties. Whenever a Bandito grows bored with one "Old Lady," he can trade her in for another. Believe it or not, the trading of "Old Ladies" is a common practice among Banditos. Members feel as if they can treat the women however they please. Some women are so caught up in the Bandito lifestyle that they do not even question or protest. For example, McIlvain once witnessed a Banditos member leading his "Old Lady" around on a leash. The woman was proudly wearing a spiked collar around her neck, while her Bandito firmly held the dog chain.[20] The Banditos force their "Old Ladies" to do anything, from selling drugs to selling their bodies for the gang.

Prospects are also used to do the "dirty work" of the Banditos, such as standing watch or fetching beers, but prospect status is still considered a privilege. Undercover FBI agent Alex Caine was brave enough to infiltrate the gang. Even Caine soon became enticed by his possible membership into the club. Surprisingly, Caine said, "I discovered, I had just as much a bond with most of the Banditos as I did with the cops. More, in fact, if you took into account my delinquent youth."[21]

In order for a prospect to become a fully vested member, the entire club must agree. Once the group has voted someone in, Banditos' initiation rites follow. Skip Hollandsworth reported on the procedure in an issue of the *Texas Monthly*. Before a new member could wear his vest for the first time, the chapter first "urinated, vomited, and defecated on it"; then the new recruit was expected to "put the vest back on and dry it out by riding his motorcycle."[22] As humiliating as that must have been, the new recruit no longer rode as a citizen; his Banditos patches, with their gold and yellow colors, distinguished him as a brother. Referring back to the Biker-Boyz, I asked Kaoz what he personally thought of the Banditos and if he had ever considered joining their club. His response to me was short, but powerful. He simply said, "Clubs like the Banditos will kill you. We stay away from them at all costs."[23]

Prior to my research, I was terrified of motorcycle clubs in general because of the things I heard about the Banditos as a girl growing up in Texas. I did not know clubs such as the BikerBoyz even existed. After meeting new people such as Kaoz, Zero, and Six-0, my viewpoint towards the biker community has changed completely. My attitude towards the biker subculture has gone from fear and intimidation, to acceptance and admiration. I've realized first-hand that the only thing bike clubs such as the Biker-Boyz have in common with gangs like the Banditos is a love for the open road, and a passion for riding motorcycles.

Prime and I were married on June 9, 2012. I now support my *husband's* decision to join a bike club 99%. (I'll leave the other 1%

to the Banditos.) Riding has become just as important to me as it is to him. I didn't realize this until we had to put the bike in the shop for some maintenance work. I could not help but miss the freedom that comes along with riding. I anticipated the opportunity to leave my worries in the wind again. What started out as simply a research paper, ended up becoming a part of my life. I now consider myself part of the biker community, and nothing else in the world matters when I let my hair down, put my helmet on, and wrap my arms around my "BikerBoy."

ENDNOTES

1. "Bikerboyz-Bikerbabez." *Bikerboyz-Bikerbabez*. Web. 26 Apr. 2012. <http://www.bikerboyz-bikerbabez-mc.com/>.
2. Ibid.
3. Bill Smith. Personal interview. 22 April 2012.
4. Kevin Ball. Personal interview. 22 April 2012.
5. Kirth Phillip. Personal interview. 22 April 2012.
6. "Bandido Army." *Gangland*. History Channel. n.d. Web. 20 Apr. 2012.
7. Thomas Barker. *Biker Gangs and Organized Crime*. Newark: Lexis Nexis, 2007. Print.
8. Alex Caine. *Fat Mexican*. Toronto: Vintage Canada, 2010. Print. 20–22.
9. Cliff Roberson. "Outlaw Motorcycle Gangs." *Police Field Operations*. By Michael Birzer. Pearson Education, 2008. 439–40. Print. 439.
10. Caine. 10.
11. Skip Hollandsworth. "The Gangs All Here." *Texas Monthly* [San Antonio] Apr. 2007: 126+. Print. 132.
12. Hollandsworth. 134.
13. Hollandsworth. 136, 226.
14. "Bandido Army."
15. Caine. 12.
16. "Texas Confidential Online." *Field Report: Bandidos MC*. Web. 26 Apr. 2012. <http://texas-confidential.blogspot.com>.
17. Judd McIlvain. "Riding with the Bandito Motorcycle Gang." *TroubleShooter*. Web. 26 Apr.2012. <http://troubleshooterjudd.com/index.php?option=com_content>. 3.

18. Skip Hollandsworth. "The Gangs All Here." *Texas Monthly* [San Antonio] Apr. 2007: 126+. Print. 131.
19. Ibid.
20. Judd McIlvain. "The Bandito Motorcycle Gang and the Women Who Love Them." *TroubleShooter*. Web. 26 Apr. 2012. <http://trou bleshooterjudd.com/index.php?option=com_content>. 1.
21. Caine. 84.
22. Hollandsworth. 136.
23. Kirth Phillip.

Jenson Erapuram

TEXAN KNANAYA CATHOLICS AND THEIR WEDDING CUSTOMS

by Jenson Erapuram

~ ~

"You are Knanaya? What is that?" I have heard these questions many times in my life—from Texans, other Americans, and a great number of Indians, too. Surprisingly, I have been asked this question mostly from people I met during my stay in Kerala, a state in India which happens to be home to the largest number of Knanaya Catholics and Jacobites in the world. Since most people are unfamiliar with the terms "Knanaya" or "Southist," it is not a surprise that most people have not heard of the history or customs of the Knanites. The history of the Knanites is vague, but it is one that begins more than a millennium ago. The Knanites, throughout their migration from Babylon to India to other parts of the world including Texas, have carried their customs with them—some customs having undergone modifications through the ages, of which the most important are observed at one important milestone in a Knanite's life; it is a milestone which may be considered important in the lives of many people all over the world across all different cultures: marriage.

All the Knanaya truly have as hints to their history are old folk songs and stories which have been passed down from generation to generation. According to a rough translation of these songs, the Knanites are the descendants of seventy-two families of seven clans, who migrated to Kerala from Mesopotamia in 345 AD under the leadership of Thomas Kinayi and Bishop Uraha Mar Yausef. They landed in a town called Kodungalloor, and the king, Ceraman Perumal, welcomed them and granted them certain privileges.[1] According to stories, Knanites inhabited the southern part of Kodungalloor, and thus, came to be called the "Southists." This story is the best known today, but it lacks solid sources. Hence, many theories have been put forward about the migration and many dates have been associated with it. Considering Mesopotamian and Indian contexts, Wilhelm Germann credits the

traditional date, 345 AD, as being the date of migration.[2] However, other historians like Diogo de Cuoto have associated dates as
late as 811 AD with the Southists' migration.[3]

The precise ethnicity of the Knanites is uncertain, though terms
like "Mesopotamian," "Babylonian," "Jewish," "Syrian," "Persian,"
and "Chaldean" are often associated with them. The term "Armen-
ian" was used by early Portuguese historians, but this seems to have
come out of confusion with the term "Arameans," Aramaic having
been a language of the Knanites.[4] There is confusion regarding the
events leading to the migration. It is said that the Catholicos of the
East in Seleucia-Ctesiphon (the head of the church in Mesopotamia
in the fourth century) came to know of the plight of the Indian
church (which had been established by St. Thomas). It had been lan-
guishing without ecclesial ministers. As directed by the Catholicos,
Thomas Kinayi, who knew much about India, organized an immigration of seventy-two Christian families accompanied by a Bishop
Uraha Mar Yausef, four priests, and a few deacons.[5] According to legends, the families were from Jerusalem, Baghdad, and Nineveh.[6]
However, Jacob Kollaparambil hypothesizes that the seventy-two
families were actually from Uruk, a city which had been engulfed by a
surrounding swamp and consequently deserted in the fourth century,
and that Bishop Uraha Mar Yausef was their Bishop.[7]

Thomas Kinayi's place of origin also is truly unknown. He is
referred to by many names, including "Thomas of Cana." Hence, it is
often mistaken that he is from Biblical Cana.[8] Jacob Kollaparambil
postulates that he was actually from a town near Seleucia-Ctesiphon
called Kynai in early times.[9] The reason behind the Knanaya vow of
endogamy seems to have been the influence of the teachings of the
prophet Ezra in Babylonia. Through the works of Baba Batra and
Quiddishin, Louis Ginzberg observes that the prophet Ezra cherished the hope of preserving the purity of the Jewish race and
inveighed against marriages between Jews and natives.[10]

The Knanaya community integrated well with Indian society.
After the destruction of Kodungalloor, they settled across Kerala
and adopted different trades.[11] They slowly adopted the language
of Kerala, Malayalam, and slowly integrated Indian elements into

their own customs. After the Coonen Cross Revolt of 1653, along with other Christians in Kerala, the Knanaya split into two separate groups: the Knanaya Catholics who pledged allegiance to the Roman Catholic Church, and the Knanaya Jacobites who pledged allegiance to the West Syrian Church in Antioch.[12] The Knanaya Catholics attended the same churches as the other Catholics and came under the same dioceses, until they were given a separate diocese, the diocese of Kottayam, by Pope Pius X in 1911, because of hostilities that arose between the Knanaya Catholics and the others.[13] The diocese was elevated to an archdiocese in 2005.[14]

Contrary to the mass immigration to India in the fourth century, Knanaya Catholic migration to Texas has happened steadily from the 1980s onwards. Unlike the religious reasons behind the immigration to India, the migration to Texas has had more to do with opportunity and favorable living conditions. The migration started when skilled workers, mainly nurses, were needed all over the U.S., including Texas. Around fifty Knanaya Catholic families were known to have settled in Houston during the late 1980s; more than 330 families now live in Houston.[15] Around 110 families currently live in Dallas-Fort Worth,[16] while around thirty families live in San Antonio.[17] As the Knanaya population in each place grew, associations were formed. Missions were established to meet the spiritual needs of the communities. The Houston and Dallas Associations have their own community centers, where, along with regular Mass and catechism classes, seasonal activities are conducted under the leadership of the executive boards of the respective associations. Because of the small size of the San Antonio community, Mass is conducted only once a month there.[18] The Houston Knanaya Catholic Mission originally came under the Diocese of Galveston-Houston, but now all Knanaya Catholic Missions in Texas come under the St. Thomas Syro-Malabar Diocese of Chicago.[19]

The Knanaya Catholics have quite a few unique traditions. Some customs have stood the test of time, sometimes undergoing slight modifications. Others have disappeared. A non-marital custom not seen in Texas is the smearing of a mixture of gold, honey, acorus and the like on the tongue of a newborn child by the child's grandmother, so that the child may have "color of gold," "a sweet tongue," "good intelligence," and so on. It is still found among the "Namboothiries," a certain caste of Hindus.[20] "Margamkali," a traditional folk dance of the Knanites, initially was a male dance, but it is associated with females nowadays. "Margamkali" is not seen in Texas, as most do not know how to perform it.

A custom which has become rare because of the unpredictable nature of death is the blessing given by Knanaya parents on their deathbed. When an old Knanaya parent feels that his time has come, he puts his right hand on each of the children and says, "God gave His blessing to Abraham, Abraham gave that blessing to Isaac, Isaac gave that blessing to Jacob, Jacob gave that blessing to my fore-fathers, My fore-fathers gave that blessing to my parents, And my parents gave that blessing to me. Now, dear son (daughter), I give that blessing to you."[21] There is also a custom of the family members of a deceased Knanite standing in a row in church while the funeral guests embrace them.[22] This is not seen in Texas. If a church is nearby, there may be a commemoration mass after the funeral. However, it is not uncommon for guests who are close relatives of the deceased to embrace bereaved family members after the funeral.

Though the wedding customs of the Knanaya have had additions over the years, especially since immigration to places like Texas, the basics have stayed the same. The way of observance of the customs usually depends on the decisions of the couple to be married, their families, and the finances involved.[23] There are several stages in a traditional Knanaya wedding. These include "pennu-kaanal," "orapeer," "othu-kalyanam," "antham-charth," "mailanjee-idal" and "kettu-kalyanam."

The first stage of a Knanaya wedding is the "pennu-kaanal," or seeing the girl. At the "pennu-kaanal," the prospective groom and his family visit the prospective bride's house, see the bride, and meet her parents. Tea is served by the prospective bride. Afterwards, the prospective bride and groom are given a chance to interact. This tradition is not exclusive to Knanites; it is seen in all the cultures of Kerala in which arranged marriage is the norm. In a truly arranged marriage, the "pennu-kaanal" is merely an evaluation of potential brides and grooms. It does not guarantee the marriage will take place. In olden times, the "pennu-kaanal" did not involve the groom. The groom's father and other male elders would see the girl and decide whether to go on to the next step.[24] Though arranged marriages still take place in Texas sometimes, they are rare because love has become a factor. When love is involved, the "pennu-kaanal" is a meeting between the families of the prospective bride and groom, and if the families already know each other, it is done for namesake.

In an arranged marriage, following the "pennu-kaanal," there is a short period of inquiry. In this period, the prospective bride's family inquires about the prospective groom's family and vice-versa. Factors taken into consideration include religious orthodoxy, family prestige, wealth, community standing, and any rumor of disease.[25] This practice stems from the notion that marriage is an alliance between two families; hence, each party must find the other party suitable. This is usually skipped in a love marriage. The next major stage is the "orapeer," or engagement. This involves the closest family members on both sides. The bride's family visits the groom's house and decides when the betrothal and marriage should take place. It involves a small banquet. Though closest possible dates are usually chosen, there can also be long periods between betrothal and marriage. This is mainly done in arranged marriages so that the bride and groom get a chance to mingle and develop a relationship before the marriage. These are referred to as "arranged-love marriages." In love marriages, the dates are decided purely based on convenience.

The "othu-kalyanam," or betrothal, is the first church-related step towards marriage. It is held at the bride's parish. During the ceremony, the priest asks both the bride and groom if they consent to marry each other. They verbally consent and shake hands before the altar as a symbol of their agreement. The priest then calls forth one paternal uncle from each side as a witness. The paternal uncles hold each other's right hand and accept the responsibility of making sure the wedding takes place. This practice exists only among Knanites and expresses the concept that the new relation is not only a relation between two people, but between two families. (Vellian and Vembeni qtd. in Mukalel para. no. 93)[26] After the ceremony, there is a banquet. In India, the banquets are held either in a pavilion erected at the bride's house, or in a ballroom, like here in Texas. Before entering the ballroom or pavillion, the bride's maternal uncle pours water on the groom's maternal uncle's hands as a symbol of hospitality. After the banquet, the groom's and bride's closest family members visit the bride's house. After a small prayer, the bride's paternal uncle presents money to the groom's paternal uncle to help lighten the financial burden on the groom's family involved with conducting the wedding.

The next major step is the groom's "antham-charth" and the bride's "mailanjee-idal." In Texas, these are held in separate ball-rooms, but sometimes they are held at the groom's and bride's houses the night before the wedding. At the groom's house or ballroom, the groom's relatives assemble. This "antham-charth" is done to "cleanse" the groom and "make him handsome." In olden days, this was done in connection with the groom's first shave (Vel-lian and Vembeni qtd. in Mukalel para. no. 98; Swiderski 25).[27] The groom's sisters prepare a platform for the groom to sit on, and one of them places an oil lamp nearby. The groom's brother-in-law seats him on the platform. The ceremony starts with a prayer. After the prayer, a folk song wishing God's protection over the new couple is sung by the guests. After the folk song, someone dressed as a barber approaches the groom, and after asking permission three times, he shaves the groom. Nowadays, the "barber" only pretends to run a shaving knife on the groom's face. Subsequently, the groom is escorted by his brother-in-law into the house to take a bath and change into white clothes.

At the bride's house, a similar ceremony takes place. The bride is escorted to a platform by her elder sister and seated. With folk songs in the background, the bride's paternal grandmother puts henna on the bride's hands and feet. When henna is allowed to dry, it leaves a coloration which remains for a couple of days. When put on the hands and feet in intricate patterns, it leaves beautiful patterns on the skin. The intricate designs are laid by professionals prior to the "mailanjee-idal." The bride's grandmother only puts on a little. This custom is also associated with beautification.[28]

"Ichappadu kodukal" is done right after the "antham-charth" and "mailanjee-idal." The groom and bride, in their respective ceremonies, are fed a special preparation of rice called "pachoru" mixed with brown sugar by their paternal uncles. "Pachoru" and brown sugar is an imitation of a Syrian confection.[29] Feeding it to the bride or groom represents fostering of the woman or man by elders before marriage.[30] The ceremonies end with dinner.

The final and most important stage of the wedding is the "kettu-kalyanam," which is the actual marriage of the bride and groom. After a prayer and blessings by the elders, both the bride and groom go to the groom's parish for the wedding Mass. In Texas, small booklets explaining the various stages of the ceremonial Mass are distributed. In contrast to a traditional procession down the aisle consisting of only the bride and groom, in Texas the procession involves flower girls, a ring bearer, bridesmaids and groomsmen, a best man, and a maid of honor—just like a traditional American wedding. The wedding Mass proceeds in the same way as a normal Malayalam Roman Catholic Mass. The groom ties a "tali" on the bride's neck. The Knanaya "tali" is different from other Indian "talis." It has the shape of a banyan leaf and has a small cross on one side made up of twenty-one beads. The number twenty-one is related with the trinity and seven sacraments.[31] A former tradition of crowning the couple,[32] does not exist today.[33] At the end of the Mass, the priest sings a song called "Barumariyam." It is a Chaldean song by which the priest prays to Jesus, the son of Mary, and blesses them in the name of Jesus.[34]

After Mass and a photo session, both the bride and groom change their clothes and everyone heads to the ballroom. Before going inside the ballroom, the maternal uncle and others perform a "nadavili" three times. They shout "nada nadayoooo" until each person's breath runs out. On the third time, the maternal uncles carry both the bride and groom to the entrance of the ballroom. There, the groom's mother dips a small piece of a tender coconut leaf in a plate containing rice and water and then makes the sign of the cross three times on both the groom's and bride's foreheads. Rice signifies posterity and prosperity, water signifies cleanliness, and the tender coconut leaf signifies holiness. The bride and groom are then seated on the stage. Together, they light an oil lamp, signifying the inauguration of the family.[35]

After this, the groom's mother, after having asked the audience permission three times, performs the "Vazhupiditham," in which she crosses her hands and places her right hand on the groom's head and her left hand on the bride's head and blesses them while a folk song related to it is sung. Following this, the groom's sister, after having washed their mouths using water in metal pots, gives them milk in a single glass to share and a single banana for both to bite as the corresponding folk song is sung. This represents their oneness.[36] The final on-stage custom is the "kachathazhukal," in which the groom presents the bride's maternal uncle, mother, and maternal grandmother fabric, or "kacha." The maternal uncle, after asking permission from the audience three times, places the "kacha" on the groom's outstretched hands, and touches the "kacha" and then the outer sides of his thighs three times. In some cases, the maternal uncle slips a ring off his own finger and puts it on the groom's finger. The same is done with the bride. It is repeated by the bride's mother and maternal grandmother, and in some cases, the maternal grandmother slips a bangle off of her hand and onto the bride's hand.

Food usually is served when the on-stage traditional Indian customs are over. Opposite to the custom observed during betrothal, the groom's maternal uncle pours water on the bride's maternal uncle's hands. A specially prepared fried chicken is given to the maternal uncle, and it is shared with everyone during the meal. This is a sign of unity. In contemporary Texan Knanaya weddings, it is not unusual for the best man and maid of honor to give short speeches wishing the couple the best. A father-daughter dance has been integrated also. After the father-daughter dance, dance music is played and the younger generation hits the dance floor.[37]

After the banquet, the closest family members of the bride and groom go to the groom's parents' house, where the bride's mother takes the bride's hand and places it in her mother-in-law's hand. This symbolizes the bride's parents entrusting their daughter to her new family.[38] The mother-in-law then takes her into the house, both placing their right foot first. After this, the bride's brother takes them to the bride's house, where the newlywed couple spends three days. On the third day, the couple goes back to the groom's house along with sweets that the bride's mother prepares. In Texas, this is followed by a honeymoon. When the honeymoon comes to an end, so do the wedding customs. Thus begins the newlywed couple's journey together.

Though the average young Texan Knanite today would probably not know the origin or meaning behind the wedding customs of the Knanaya, he or she would most probably try to find their meaning at least when the time for his or her marriage has come, and would try to have them observed at the time of his or her marriage (even if only as a small part of today's diversified marriage ceremonies). However, many would argue that the customs are on their way to extinction, just like the endogamous Knanaya community. For the time being, however, the Knanaya community in Texas seems to be on the rise, and the customs of the Knanaya community continue to be observed. Whether the size of the Knanaya community and observance of its customs will, in the future, grow, stay the same, or decline remains to be seen.

ENDNOTES

1. Fr. Lallu Kaithram, Kester and Team. *Knanaya Songs. Knanaya Voice.* Knanaya Voice News, 3 Jan. 2009. Web. 1 Nov. 2009. <http://www.knanayavoice.com>.
2. Jacob Kollaparambil. *Babylonian Origin of the Southists Among the St. Thomas Christians.* Robert F. Taft, ed. Roma: Pont. Institutum Studiorum Orientalium, 1992. Print. 92.
3. Ibid. 93.
4. George Menachery, ed. "History of Christianity after the Apostolic Times." *The St. Thomas Christian Encyclopaedia of India.* Vol. 1. Madras: B.N.K. Private Ltd., 1973. Print. 6.
5. Kollaparambil. xxiv.
6. L. W. Brown. *The Indian Christians of St. Thomas.* Cambridge: Cambridge UP, 1956. Print. 71.
7. Kollaparambil. 60.

8. Ibid. 1; Richard M. Swiderski. *The Blood Weddings The Knanaya Christians of Kerala*. Madras: New Era Publications, 1988. Print. 53–54.
9. Kollaparambil. 1-2.
10. Ibid. 31.
11. Abraham Mukalel. "The Existence of the Knanaya Community and The Knanaya Catholic Community." Thesis. Pontifical Institute of Theology and Philosophy, Alwaye, 2000. *Knanaya Catholic Community*. 2003. Web. 09 Nov. 2009. <http://www.knanayacatholics.com>. Quote from Mathew Melandassery. Para. 47.
12. E. P. Mathew. "The Knanaya Community of Kerala." *The St. Thomas Christian Encyclopaedia of India*. Ed. George Menachery. Vol. 2. Madras: B.N.K. Private Ltd., 1982. 74–75. Print. 74.
13. Merry Del Val and Pius X. "The Papal Bull." Letter to Knanaya Community. 29 Aug. 1911. *The Archeparchy of Kottayam*. 1995. Web. <http://www.kottayamad.org>.
14. Antony Kollannur and Varkey Vithayathil. "Decree of elevating the Eparchy of Kottayam to the Metropolitan See." Letter to Mar Kuri-akose Kunnacherry and Mar Mathew Moolakatt. 9 May 2005. *The Archeparchy of Kottayam*. Web. <http://www.kottayamad.org>.
15. Jimmy Kunnasserry. Telephone interview. 9 Nov. 2009; "Knanaya Catholic Mission of Houston." *Knanayaregion.us*. Abraham Mutho-lath, ed. 4 Nov. 2009. Web. 11 Nov. 2009. <http://www.knanayaregion.us/houston_mission.htm>.
16. "Knanaya Catholic Mission of Dallas." *Knanayaregion.us*. Abraham Mutholath, ed. 11 Apr. 2009. Web. 11 Nov. 2009. <http://www.knanayaregion.us/dallas_mission.htm>. Para. 3.
17. "Knanaya Catholic Mission of San Antonio." *Knanayaregion.us*. Abraham Mutholath, ed. 11 Apr. 2009. Web. 11 Nov. 2009. http://www.knanayaregion.us/san_antonio_mission.htm>.
18. Rev. Fr. James Cheruvil. Telephone interview. 7 Nov. 2009.
19. Ibid.
20. Mukalel. Para. 80.
21. Jacob Vellian. "Jewish-Christian' Community." *The St. Thomas Christian Encyclopaedia of India*. Ed. George Menachery. Vol. 2. Madras: B. N. K. Private Ltd., 1982. 73–74. Print. 73.
22. Jacob Vellian and S. K. Vembeni. *Kalyanathinte Kalchilamboli*, qtd. in Mukalel. Para. 82.
23. Lucy Mathew. Telephone interview. 16 Nov. 2009.
24. Mariam Korah. Telephone interview. 13 Nov. 2009.
25. Swiderski. 21.
26. Vellian and Vembeni. *Kalyanathinte Kalchilamboli*, qtd. in Mukalel. Para. 93.

27. Vellian and Vembeni. *Kalyanathinte Kalchilamboli*, qtd. in Mukalel. Para. 98; Swiderski. 25.
28. Swiderski. 24.
29. Ibid.
30. Mukalel. Para. 103.
31. Mukalel. Quote from P. M. John Pullapally. Para. 104.
32. Mukalel. Quote from Johnson Plakkoottathil. Para. 109.
33. Mukalel. Para. 109.

chilamboli, qtd. in Mukalel.

Nov. 2009.

ted in Missouri City,
aya Catholic activity
hosting meetings and
holic Society

Downtown, featuring Hemphill Drug Co.

HEMPHILL: REVISITING SMALL-TOWN TEXAS

by Sue M. Friday

When I was a little girl in the 1950s, the town of Hemphill was magical, a movie set for a turn-of-the-century film. Thriving shops surrounded the large courthouse, men in khakis and overalls, their Stetsons pushed back, played 42 under a large old cedar tree or sat on the bench talking politics and chewing tobacco. Women in print dresses and lace-up black shoes carrying pocketbooks on their arms met and visited. Only skirt lengths and the dusty pickup trucks lining the curbs were truly modern. Exchange them for longer dresses and horses and wagons and my great and great great-grandparents would have felt right at home.

My sister Patsy and I stayed on my grandparents' farm every summer to get away from the polio epidemic in Shreveport. Saturday was town day. Grandma gathered up her butter and eggs, Grandpa loaded tomatoes and peas, and off we went to peddle produce and purchase the few things the farm didn't provide. While Grandma shopped, we went with Grandpa to Charlie Rice's feed store. "Get those girls a cold drink!" he would tell a helper who went to the drink box and slid out a 6 oz. Coke for me and a Nu-Grape for Patsy—always a treat, as we only made Kool-Aid (cheaper) at home. We sipped from the icy bottles as we wandered around helping Grandpa choose the right print on the chicken feed sack. Grandma was teaching us to sew on her treadle machine, and two matching sacks made a dress. If Grandma needed a prescription filled, we sometimes went to the soda fountain in Hemphill Drug and had a coke float or shared a real milkshake. If we had earned the money as Grandpa's "helpers," we could spend ten to fifteen cents on a comic book.

All of this sounds so idyllic that, even now, I wonder if it was real. Were all the stores truly filled with merchandise and people? Was every parking space taken? Some years ago I asked Cousin Clement McDaniel if he would draw out the square and list the stores from that time. Clement, who died this year at the age of 98, called his nephew, Sabine County Historian Weldon McDaniel, and asked him to do it instead. Weldon is the go-to person for the facts and, like me, was a child in the '50s. Sure enough, he drew the square as I remember it: a post office, two drugstores, dress shops, grocery stores, appliance stores, Winslow Clinic, three small cafes—everything shoppers would need to keep them from going anywhere but Hemphill. With just over 900 inhabitants within the city limits, Hemphill and the surrounding area supported two car dealerships on or near the square and another out Highway 87N. Plymouth/Dodge, Ford, and Chevrolet. This was a time well before cars were sold from any other country but ours.

My favorite store was Fult's Five and Dime, filled with aisles of cheap trinkets to dazzle a young girl. The Nifty Frock Shop and Elliott's Dry Goods were both elegant and too expensive, except for special occasions. Cousin Peggy told me that her mother, Aunt Verdie McDaniel, was too modest to try on "store bought" dresses and sent Uncle Norman into the Nifty Frock Shop to buy for her. We were all modest in the '50s. My mother and grandmother had an intense discussion on whether or not my sister and I were too old to wear shorts to town, Grandma being very much against our doing so. I was seven and Patsy was five.

And now, after several decades of being away, I find Hemphill somewhat the same, but changing. The older men who socialized on the bench under the cedar tree beside the courthouse (called the Hookworm Bench), have moved to the café side of Lane's Grocery. It's air-conditioned and the coffee is free. They share the same yarns and stories, but these men were children in the '50s, like me. Brookshire Bros. Supermarket (*Welcomes Fishermen*) has taken the place of multiple grocery/gas stores. Drug stores and

The courthouse, and the cedar tree where men socialized

doctors' offices have moved out Highway 83S near the hospital and nursing homes. Retail is mostly along 87N in Beanville (named for Bienville, one of LaSalle's men). According to the city limits signs, the population is now 1198. Not much difference, although people settling on the shores of Toledo Bend Lake have caused the overall Sabine County population to jump.

The most noticeable change is around the square. It is almost deserted, and this saddens those of us who remember it as a thriving gathering place. I spoke at length to Donna Alexander, owner of The Clothes Horse (*All Women are Created Equal & Then We Accessorize!*). The Clothes Horse is the most successful of the retail shops on the square, and draws customers from most of East Texas. Donna moved her shop to the square almost three years ago. She has seen her business decline the last two years with the recession, but not by much. What has hurt her most is the closing of two restaurants, The Bistro and The Feed Store. Women who drive to Hemphill for her clothes have no "lunch" spot. The

Antique Connection, which had been on the square for years in the old Hemphill Drug site also closed when the owners decided retirement and an Internet business looked better than the day-to-day grind of keeping a store open. The Antique Connection was a secondary site for the women who drove in.

A recent circuit of the retail shops on the square did not take long. Besides The Clothes Horse there are five: Pat Roberts' Healthy Solutions, Regina Johnstone's Cedar Tree Nest Quilts, Helen Bordelon's dress shop Prim'Z, and J & A Antiques, a twenty-dealer co-op. I'm not including the NAPA store, as that's a special purpose store rather than a browsing place. Several of the ones listed are open less than four days a week.

Hemphill must still be magical, because without a major industry there doesn't seem a logical explanation for its continued existence. Statistics that describe the town are not encouraging. The median age is a couple of years older than the rest of Texas; the median household income is substantially lower—$24,014 versus $48,259. The median home value is $50,151, and for the rest of Texas it is $125,800. Like small towns all over Texas, Hemphill is there because people want it to be. And because there is an active core of believers who work to keep it going.

They try a little bit of everything. Sometimes there will be flowering baskets around the square. The quilt store sponsors an annual "Airing of the Quilts" in which beautifully made quilts are hung like banners along the sidewalk. Sometimes there will be a craft fair in which locals bring hand-made products and food and set it up all around the courthouse.

There are parades for Deerfest, the rodeo and homecoming, although they don't seem the same since Audrey Dean Leighton died several years ago. Known as "Audra Dean," he graduated as valedictorian from Hemphill High School in 1968, and then went on to become a self-described global twirler. He made it his mission to take his baton and lead every parade around the square. The first time I saw him was in Brookshires, and he scared

Audrey Dean Leighton, "Audra Dean," leading his last parade

me: a grown man dressed in short shorts, laced up knee-high boots, with a grizzled beard flowing to mid-chest. I saw him lead his last parade of horseback riders, young beauty queens throwing candy from the back of pickups, and the Hemphill High School marching band in full uniform. He marched in front and an audible titter rippled through the crowd as he went by. "There's Audra Dean!" as if the parade was complete. And actually, he was very good with his baton, sending it spinning high in the air and using all the other twirler moves.

Other well intentioned projects end on a sad note. A group formed to save the historic Pratt house, one of the last turn-of-the-century mansions, from being torn down to make room for the First Baptist Church's family life center. The church donated the house and money was raised to move it to a location at the back of the city park, but then vandals set it on fire. Made of heart pine, it went quickly.

On one trip, at the invitation of Weldon McDaniel, I joined the morning group at Lane's for breakfast, free coffee, and a roundtable discussion about Hemphill. Donna Alexander had told me that throughout Texas historical tourism is a major industry. Hemphill retains a nineteenth century feel in the square around the central courthouse with its historic jail museum and old store fronts. The Lane's group, all Hemphill natives, was in general agreement. Robert Hamilton, Hemphill's mayor for twenty years and a Lane's regular, said the city is already about to make a major step, installing public bathrooms and a pavilion. And simple as that is, like a good restaurant on the square, basic tourist accommodations are essential.

Weldon McDaniel said declaring a two-block-deep area around the square a historic district opens the door to grants and other help in restoration. The consensus seemed to be that it would never happen, as property owners don't like to be told what they can and can't do. Many of the new buildings are metal and no one wants restrictions that would require façades in keeping with the historic character of the square. Even the History Center just off the square is a metal building.

Besides the mayor and historian Weldon McDaniel, Carl Beall, whose grandfather owned the Star automobile dealership in the '20s, school board member Weldon Elliott, Millard Jordon, and J. W. Gooch are all regulars at Lane's, and all care deeply about Hemphill. I asked for a vision statement for Hemphill's future. Millard emphatically said he liked it like it is, and all seemed to agree and joked about not wanting change. But they also realized that what they really wanted was to see it like it was when we were kids.

They said that although there are a few ranchers like Weldon Elliott, the farmers who once provided Hemphill's income have about disappeared. Many of the people who keep Hemphill going are retired and live on Toledo Bend Lake. Others come for the hunting and fishing. Almost 80% of the land in Sabine County is national forest land, which provides habitat for deer as well as supports a timber mill in nearby Pineland. There is peace, quiet, and a great deal of natural beauty.

Another asset is the school system. Weldon Elliott said that they have a graduation rate of over 80% and no debt. But, of course, once the students graduate there isn't much for them to do in Hemphill. The jobs are elsewhere, and all the breakfast group would like to see more opportunities for keeping their children and grandchildren closer.

In February of 2003, debris from the Space Shuttle Columbia fell over much of Sabine County, and the bodies of the seven astronauts were found there. The new Patricia Huffman Smith NASA Museum has opened next to the library in honor of the fallen heroes. It brings in almost 400 visitors a month and will bring more once shuttle flight simulators are installed. But once visitors are there and tour the space museum and the history museum at the jail (if it is open), they have no place to stay and no restaurant that can accommodate a large group.

They mentioned the opening of two new restaurants just off the square: Proctors BBQ (*Smoked with Time N Love*) and Dinner Time Casseroles To Go, a five-table lunch-only eatery that specializes in take-out dishes. And then we talked about alcohol. Hemphill and most of Sabine County are dry, but there is a new push to vote in beer and wine. J. W. Gooch said he felt that the ability to have a drink with dinner would support the efforts of restaurants to make a go of staying open. And though all agreed it would make a difference and perhaps lead to a reopening of the two sites on the square, few around the table would endorse the idea. Traditions die hard in Hemphill.

Ultimately, we concluded that Hemphill will survive, but probably not change a great deal. People will continue to come "home" once they retire. Those who come for the hunting and fishing bring spouses who want a place to shop or eat, and that will support some businesses. An aging population needs health care, so that industry will continue to exist. If alcohol is voted in, the square may become more active. And if Hemphill stays as it is, a lot of people think that's just fine.

Beto Villa 45-rpm cover

MÚSICA TEJANA RECORDING PIONEERS

by Alex LaRotta

Unique to Texas, amongst its diversity in cultures, geography, and folklore, is the independent recording industry born from America's post-World War II economic boom. What follows is an in-depth documentation and history of the Tejanos that pioneered a statewide recording industry, independent of the monopolistic "big five" record company collective of New York and Chicago. Starting with Armando Marroquín's first locally produced *conjunto* record in 1945 and going up until the end of the independent era with the synthesizer-driven *Tejano* boom of the late 1980s, this study will focus on the peoples, places, genres, and recording technology throughout Texas within this forty-plus year time frame.

Texas, naturally, was a popular destination for record company talent scouts during the advent of "folk music" record production during the early twentieth century—tall tales of the singing cowboy, Mexican balladeer, and African-American bluesman helped steer interest to the Lone Star borderlands. It wasn't until the late 1920s, however, when record companies developed mobile makeshift studios, that "Tex-Mex" music (or *música tejana*, as it will be referred to herein) soon developed an in-demand sensation throughout Hispanic Texas. *Música tejana's* first recording stars were Lydia Mendoza and Narciso Martinez, both of whom are widely credited with pioneering the classic accordion and *bajo sexto* instrumentation found throughout the South Texas *conjunto*—a hybrid music, typically associated with working-class migrant farmers, inspired by the German-Texan polka and various north Mexican musical traditions. By the time the Great Depression swept the Southwest in the early 1930s, coin-slotted jukeboxes had become a popular, cost-effective form of entertainment, and were widely distributed in beer joints, cantinas, and dance halls across the country. This demand effectively incited a boom in popular/folk music production, particularly in an increasingly industrious and ethnically diverse Texas.

The Early Years of the *Música Tejana* Recording Industry: 1945–1963

Armando Marroquín was born September 12, 1912, in Alice, Texas. Nestled in the South Texas plains between San Antonio and the Rio Grande Valley, Alice is widely recognized as the "Birthplace of Tejano Music" (officially, as of 2001, by the Texas Legislature), mostly owed to the diligent efforts of Marroquín and his fabled Ideal and Nopal record labels. Before Ideal Records, Marroquín cut his teeth as a jukebox distributor, looking for *conjunto* records to satisfy the growing frenzy throughout the Southwestern borderlands. Historically, Ideal Records is considered the first Mexican-American owned label to produce records by a Mexican-American artist in the United States. But Marroquín's groundbreaking feat didn't come easy, as he later explained in an interview with Tejano historian Ramón Hernandez. "There were no (locally produced) records, just what people brought in from Mexico. So I got the idea of making our own Texas recordings. No one pressed records in Texas, so I found a place that pressed records in California and circa 1943 to 1944, I started recording local artists for my pianola (player piano) and sinfonola (jukebox) business."[1]

Marroquín's first known recording of Tejana sister duet Carmen y Laura (Marroquín's wife and sister-in-law, respectively) and their breakout "Se Me Fue Mi Amor" was recorded in 1945 in his living room, with his neighbor and friend Isaac Figueroa on accordion. "He first had them pressed in Los Angeles on Four Star Records because Four Star apparently did a lot of custom work," confirmed Arhoolie Records president Chris Strachwitz, who knew Marroquín well in his later years and reissued the bulk of Marroquín's recordings on Arhoolie's *Tejano Roots* CD series. "They put them out on their label (Four Star) until he got together with Mr. Betancourt."[2] It was shortly after Marroquín partnered with San Benito-based music entrepreneur Paco Betancourt that South Texas became a hotbed of recorded music.

From 1946 to 1958, Ideal Records produced hundreds of recordings from local talent across South Texas, becoming one of the most prolific labels in Texas music history. Texas-Mexican groups from San Antonio, Del Valle, McAllen, San Benito, Gonzalez, and many other Hispanic communities throughout South Texas came to record with the famous local producer. Perhaps most important for *música tejana* preservation is the fact that practically all types of regional Mexican and border music—particularly pre-war *corridos, rancheras, norteño, conjunto,* and polkas—were well-represented throughout these historic recordings. Before the advent of professional recording studios found later in Texas's major cities by the 1960s, Marroquín recorded talent at his home in Alice as a do-it-yourself sound enthusiast. Marroquín initially recorded musicians in his living room, but quickly moved his operations (at the discretion of his doting wife, Carmen) into his two-car garage, using bed mattresses as sound isolation and two microphones that were plugged into an Ampex 300 tape machine.[3] Before the advent of the popular Ampex tape machines in the late 1940s, Marroquín likely used a Rek-o-Kut brand turntable to record direct to acetate for the first few years of production.

But Marroquín and Betancourt didn't just record their own records; they eventually got to the point where they were pressing them too, effectively cutting out the far-removed pressing plants on the west and east coasts. "We were at war with Japan and Germany so we continued ordering records from California and New York," recalled Marroquín, "until Paco brought the necessary equipment and opened (one of) the first record pressing plant in Texas."[4] Though they likely didn't think much of it at the time, their actions were the first steps towards creating a self-sufficient statewide music industry—an industry that would grow to a multi-million-dollar trade by the end of the 20th century.

Paco Betancourt had already established himself amongst South Texas's elite entertainment entrepreneurs by the time Ideal Records was formed in 1946. Betancourt founded Rio Grande Music Company thereafter, where he distributed records along the Southwestern border towns for major recording companies like

Blue Bird and OKeh Records. By the mid-1930s, Betancourt—like his future business partner Marroquín—had invested in a network of jukeboxes in and around the Rio Grande Valley and was looking for a way to fill them with *conjunto* records. Though demand continued to grow for homegrown border music, the major labels had effectively discontinued their ethnic and "race" series by the time America entered World War II. Mostly due to material rationing for the war effort and a devastating musicians' union strike in 1942 that crippled the recording industry, folk records were shelved for a limited run of big band and classical records. It was precisely this shortage in record production, however, that would later fuel the independent record label revolution.

Around the same time, and just some forty miles west of Betancourt's Rio Grande Music operation in San Benito, Arnaldo Ramírez was dabbling with home recording in McAllen, Texas. Likely influenced by Betancourt and Marroqúin's newly formed enterprise, Ramírez was quick to capitalize on the burgeoning record market. In 1947, Ramírez recorded accordionist Pedro Ayala in his living room for the New York-based Mida label for a recently initiated (yet short-lived) "Mexican-Series," though the label was more closely identified with Afro-Cuban and tropical music. Just one year later, Ramírez founded Falcon Records in McAllen, which would soon climb the ranks as a music powerhouse in the heart of the Rio Grande Valley. For over forty years, Ramírez's Falcon imprint—and its various subsidiary labels, nine at its most active—would dominate the *música tejana* market, rivaling Ideal as the kingpin label of South Texas.

Though many urban Mexican Americans largely considered Texan *conjunto* and Mexican *norteño* music to be low class, blue-collared music (a stigma that still exists in various fashion to this day), innovative bandleaders of the post-war music world soon hybridized the *conjunto* format with *orquesta*-styled dance music so as make it more "tasteful" for urban audiences. Narciso Martinez and Beto Villa were making names for themselves as renowned *orquesta* bandleaders, selling thousands of records and filling up concert halls throughout the Southwest. It wasn't long until migrant workers brought the *ranchero* sounds to the big city lights of San Antonio. Much like Nashville to country and Chicago to the blues, San Antonio became the urban epicenter of the *música tejana* world. While Falcon and Ideal (and later Nopal) still reigned king in South Texas, San Antonio became the headquarters of the independent label explosion.

One of the very first *música tejana* imprints from San Antonio was Manuel Rangel's Corona Records, considered the grandfather of the Alamo City labels. In 1947, Rangel produced the very first recording of famed accordionist Valerio Longoria in his one-room electrical repair shop, converted into a makeshift recording studio. Under Rangel's direction, Corona produced hundreds of records for both local and regional talent, bringing the borderland sounds into the big city. Corona continued producing on through the "*La Onda Chicana*" phase of the 1960s and 1970s, to later have his son, Manuel Jr., continue his successful enterprise. Manuel Rangel, Jr., soon became one of San Antonio's most well-known record distributors, helping solidify San Antonio as the hub of the *música tejana* industry.

To be sure, Rangel's biggest competitor in San Antonio's early record industry was Hymie Wolf and his short-lived but highly influential Río record label. In the late 1940s, Wolf opened the Río Record Shop—converted from a liquor store that he previously owned and operated—and founded Wolf Recording Company, the "Home of the Río Record." For well over a decade Wolf produced hundreds of records, until his untimely death on October 10, 1963.[5] Río records are known for containing some of the best San Antonian *cantina* music, made popular from its lively mariachi-styled roots music.

LA ONDA CHICANA AND THE BIRTH OF "TEJANO": 1963 TO EARLY 1980S

La Onda Chicana, or "The Chicano Wave," is a broad term often used to describe both Mexican-American music and the "brown

power" socio-political movement of the 1960s. These two phenomena were often intertwined, as music eventually *became* political for reform-minded "Chicanos" (young, activist Mexican-
Americans) swept up with civil unrest of the 1960s. For the pur-
poses of this musical history, however, we can broadly identify *La
Onda Chicana* as the hybridization of borderland *conjunto* music
and American R&B and rock music, rooted in the early 1960s.

Dallas-based record producer Johnny Gonzales signed Jose
Maria "Little Joe" Hernandez and his Latinaires to a record contract with his newly established El Zarape Records in 1963. Later
that year, Little Joe released "Crazy Baby," a regionally popular
45-rpm doo-wop single that garnered much attention on the local
radio circuit. In 1964, El Zarape released Little Joe's *Por un Amor*
LP—the first stereophonic LP in *música tejana* history—featuring
the smash hit single "Amor Bonito," which had effectively
launched the young group into *música tejana* stardom. With the

Advertisement for El Zarape Records

pioneering efforts of entrepreneurs like Gonzales and Manuel Rangel, *música tejana* record distribution soon went as far west as Los Angeles, and as far north as Chicago, respectively the second and third biggest markets outside of Texas by 1970.

"I went to Mexico City since I was associated with CBS International," recalled Johnny Gonzalez (founder of the El Zarape Record Company), "and they advertised my name and my label in all the newspapers in Mexico City and it said 'La Onda Chicana has come to Mexico: Johnny Gonzalez and El Zarape Records.' And they distributed my records in Central and South America, Spain. . . I would get royalties from a lot of countries. I would get recognition for Tejano music."[6] Some music historians, notably Joe Nick Patoski in his biography of *Tejana* sensation Selena Quintanilla, consider Johnny Gonzalez as the originator of the "*La Onda Chicana*" term and subsequent movement. Though there's a general lack of consensus on who was most responsible for advancing the movement, Johnny Gonzales and his Dallas-based El Zarape Record Company are certainly owed a fair share of the glory.[7]

By 1963, Little Joe had released at least one 45-rpm single (a cover of Stax recording artist Rufus Thomas and his popular R&B hit single, "The Dog") for Benjamin Moncivais' Austin-based Valmon Records, a jewelry store-turned-record company located in the heart of Austin's east side. Little Joe's own Buena Suerte Records of Temple, Texas—which he founded with his two brothers in 1968—along with Moncivais' Valmon Records were amongst the first *música tejana* labels to extend out of its traditional South Texas roots into Central Texas. Meanwhile, Johnny Gonzalez's El Zarape and Luther de la Garza's Capri Records were two of the most successful *música tejana* labels of the Dallas-Fort Worth Metroplex. Along with Capri, de la Garza had a string of successful record shops and jukeboxes, and also owned the popular Hi-Ho Ballroom nightclub in neighboring Grand Prairie, Texas.

Little Joe's polka-*ranchera* "Las Nubes," taken from his 1972 *Para La Gente* LP, became a huge hit and later served as an anthem for Cesar Chavez's United Farm Workers organization and the wider migrant labor movement closely associated with Little Joe's fan base. In addition to traditional polka-*rancheras*, Little Joe's Buena Suerte Records issued an assortment of *cumbias*, ballads, country, rock, and even soul/funk music from a variety of talent across Central Texas. From their early days in Temple, Little Joe and the Latinaires (later called "La Familia") would go on to become one of the most iconic and prolific *música tejana* bands in history.

"TALK TO ME": SAN ANTONIO AND THE "WESTSIDE SOUND"

One of the most instrumental figures behind San Antonio's centrality on the *música tejana* industry is Bob Tanner and his TNT Record Company, recording studio, and record pressing plant. Tanner opened his pressing plant in 1947, one of (if not *the*) first in the state to do so. Located just north of downtown San Antonio, Tanner's studio and plant became an all-inclusive record-producing machine. Even by today's standards, Tanner's innovative integration of the entire record production process is impressive, particularly in context of the early days of independent record production. Naturally, Tanner's plant became the go-to production house for the majority of Texas labels, with 80% of their output dedicated to *música tejana* labels by 1973.[8] Six years after the start of his pressing plant, Tanner decided to go into the recording side of the business when, in 1953, he founded his TNT Record Company, which mostly dealt in country and western. Tanner did release some *música tejana* on his label, however, as well as R&B, pop, and blues.[9]

Idelfonso "Sunny" Ozuna was born September 8, 1943, in San Antonio, Texas. Ozuna, along with Little Joe, Ruben Ramos, and Augustin Ramírez, is one of the key musicians of the *"La Onda"* generation. Apart from the previously mentioned artists, Ozuna was instrumental in the formation of San Antonio's now-legendary "Westside Sound"—a hodge-podge of *conjunto*, polka, soul, R&B, blues, and rock, as interpreted by (mostly, but not conclusively) young urbanite Mexican-American musicians. Prominent Texas musicians like Sunny Ozuna, Doug Sahm, Flaco Jimenez, and Spot Barnett dutifully represent San Antonio's fabled "Westside Sound." Nightclubs, concert halls, and beer joints across the city soon set the stage for what is largely considered the "golden age" of San Antonio music during the 1950s and 1960s.

Sunny and the Sunglows' first 45-rpm release was issued for local KMAC disk jockey Joe Anthony and his Harlem Record Company, established in summer of 1959.[10] Other small labels soon sprang up around the city, inspired by Manny Guerra's popular Sunglow and Anthony's Harlem record companies. Manuel Rangel, mentioned earlier for his post-war Corona label, developed his hipper, doo-wop-oriented Rival label in 1959. Jesse Schneider's Renner and Emil Henke's Satin records were also big players in the "Westside Sound" era. But Manny Guerra's biggest competition in town must have certainly been Abe Epstein.

Abe Epstein, like the most successful producers of his time, was quick to integrate his recording companies, publishing firm, and recording studio into a successful media conglomeration. Epstein founded his Jox, Cobra, and Dynamic record labels in the early 1960s, and housed his four-track Ampex tape machine in a small studio on General McMullen Drive, in the hub of the bustling west side. Today, Epstein and his hundreds of record releases on his various labels are the veritable bread and butter of the early "Westside Sound" in San Antonio. Westside legends like The Royal Jesters, Dimas Garza, Henry and his Kasuals, and Sunny and the Sunliners are just a few of the local pop groups that Epstein produced over the years.

Sunny's biggest and career-defining hit was his 1962 "Talk To Me," released initially on Sunglow Records and later reissued and distributed nationally by Houston music mogul Huey Meaux and his Teardrop record label. "Talk To Me" would go on to become one of the biggest hits of the *"La Onda"* era—a slow-moving sweet ballad that embodied the exceedingly popular "Chicano Soul" sound of the 1950s and 1960s, which extended from Los Angeles to San Antonio. Sunny's six-decade-spanning music career would take to him to the highest echelons of the *música tejana* world, making him one of the most revered and adored musicians of the *"La Onda"* generation.

"Synthesization": End of the Independents, Return to the Majors

"Tejano Music," a term most associated with synthesizer-driven *música tejana* of the early 1980s (and that continues to represent practically <u>all</u> *música tejana* today), solidified its commonality in the industry with the first Tejano Music Awards in 1980. *La Onda Chicana* was flying high by the mid- to late 1970s; big brass-filled *orquestas* were the most popular groups of the era, but the industry was beginning to change. Polka-*rancheras* proved the most popular song format, with Little Joe and Sunny popularizing "el grito" as a standard feature in the music—with the iconic "ay yi" yelp heard in many *música tejana* songs of that era. As music duplication technology became widely accessible to the public—primarily reel to reels and blank cassette tapes in the late 1970s—piracy and bootlegging became a worrying concern for the music industry, most especially for vulnerable independent producers. At the same time, electronic instruments like the synthesizer and drum machine were replacing traditional rhythm and brass sections, forever changing the soundscape of the Texas-Mexican *orquesta*, as smaller electro-combos soon replaced traditional big bands. Moreover, affordable digital recording consoles were replacing the bulky (and costly) analog tape machines of yesteryear—the industry, in essence, was shrinking.

And all the while, major labels in New York and L.A. were looking to capitalize once again on this regional "ethnic" music that had largely been ignored by the music industry for the last forty years. Likely enamored with the success and marketability of *música tejana* in the 1970s, and the overall success of tropical Latin music in the U.S., majors such as EMI, Capitol, WEA, CBS International, and Sony Discos International set up recruiting offices in San Antonio and Houston to attract fresh new talent. The old independents were hit hardest by this rapid transformation.

The turn of the 1980s marked a new era in *música tejana*. With recession and bootlegging on the rise, once-successful producers were struggling to pay staff and keep lights on in the studio. "I got hit a lot by the bootleggers," recalled Johnny Gonzalez, of the last days of his El Zarape Records empire. "I leased the company because I couldn't keep up with them [bootleggers]. I busted a few in Brownsville, Oklahoma, Midland. That's one of the reasons I got out of the business; the other record companies didn't want to come forward and sue these people. It was too tough to do it alone."[11] The *música tejana* industry, for better or worse, had changed dramatically.

By the mid-1980s, *música tejana* was one of the last Latin genres to "cross over" to mainstream appeal, but all that would soon change. Selena Quintanilla-Perez, known affectionately as "The Queen of Tejano," and a new generation of *música tejana* artists would take this music out of Texas and across the world. At her height, Selena and her Dinos had fans as far north as New York and Canada, as far south as Argentina, and a growing fan base in Europe and East Asia—an accomplishment no *música tejana* artist had yet accomplished. Selena, La Mafia, Grupo Mazz, Laura Canales, and Emilio Navarro are some of the biggest names of Tejano music of the 1980s and 1990s, though much credit is owed to the wider distribution networks of the major labels, music videos, and direct access to international retail conglomerates such as Walmart, Best Buy, and Target. Of all the successful Tejano bands of the 1980s and 1990s, Selena y los Dinos were the biggest of them all.

By the 1980s, the Colombian *"cumbia"* became a standard musical style within *música tejana*, especially embraced by young, pop-oriented Tejano bands attempting to cross over to the larger Latin music markets, particularly in Mexico. It was precisely Selena's infectious electro-*cumbia* and smoothed-over commercial sound that launched her into crossover pop stardom—her affable personality and overt sexual prowess would eventually lead to her nickname in the press as "The Mexican Madonna." It would take her signing with Los Angeles-based EMI Latin Records in 1989, after having started with a local record label in San Antonio, to eventually go multi-platinum. Selena's 1994 *Amor Prohibido* remains her best-selling CD album to date, with over 1.5 million units sold worldwide by 1997.

Tejano remained immensely popular throughout the better part of the 1990s. But Selena's tragic death on March 31, 1995, is a date some Tejano aficionados remember as "The Day Tejano Music Died." Since that fateful day, many say that Tejano never fully recovered to its former popularity. Album sales in the Tejano market, much like in other genres, have consistently slumped since the late 1990s web-based MP3 file-share revolution.

Since its commercial inception in the early twentieth century, *música tejana* has had an extraordinary history. From the post-war jukebox kings of South Texas to the multimillion-dollar producers of New York and L.A., *música tejana* owes much to the efforts of these behind-the-scenes industry innovators. A once regional, working-class music was soon exposed to the world by way of pop sensations like Selena, leading to multi-platinum album sales and *conjunto* crazes in Japan, Germany, and China. Moreover, this "cross-pollinated" native genre is unique yet intercultural. From the Austro-German polka to the *norteño* of northern Mexico, this musical fusion is a defining feature of Texas folkloric music culture.

ENDNOTES

1. Armando Marroquin. Interview by Ramon Hernandez, Hispanic Entertainment Archives.
2. Chris Strachwitz. Interview by author, October 27, 2011, San Antonio, Texas.
3. Ramon Hernandez. "Armando Marroquin Biography." Hispanic Entertainment Archives.
4. Ibid.
5. Chris Strachwitz. Liner notes to *Tejano Roots: San Antonio's Conjuntos in the 1950s.* Ideal/Arhoolie CD-376, 1991.
6. Johnny Gonzalez. Interview by author, November 30, 2011. San Antonio, Texas.
7. Joe Nick Patoski. *Selena: Como La Flor.* Boston: Little, Brown, and Company, 1996. 145.
8. Charlie Brite. "Texas Pressing Plant Sold; Facilities To Be Updated," *Billboard*, August 23, 1973. 23.
9. Ibid.
10. Wired For Sound. "No Color in Poor": San Antonio's Harlem Label." http://wired-for-sound.blogspot.com/2011/09/no-color-in poor san antonios-harlem.html (accessed November 28th, 2011).
11. Johnny Gonzalez.

Lucy Fischer-West

"BUT *MISS,* MY FAMILY DOESN'T *HAVE* A SAGA!"

by Lucy Fischer-West

I have been telling stories for as long as I can remember. More specifically, I have been telling *my* story since the third grade. My homeroom teacher, Miss Ross, was also the librarian, so I was surrounded with books. I came from a home filled with books and scant other furniture except for the antique bookcases they were kept in. It wasn't that we could afford rare or expensive antiques; those bookcases had been acquired at a second-hand shop in the northeastern United States, where my father spent his first years after arriving in the United States from Germany, landing in America with about five dollars in his pocket in 1912, at the age of twenty one.

By the time I got to 3rd grade in El Paso's Zavala Elementary School, I had already gone through Kindergarten, and first and second grade at *Escuela Agustín Melgar*, a small primary school across the Mexican border in Cd. Juárez where my mother taught. When Miss Ross gave us the assignment to write the story of our lives, I couldn't imagine completing it based on my short existence. So, I started by telling my parents' story. Over forty years later, I began *Child Of Many Rivers: Journeys to and From the Rio Grande*[1] the same way, not because I hadn't had a life beyond that of being my parents' child, but because they were interesting people with stories of their own, and they shaped who I am.

My transition to schooling on the American side of the border was relatively smooth thanks to excellent teachers at Zavala Elementary through seventh grade, then going on to Lydia Patterson Institute, many of whose students came from across the border first to learn English and then to get their high school education. I was in the minority there, much as I had been at Zavala. I was fully bilingual as the result of my upbringing. When I addressed my father, I spoke English; my mother and I communicated in Spanish. My parents learned to speak each other's language eventually, but in their conversations she spoke Spanish to him and he responded in English. I could read both languages by the age of five. Facility of two languages is one of the many blessings my parents imparted on me.

In 2003, I began teaching freshman English at Cathedral High School, an all-boys Lasallian Catholic school. A great many of our boys come from across the border in Juárez, attending parochial school before coming to us to get an American high school diploma, with the intent of attending a university in the States. They have excellent skills in science and math, and a good foundation in the humanities. What they sometimes don't have is English language skills, nor any perspective on American—or English— history, because they don't have much exposure to it in a Mexican education. I discovered very quickly that part of their frustration in reading out of our anthology was that they not only lacked the vocabulary, but they also lacked the knowledge of the cultural settings of the stories they were reading. Believing that literature and history—and folklore—go hand in hand, I routinely gave my students background on the stories they were reading to give them a better foundation for understanding them. I also threw in a healthy dose of proverbs in both languages.

Eight years ago, when I began teaching world history, I had a further epiphany: many of my students had no sense of time. In an early-year quiz, their answers made it evident that whether their previous schooling had been in El Paso or Juárez, some hardly knew what century *they* were living in, much less when their parents had been born, or what historical periods or events their grandparents had lived through. I begin the year by teaching local history, going back to prehistoric times, sharing with them how the Rio Grande changed courses several times and wreaked havoc with our international boundary. I explain how El Paso came to be, what influences shaped it, and what was going on in other parts of the world as El Paso was evolving. I then explain why my classroom has signs posted all over that say "World History Begins With You."

I pull out my copy of PTFS Volume LX and read to them from *The Family Saga*, starting with an excerpt from Francis Abernethy's Introduction: "A family legend is a type of folklore. It is a traditional prose narrative that has a historical setting and real people as characters. The legend is passed down in the family through the oral tradition, by word of mouth, from one generation to another. As with all folklore, the story exists in variations, its author or first teller is anonymous, and it fits a formula in being true to the spirit of the family but not necessarily to the facts of history."[2]

I share with them the book's table of contents to give them some ideas as to what kinds of stories families tell and retell, reading, among other offerings, "Illegal Entry" about my father's arrival in America in 1912, and "Thanks to a Psychic in Shanghai" about the fortune teller who predicted my parents' marriage. However much I had valued the stories told to me by my parents, these two pieces were the first written accounts of those events. At my dinner table, the telling of the tale as to how *I* came to grow up in El Paso always included their meeting in that Juárez bullring. As my book *Child of Many Rivers* developed, I found myself marveling that relating the story of my parents' lives encompassed the passage of a century—the historical framework of their lifetimes spanned a hundred years, from my father's birth in 1891 to my mother's death in 1991. Separately, their lives were affected by World War I, the Mexican Revolution, the Great Depression, and World War II. Together, they settled on the El Paso-Juárez border with me as their only child and we shared several more decades of world events. When I say that I grew up a fortunate child, it is an understatement. What they gave me far surpassed anything of a material nature that existed then, or now.

"The family saga," Abernethy says, "is *not* history. It is *not* an accumulation and an evaluation of factual and documented details, because most families have few facts and very little documentation. But even though the stories are not history, they are shadows of history, which in one sense is more important than the details." I love that phrase, "shadows of history." It is the concept of what I try to convey to my students—that their world history text tells them the facts and figures, but not the stories of the people who lived the time periods and events we study. To continue quoting Abernethy, "A list of ancestors and how long they lived and whom they begot and how long they lived is important factually, but it does not interpret; it does not reveal a family's spirit nor what it believes nor how it thinks. A genealogical list tells *what*, not *why* and *how*; and the *what* is the beginning, the first step, the introduction. The *why* is the reason for being. And the *whys* of a family are revealed in the family's legends."[3]

With my own story, I give them a photographic and narrative journey of my family history that spans those hundred years and I explain the importance of personal journals and oral tradition in recording family legends. It is people that make history, I tell them, and you, as a person, have a history and are connected to events long past. They really don't believe me of course. I have to convince them: I send them home to do field research—to search for the stories told by their oldest living relatives. They are assigned the *pleasure and privilege* (I don't call it a task) of collecting at least three stories and connecting their family sagas to world history events. They do both written and oral projects, introducing their classmates to their family tales. The last element is creating mini-posters to illustrate those connections between world history and family sagas. Even if it is only in placing their stories in the particular time period in which they happened, they acquire some sense of time. They also discover their links to generations that have, each in their own way, made history.

As in the case of any classroom, the results are varied. Some students already have a sense of where they came from, what their families have lived through. Others delight in the exploration and discovery. And, alas, still others do as little as possible to get through the assignment. But they all learn a little more about themselves, and each other, even those who come back three or four days in a row telling me, in their most plaintive voices, **"But *Miss,* my family doesn't *have* a saga!!!!"**

Herewith are some stories our boys have brought to my classroom, beginning with one that would fit into Abernethy's "From the Old Sod to the New World" category. Fabian Yepo wrote, "In 1915, the war between China and Japan was raging and my great great grandfather was in distress. He had to choose one out of four children to send as a refugee to Mexico. My great grandfather Yep Yong, (or so we think was his original name) was chosen and sent at the age of 14. He never got to see his siblings or parents ever again and had no idea what was going to happen. As he arrived, the Mexican officials asked him what his name was. He answered and left the officials clueless as to what he had said, so they gave him a name based as to what they understood: 'Francisco Yepo.'"

Francisco Yepo worked picking crops on a farm where he saved the minimal pay he received for his work. "At the age of 19 he left for Juarez to become a businessman. He worked in a shop and got to know how things worked. Nearby in another shop worked a Chinese woman who caught his eye. My great grandfather and she dated for some years and married in 1941. Together with another man, my great grandfather opened a grocery story called *La Morenita.*" In time, Fabian's great-grandfather bought out his partner and eight years after *La Morenita* opened, he opened *La Nueva Central*, which became a restaurant well known and loved by the people of Juárez. "Actors and politicians went there to eat, and because of that, my great grandfather became a respected and well known man. He worked even when he was old, but his primary intention was to teach my grandfather how to take care of the business. Even though he eventually got the hang of it, he still didn't have the same intelligence as my great grandfather." I had to laugh at this last sentence because his grandfather, Francisco Yepo, was one of my mother's favorite, and smartest, students in fourth grade at *Escuela Agustin Melgar* where I started school. My mother and I shopped at *La Morenita* and ate at *La Nueva Central* frequently. We border children who share an international boundary frequently find intergenerational connections to each other.

"My great grandparents," said Jose Alberto Almada, "had to come from Armenia because of the First World War in the neighboring countries of Turkey and Russia. In 1915 Armenia became a part of Russia and that name disappeared until 1976 when Armenia became independent again. On the way to America, one of the two kids died about two weeks before arriving and my great grandparents had to throw him into the ocean. They arrived in Mexico in 1924 and tried to cross into the U.S. to go to New York where they had family, but had no permits or passports so they stayed here. The first baby was born in 1925; she is my Great Aunt Rose. Right now, only two sisters are alive to tell their grandchildren their stories."

Sam Przybyl's great-grandmother "came to the United States from Poland when she was 20 years old in 1922. She travelled on a large ship in the steerage compartment and arrived at Ellis Island in New York with the clothes on her back, two silver spoons, and a small pot. She spoke no English and had a piece of paper pinned to her clothes that had the words 'Buffalo, New York' on the front and the name and address of her brother who had already come to the United States. She made her way across the entire state (about 500 miles) by train without speaking a word and just relying on the kindness of people who made sure she got on the right trains to Buffalo."

One of the joys of this project is to see the admiration and respect that comes through when boys share stories of favorite ancestors. Some are shy, quiet boys whose words light up the pages. Such is the case with Matthew Conner Adrain Hallmark's stories of his grandfather, Kenith Adrain Hallmark, born in Athens, Texas, on December 30, 1939. "From the very moment he was born, my grandfather had a rather unconventional childhood. He was born into a family that was not desperately poor, but then again, they did not have much money to just throw around. In fact, sometimes he had no way of washing his clothes, so my grandfather was forced to hitchhike to his aunt's house where he could wash his clothing. Then, he would hitchhike all the way back home, miles away. He dropped out of school in the 8th grade so he could help his dad care for horses and continue building the Hallmark legacy. You see, my grandfather grew up country. It didn't matter if there was rain, sunshine, or snow, my grandfather always had on a long sleeve button-up shirt, blue jeans, cowboy boots, and a cowboy hat. After dropping out of school, my grandfather had to help his father break wild horses. My grandfather often fell, or rather flew, off these horses, cutting and scraping his face, hands, and head open quite frequently, leaving huge gashes and wounds. Meanwhile, his father would scream and yell at him to get back up, try again, and successfully break the horse.

"My grandfather continued to help his father care for horses for several more years, until he followed his uncle's footsteps and became a professional jockey at the age of 18. He raced in the All-American Derby, Belmont Stakes, and Churchill Downs, in long distance and short distance races. He won many trophies, which I enjoy looking at when we visit him. My grandfather was

Matthew Hallmark's depiction of his grandfather, jockey Kenith Hallmark

very successful as a jockey, not to mention that he was also trading and training horses during this time. He was always determined to get first place, stayed persistent when things were
tough, and showed true passion for his job. In fact, my father
often says that my grandfather was more passionate and patient
with horses than he was with human beings. He truly loved
horses. While others hired medics to care for their horses and
make special creams, he made his own creams and medicines
which worked well and helped the horses run better.

"After making such a huge impact on the world of horse racing, and leaving his mark as a jockey, at the age of 72, he is a truck
driver and resides in Hawley, Texas a small town near Abilene. He
is changing lives to this very day. Because of the drive within him,
his persistence, and his determination to succeed, he pushed my
father to succeed, and pushes me to do my very best. My father
and I and most others in my family would not be who they are or
where they are if it weren't for my 'Pa'."

The Rio Grande's changing course and the Mexican Revolution have been two major influences on border life throughout the
years. When I make this assignment, I know that our boys will have
ancestors whose stories connect them to Pancho Villa, Mexico's
bandit-hero. The following is Jorge Luis Ruiz's account of his
great grandfather's encounter with Pancho Villa: "Andres Bunsow
was born in 1888 in Germany. When he was older, he moved to
Mexico to start a new life. There, he met my great grandmother;
they had trouble understanding each other mainly because one
spoke German and the other Spanish. In Chihuahua he opened a
store called Nuevo Mundo, which means 'new world.' This store
had stuff from Germany and one day Pancho Villa walked in. He
said he wanted a dress for his girlfriend. But Andres said it was
already reserved, so they got into a fight and finally Pancho Villa
said that if Andres did not give him the dress he would burn the
store." Villa did burn it down, and Andres was left with nothing.
He and his wife moved to El Paso to "start all over again."

Ricardo Uribe had more details in his story than most of my
students: "My great-grandmother was born in 1900. Her name

was Emma Rodriguez, but everybody called her Mama Emma. In 1910, when she was ten years old, Pancho Villa came to Juárez and besieged the city when everybody was sleeping. She and her family lived in the post office because her father, Everardo Rodriguez Camargo, was the chief of the mail. So, in order to save the post office goods, her father hid under the floorboards with all the money, stamps, and mail. He was there for at least three days. Mama Emma's brother came from El Paso to give him food every day.

"The fighting between the Villistas and the Federales started at dawn. Then they ceased firing so that they could pick up the dead and the wounded and for civilians to leave the city. Mama Emma, her mother, sisters, and brother fled to El Paso. She never forgot that on the way to El Paso there were dead people on the ground as well as wounded people calling for help. Three days later Don Enrique Acevedo went to rescue her father from under the floor. They dressed up with American Smelting overalls, helmets, and lamps hiding the [post office] money and goods in their clothes. Her father said that it was the only time that the Mexican Post Office was running from El Paso, Texas."

Pablo Orrantia had this story of his maternal great-great-grandfather: "Jose D. Gonzalez was born in Quintana Del Rio, Spain and was sent to Veracruz, Mexico to avoid starvation. He worked in the fields with ranch animals and crops, worked hard, established a general store and became rich and successful. There were unfortunate circumstances that would disturb his life every once in a while. He lived during the time of Pancho Villa. This was dangerous because Villa did not like Spaniards. So every time Villa came, he would take all his money and cows, and would have to hide or flee until Villa left."

From the paternal side of the family, he told of his great-great-grandfather Cruz Arzola: "During the time of Villa, he lived with his daughters in San Pedro, Durango. Villa would come through and he would have to hide his great grand-aunts. . . . by digging a deep hole in the pig corral. The hole would be covered up with boards and the pigs would walk over it like nothing. My great-great grandfather would gather all the neighborhood women and put them in the hole that was very hidden. One time one of the ladies didn't get into the hole and was caught and raped. Even though this happened, my great-great grandfather was thanked for hiding the women."

In any given year, in any given class, there are many tales of ancestors involved in the 1910 Revolution, some pro-Villa, some not. Chris "Blacksmith" Juarez's grandfather provided food for Villa and others who fought with him. Jerry Alvarez told of his paternal great-great-grandfather who fought alongside Villa and Emiliano Zapata: "Just after he had sat for a picture beside a cannon wheel, he walked in front as the cannon was fired. He lost his left arm as a result of the accident." Pete Galvan's grandmother was Pancho Villa's nurse. Octavio Celaya's family fought against Villa, and Manuel Papadakis's family land was stolen by Villa. Samuel Pichardo's family had to hide from the Mexican hero-bandit in order to survive. Stephen Romero's great-grandfather, who was a telegraph operator, was abducted by Villa so he could intercept messages from the Mexican forces.

Vicente Lopez had a family story of a Villa gold barrel purportedly buried in walls but never found, he said, "even through the help of the Satanic Ouija board." Pablo Bustamante's grandfather fought Villa on a roof and Pedro Alvillar's ancestors fled to the border. Alejandro Baca's family supped with Venustiano Carranza, and Alex Perea's great-grandmother danced with Villa, while Abraham Vizcarra's grandfather fought alongside the *"Centauro del Norte."* "My great-great grandmother gave birth to Pancho Villa's son who is my great grandfather on my maternal grandmother's side," proclaimed Victor Reyes in his presentation. Nobody could top that one. That was in 2006.

On the day my current students did their oral presentations, Julio Meza related how Villa's men forced his great-grandmother's family "to walk barefoot through the desert several kilometers, then forced them to dig their tomb without pity, whipping them and making fun of it." Once they were done digging their graves, they shot them in the head. Franz Felhaber, the next student, finished that day's presentations saying that his great-uncle José Saénz Pardo and his brothers had shot Pancho Villa to death in Parral.

In his paper, Mark Gonzalez had courtship tales and marriage tales, "My grandparents on my dad's side are Maria Benavidez and Clemente Gonzalez. Grandpa was born on March 18, 1927 and Grandma was born on December 18, 1927. It was love at first sight at a school dance when my grandma took one look at my Grandpa and thought he looked intelligent because he wore glasses. To this day, my Grandma likes to joke around by saying that she was deceived by the glasses. My great grandparents on my mom's side were Cecilio Trejo II, born on October 18, 1896, and Fidela Moreno, born on September 23, 1893. . . . In order to dodge the [World War I] draft, Cecilio fled to Mexico. It was in Mexico that he met Fidela. They fell in love and wanted to get married in the United States. To cross the Rio Grande, Cecilio put Fidela in a large washbasin and pushed her across the river into Texas where they later married. [My paternal great-grandfather] Aurelio Benavidez was born on May 5, 1872, and he took my great grandmother Delfina's breath away as he rode into San Antonio on his black stallion. . . . [She] left the convent to marry my great grandfather. I am thankful that she left the convent because if she hadn't, my Grandma Gonzalez would never have been born; therefore my father would never have been born, and finally I wouldn't be here right now presenting this report!!"

Connecting past history to local history, Carlos Martinez related the following story of his great-grandfather, who was a bricklayer: "He worked in the remodeling of Sacred Heart Church. He laid down the brick foundation and his brother worked on the doors of the church. The church still stands today with the same foundation that he laid in 1929." In the '40s, his grandmother worked at Fort Bliss Laundromat, getting to her job via the streetcar. "She saw the work camps where Italian, German, and Japanese prisoners were held. In her workday, she would witness when the Italians would be taken out to New Mexico into the farms to do labor and be paid $1 a day. She was not allowed to talk to them or be seen turning her head to see them but she was still able to infer that they were good people. She left two years later for a job at ASARCO. There she shoveled metal. The women working there organized a strike with the help of the labor union to raise their wages from $1.05 an hour to $4.99 an hour. As the men came back from WWII, the women were forced to give up their jobs to the men."

When writing about ancestors who have been caught up in wars, I have had students who did the minimum, like one who wrote that his "great great great grandfather had been in Napoleon's army" but had no further details than that. Ryan Smith, however, was much more thorough: "The account of my family's history begins with my maternal great grandfather, born on October 17, 1892, who is the oldest known of my relatives whose history can be somewhat verified. During the conflict that was going on before the United States entered World War I, some of his twelve siblings brought an unexploded bomb to their farm and it exploded and killed some of them. This caused his father to urge him to go to the United States. His original name was Orlando Eduardo Miguel Ciamano, but after he stowed away on the ship *Venezia* and arrived at Ellis Island on March 30, 1911, he was given the name Orlando McGill."

Orlando McGill worked "as a bridge builder, and traveled across the country working on the Golden Gate and Brooklyn bridges. He enlisted in the Army on June 5, 1917 and served as an infantryman in France during WWI. While there, he was wounded two times. The first time, he was shot across the back by a sniper's bullet, and the second time his right calf was torn off by an exploding shell in an artillery battle. After he was wounded the second time, he survived for three days in a ditch until he was rescued by the people who had come to the battlefield to dispose of the bodies."

"My great grandfather Gonzalo Sotelo," wrote Oscar Sotelo III, "was a machinist for Southern Pacific Railroad and made enough money to give my grandfather and his four brothers and

Oscar Sotelo's grandfather chose photography as his trade in the Army

one sister the basic necessities, but they had no college money for their future. So my great grandfather signed approval to send all his sons to the Army to learn a trade instead of graduating from high school. When my grandfather joined the army at 17, he randomly chose photography as his trade in the Army. The Army taught him everything about still photography to reel-to-reel video recording and he photographed from the ground and from helicopters."

As an army soldier, he became a military photographer during and after wartime. "He witnessed and photographed the war and its aftermath during his career in the Army, from soldiers in action, to the casualties of war, to the destruction of cities and towns, to ceremonies of important military events, and military successes and failures. My grandfather Oscar said that he felt guilty that he survived over all our fallen heroes who did not. He said it was not fair that they did not get a chance to go home to their families after the war. He does not like to talk about his past as a soldier because it still scares him." He continued to work as a civilian photographer at Ft. Bliss for forty years. "As a civilian, he had the high security clearance whereby he had important assignments like being dropped into the nuclear warhead silos in the Dakotas to photograph the stability of the silos' inner walls." Mr. Sotelo is ninety-three and still residing in El Paso where he was born and raised.

"My Grandpa Gibson," reported Dalton Bowling proudly, "jumped out of a jet plane with a parachute in the middle of a battle in WWII at Normandy on D-Day." "My Grandma," said Vincent Minjares, just as proudly, "sewed parachutes for the men in combat in WWII." Jerry Alvarez said his grandpa, Arturo Gonzalez, "told stories about WWII and how he escaped near death experiences in battle or when his ship sank . . . my grandpa and four other sailors were the only known survivors. They walked a few miles into an island of the Philippines to look for a Chinese camp. As they went further into the island they came upon a road and followed it, but they started to see tall stakes with heads of men at the top. My grandpa and the four other soldiers knew that this was the warning sign of the guerrillas. They started to run because they had no fire power and the guerrillas were after them. As they ran, they came to a dried out riverbed filled with dead bodies. My grandpa and the others jumped in and threw dead bodies on themselves to hide. [The guerrillas] finally gave up and my grandpa and the others got out and ran to the Chinese camp they were looking for."

The following is an offering from Sean Miller, a current student: "On March 19, 1947, a baby boy was born. A boy who had no idea that he would grow up to receive the most coveted award of the United States Armed Forces. A boy who would be so brave and show so much courage to completely disregard his own well being to save others. That type of courage is found deep within, and only comes out when there lies an extreme adversity that one finds themselves in, and only has minutes, or even seconds to react.

"My Great Uncle Gary Lee Miller joined the army in Roanoke, Virginia in 1967. Just two years later he found himself serving as a first lieutenant in Company A, 1st Battalion, 28th Infantry Regiment, 1st Infantry Division in the Vietnam War. He found himself in Binh Duong Province in the Republic of Vietnam on the 16th of February 1969. While he was serving as a platoon leader at night, his company was ambushed. After enemy contact was over, and my Great Uncle thought that they had either retreated or had been killed off, he led a reconnaissance patrol to search for enemy casualties. He and his group were suddenly attacked and he was seriously wounded. The group fought back with a force greater than that of their enemies. An enemy grenade was then thrown into the midst of the reconnaissance group. My Great Uncle located the grenade in the dim light and threw himself upon it, smothering the blast of the explosion. He saved nearby members of his patrol from serious injury and death.

"My Great Uncle Gary Miller was awarded the Congressional Medal of Honor posthumously. A part of the Medal of Honor Citation reads: 'The extraordinary courage and selflessness displayed by this officer were an inspiration to his comrades and are in the highest traditions of the U.S. Army.'"

1st Lieutenant Gary Lee Miller's parents receive his Congressional Medal of Honor posthumously from President Richard Nixon

Just as my students bring stories of acts of courage for their country, they bring accounts of great faith, such as this one from Pablo Herrera: "When my grandmother Consuelo Plascencia was pregnant with my uncle, her left side was paralyzed because of liquid that went to her brain. My grandma had to be under constant X-rays for tests and the doctors covered her abdomen trying to protect the baby from radiation. Because of the high amounts of radiation the baby was exposed to during his first months, it was a high possibility that he would be born with physical deformations. When doctors informed my grandma about that, she went to the church in Amatitán, Jalisco and promised to 'El Señor de la Ascencion' that if He let her baby be born healthy, she would walk on her knees all the way from her house to the church through the cobblestone streets. Three months later, my uncle was born healthy and my grandma fulfilled her *manda* by walking 500 meters to the church."

Luis Lazalde's depiction of the Cristero War

As a teacher, I wouldn't be worth my salt if I didn't learn from my students. Luis Lazalde shared what he knew about *La Guerra de los Cristeros*, the Cristero War in Mexico. "At the time that the Constitution of 1917 was signed, Venustiano Carranza was the President of Mexico and he enacted anti-clerical laws which were later enforced selectively by Alvaro Obregon. . . . However, in 1924 a fervent atheist by the name of Plutarco Elias Calles became President and enacted all the anti-clerical laws with the utmost enthusiasm. Up until that point, the Catholics of Mexico had resisted the government's laws peacefully. Then, on August 14, 1926, the government sent agents to Zacatecas to purge the area of Catholics, including my great-grandfather. While my 26-yr old great-grandfather was tending the fields, some government agents snuck up behind him and beat him. They used whips and sticks and hurt him horribly. He managed to somehow escape the thrashing and limped off to his house. When he got there, badly bruised and bleeding, he told his wife it was time to go. That night, they left Zacatecas with only the clothes on their backs. He left his parents and siblings behind and never went back."

Pedro Gonzalez Bello, who came to Cathedral High School as a sophomore in his first year of American schooling, wrote his family history in Spanish, at my request, for I didn't want the limitations of vocabulary to hinder the telling. The following is my translation: "My grandmother is from the small town of Jalostotitlán, Jalisco. During the Cristero War she was seven years old. When word would come that the *federales* were nearing the town, the church bells were rung as a signal for people to hide. The Cristeros would take control of the church while the *federales* would take over City Hall. Then the shooting would commence. It was not unusual for the *federales* to seize ranches, steal horses and kill livestock, abuse servants, destroy houses, burn down ranches, rape the women. On one occasion my grandmother's great-uncle was nearly lynched.

"My grandmother, however, remembers the incidents from a child's perspective, like a pleasant dream: 'When the church bells rang, the servants would scramble to get provisions packed on mules—mattresses, blankets, and food to sustain them. The family and servants would go into the hills into a large cave, one whose opening was hidden by vegetation, and so small that even she had to stoop to enter it. At the cave's exit was an arroyo where they would bathe, wash dishes, and get their drinking water. They stayed in the cave until it was safe to go back.' That's how my grandmother remembers the era.

"I did not know anything about the following until I did this project," Pedro said. "My paternal grandfather had a cousin, Toribio Romo González, born in 1900 to a very devout Christian family. At the age of twelve he entered the seminary and when he became a priest, he dedicated himself to teaching catechism, ministering to the sick, conducting masses and marriage ceremonies, all of which were against the law at the time. He lived in a tequila distillery where the owner allowed him to conduct masses in a makeshift chapel.

"One night the *federales* arrived with Cresencio Landeros, a trusted friend of Father Toribio's. They had threatened to hang him if he didn't follow their command. Sr. Aguirre, the distillery owner, answered the knock at the door thinking Cresencio was alone. The *federales* barged in looking for Father Toribio, shouting 'There's the priest. Kill him!' The rifle shots rang out along with their voices. 'Death to the priest. *Muera el cura!!*' Padre Toribio died in his sister's arms that night of the 25th of February 1928."

"On May 21, 2000, Pope John Paul II canonized a group of 24 Mexican martyrs from this period. The avenue of the Church of Santa Ana pays tribute to them. Padre Toribio's remains are in the church that is dedicated to him."

Imagine that—starting a school year with students who don't think they *have* a family saga, and having one student discover that he's related to a saint! It's no wonder I love teaching as I do.

[All students cited in this paper attend or did attend Cathedral High School in El Paso, Texas. The collection of these family stories took place during the 2006–2007, the 2009–2010, and the 2012–2013 school years. The project is ongoing.]

ENDNOTES

1. Lucy Fischer-West. *Child of Many Rivers: Journeys to and from the Rio Grande*. Texas Tech University Press: Lubbock, 2005
2. Francis E. Abernethy, Jerry Bryan Lincecum, Francis B. Vick. *The Family Saga: A Collection of Texas Family Legends*. Publications of the Texas Folklore Society LX. University of North Texas Press: Denton, 2003. 3.
3. Ibid. 4.

Urban Legends, Ghost Stories and Towns,

and Searching
for Lost
Treasure

Gretchen Kay Lutz

LIVING AN URBAN LEGEND: GALVESTON BALL IN THE EARLY 1970S

by Gretchen Kay Lutz

"What brings you to the Treasure Isle?" The interviewer for the Galveston Independent School District smiled sardonically. He had a good idea why a young married woman right out of college was looking for a teaching job in Galveston. The interviewer presumed I was the wife of one of the new medical students at the University of Texas Medical Branch. I was one of the scores of young teachers who came to Galveston not because the district had a reputation for good schools or because Galveston itself was a pleasant place to live. I was in Galveston to put my husband through medical school. Teaching in Galveston would be just one of the sacrifices I was willing to make to see my husband become a doctor.

Galveston in 1970 was not what it is today. George Mitchell's restorations on the Strand and Tilman Fertitta's Landry Company developments on the Seawall had yet even to be conceived. Always decadent, never much for middle class respectability, Galveston had lured tourists with elaborate, albeit illegal, gambling casinos where famous entertainers played. When the state of Texas shut down wide-open Galveston in 1950, all that could rightly be termed the Treasure Isle disappeared. Still, for my husband and me, Galveston was where medical school was, so we resigned ourselves to a life there.

Because my spouse was accepted by UTMB at the last minute, I was late among teaching applicants. Although I had always envisioned myself teaching high school English, preferably seniors, I felt myself lucky to get the one job that was left—seventh grade English at Weis Middle School.

Weis was one of the three or four air-conditioned school buildings on the island. Friends pointed out that Weis was in the only neighborhood in Galveston that could be termed both "modern" and "nice." Weis was to most observers the best middle school on the island. Everyone said, "Just be glad you are not going to teach at Ball High." Because I had always planned on teaching at the high school level, I questioned why the only upper school on the island would be so undesirable. Galveston itself was a rough town, but Galveston Ball was even rougher, I was told. After all, there was the story of the football bus.

At the time, I did not know the characteristics of an urban legend and therefore was not skeptical when I heard person after person among my medical school friends tell the tale of the night Ball High students overturned a visiting school's football bus. The Ball High students were purported to come chanting threateningly to the hapless opponent's bus in the stadium parking lot. Then, it was told, the Ball kids surrounded the bus and started pushing the bus from all sides, causing it to rock back and forth. Finally, the force of the Ball hooligans was too much; the bus full of opponent students turned over. Sometimes it was said it was the band bus, where instruments were crushed. Sometimes it was cheerleaders and the pep squad, with panicked girls squealing and crying. Sometimes it was even the opposing football team itself, humiliated, yet afraid to come out to fight.

The story would end in various ways according to whose "friend of a friend" had been a witness. The name of the opponent would change from teller to teller yet remain plausible—LaMarque, Texas City, Alvin, Spring Branch. Although this vagueness over just who the victim was should have caused me to doubt that the bus incident was a true story, tale tellers told the story with such earnest sincerity, that despite my having wanted a high school teaching job most of my life, I became resigned and even a bit relieved not to be going to Ball High to teach.

It was not until years later, when I studied folklore and came to know that urban legends reflect our collective hope or fears, especially our fears, that I came to know that the oft-transmitted story of the overturned school bus was just a story—an urban legend borne out of fear of what a huge, newly-integrated high school would be, something quite different from the bucolic-seeming high schools of our own reminiscence. But believing the legend, I was content and relieved not to be going to Ball High School for my very first year in the classroom.

In late August I took my place with the seventh grade English students. I saw almost immediately that it takes a special kind of person to succeed in teaching thirteen-year-olds. I was not that person. There is much misery in the seventh grade—the kids for a large part of their day are miserable, and because of that, they make others around them miserable, too. Just when they are most vulnerable to cruelty, they themselves are the cruelest.

And at the very beginning, I never got the hang of how a teacher has to regiment in minute detail the activities of the students. I could not just send my class to the library, following a short distance behind. I learned the hard way that middle schoolers without intense scrutiny cannot go from room to room without incident. I discovered I had to line the students up single file and march them, with my walking up and down the line like a drill sergeant. Once, after practicing the march three or four times back and forth from classroom to library, my group and I returned to find a note written anonymously on the blackboard. "F—- the Library," it read. I could not have agreed more.

And then there was my lunch duty: Boys' restroom. Soon my experience taught me that the paradigm of middle school was two little boys running full blast down the hall, trying to kick each other in the groin. For me, the whole attempt to impose the values of middle class respectability upon the children of Galveston Island was just too daunting.

At Weis, frustrated as I was, I was, at least, among fellow travelers. A group of us young teachers started going to happy hour at the Pizza Inn across the street. We began by going right after school every Friday. As the year progressed, we were going every Thursday and Friday. Still further into the year, we were at the Pizza Inn every Tuesday, Thursday, and Friday.

I remember one Wednesday in February. It was one of those wet Galveston days of cold, grey drizzle. Walking into the apartment from school, I wanted something to warm me, so I boiled water for a nice cup of hot tea. I poured the boiling water into the cup and then opened the cabinet to get a tea bag. Searching the shelves, I noticed a half-full bottle of whiskey. I went to the sink, poured out the hot water, and filled my tea cup with Jack Daniels. Before I drank, I paused. "What have I become?" I asked myself, melodramatically. Grimly, I acknowledged with conviction that I had to get out of middle school. Despite all the warnings, despite the legend of the overturned school bus, I was going to go to Ball High.

Opened in 1884, Ball was the first public high school in Texas. In 1968, Ball had merged with Central, Texas' oldest African-American high school, so that by the time I came there in 1971, Ball, with 3600 students, was the largest high school in Texas. When I went up the school's front steps for my interview, I was excited yet apprehensive—what if Ball High turned out to be just as scary as everyone feared?

Unlike Weis, with its harsh fluorescent lights, Ball, a building in Mid-Century design, had the recessed lighting customary of the 1950s. I was astonished to see no students being marched from place to place by their authoritarian teachers. It was lunch time, and students were gathered into small groups merely talking—no pushing, no hitting, no running. A student approached me and asked if she could help me. She showed me the way to the principal's office, and guessing that I was a job applicant, she bade me good luck.

So far, Ball High seemed disarmingly benign. The principal seemed both surprised and flattered that anyone would want to leave air-conditioned Weis in the nice part of town, to come to his hot, decidedly not air-conditioned school, with every possible kind of student one could find on the island. "You are in luck," he said. One of the teacher's husbands had gotten a residency out of town, leaving an opening in eleventh grade English. He offered me the job on the spot. I was thrilled to accept. As I walked back to my car, I started imagining what work of American literature I would start with—maybe *Huckleberry Finn*. We would sit out on the front lawn in a circle, putting ourselves on the raft with Jim and Huck. Fall could not come soon enough.

Reality never quite has the glow of the imagined good thing, but the reality of Ball High was, for me, so much preferable to being with seventh graders that I grudgingly accepted things like the fact that I had forty-two students in a classroom designed for twenty-five. I reluctantly accepted the fact that the rudimentary computer system could not level classes for another six weeks. I also accepted the fact that I had to walk through the student ciga-rette smoking area on the way to my classroom.

It was not as bad as it seems. The students themselves in that class of forty-two, good natured about the over-crowding, arrived early in order to have a desk. The smoking area was rendered less odious because some of my veteran teaching colleagues, who were smokers, would greet me as I passed through, occasionally offering me tips about how to survive as a high school teacher.

The apt advice, "Don't sweat the small stuff" was a kind of inside joke in our sweltering, un-air-conditioned building. I remember that during my first week at Ball, I was grading a stack of papers while my students worked at their seats. Suddenly, water began pouring on to the papers. Startled, I looked up, hoping to find the leak in the roof so that I could report it. There was no leak, I quickly realized. The water flowing onto my papers was coming from my own hair; it was literally the sweat of my brow.

I came to quietly accept the heat until one day when I was rid-ing with my carpool of other medical students' wives. Before I got into the car, I stepped in a pile of dog doo. Trying to clean the mess off, I scraped and scraped my shoe on the grass outside my apartment. When I got into the car, however, the smell was over-powering. Everyone cried, "Ooh, get that out of here," but we were about to be late, so we endured all the way to school.

When I got inside my classroom, I was relieved that I did not smell the dog poop anymore. The day passed pleasantly enough without incident. At the end of the day, I joined my friends in the carpool, where we were almost overcome once again by the excrement smell. And then I realized that the offending odor had not gone away at all. Instead, the other smells of Galveston Ball High School had been so pungent that my little dog poop contribution got lost in the general stench.

The experience at Ball was not all easy and amusing. Integration for racial equality was an ongoing process, not something that just happened by fiat. In those very early years, some of the African-American young ladies protested that the dancing style of the Tornettes drill team was just too white for them. They may have had a point. The Tornettes were modeled on the Kilgore Rangerettes, right down to their red, white, and blue outfits, which were remarkable in that purple and gold were the official Ball High colors. A year passed with no blacks trying out for the team. The next year, a few African Americans auditioned, made the squad, and by my third year at Ball, the cadet colonel and fully a third of the young ladies on the dance squad were black.

Sports teams integrated more readily, but because Central had had its own staff of coaches, there was tension among the adults over who would be in charge at Ball. Within a few years together, however, coaches and players seemed reconciled, especially so because the football and basketball teams were successful—more successful, in fact, than they had been when Ball and Central were separate schools.

Still, the Ball High bad reputation remained. And there were some very tough, serious, sometimes life-and-death adult situations that our students had to face, problems that just did not come up at a place like Weis Middle School. To get us ready for the Ball High teaching experience, Principal Jim Watson held an annual faculty assembly where he introduced old and new faculty by roasting members of the returning faculty. I remember that he would pretend to be looking at a teacher's transcript, commenting on the courses she took and the grades she made. Watson, of course, knew whom he could kid and whom to avoid. The crowds of old heads roared to hear their friends skewered. Then Watson, today perhaps best known for having been Nolan Ryan's baseball coach, got serious. He warned the new teachers that at Ball High School, they were going to see some things they just were not going to believe. To survive, they had to be ready to roll with it. To succeed at Ball High, the most important quality a teacher could have was a good sense of humor.

Watson's was a point well taken. Because Ball was such a large school, we had two separate campuses separated by two city blocks. Students had to cross two streets to get to class. Twice, while I was walking among the students as they were passing, a student, not realizing I was a teacher, offered me a marijuana joint. My response: I could either make a big deal and risk starting a riot in the street, or just pretend I did not hear. I took the calmer way out. One may question that today, but it was, after all, the 1970s.

One day, while I was teaching my class, a student who was the president of the Rah Rah Committee, the spirit organization I sponsored, stopped by my door and motioned me outside. I was a little miffed at being interrupted, thinking he wanted to talk about making spirit decorations while I had a class waiting. I frowned at first as this student told me, with a confidential tone, that there was someone walking along the roof, mooning the passing traffic. I responded, "What do you want me to do? Do you want me to get the principal?"

"Oh, no. Nothing like that. I just thought you would want to know."

My Rah Rah president, who went on to become science writer for the *New York Times*, understood without being told the mystique of Ball High. Every day another student from the class next door would come to me to ask, "Is this the Hotel California, or is that Mr. Meischen's class?" Even, the students, or maybe *especially* the students, knew that the way to get along at Ball High School was to have a sense of humor.

Still, to outsiders, especially those who had heard the overturned bus story, Ball was perceived as a rough, tough school.

They reasoned Ball High teachers must be really tough, too. That was not necessarily the case, but we reveled in that mystique, and in the swagger, the reputation that went with prevailing day after day in a difficult situation. When one of us would worry aloud about the consequences of displeasing the administration, we would invariably answer with what had become a cliché among us: "What are they going to do? Send us to Vietnam?"

Sometimes we Ball High colleagues would attend Houston-area teachers meetings. At such meetings it was typical for each small group to give the name of the school they represented. Groups would respond with the name of some Houston suburban or mainland high school, and no one would pay much attention, until we fresh-faced twenty somethings would respond, "Galveston Ball." Suddenly, there would be a gasp from the crowd, followed by a murmur: "Those young teachers are in charge at the school where the students turned over the school bus? Could that be?"

Well, no, that was not exactly fact. Yet it was, in a more important sense, truth—truth about what really matters. Like Galveston Island itself, Ball High was unique. In forty years of teaching, I was never to experience a school like it again. The truth about being a teacher at Ball HS in the 1970s, we learned, was, as Principal Watson had advised, to have a great sense of humor, because we were going to see some things we were just not going to believe, or sadly, were never going to see again.

So, in my own recollection, the school bus urban legend of Ball High School, which proved to be not at all indicative of what that place was really like, has been replaced by a nostalgia for a time in American culture and a time in my personal life when the unknown future offered more to be welcomed than feared. My world today is populated by new, contemporary urban legends, the sort of fear-inspired conspiracy theories that enjoy, and I use that term ironically, a vigorous folk circulation on the Internet. From what we see in email and on Facebook, we folklorists come to acknowledge that the folk are as alive in twenty-first century, middle class, sophisticated, educated America as they were in an imagined, more benighted time when the "folk" were primitives who circulated storied to explain to themselves their world.

Just as the false story of the overturned school bus influenced how a generation saw the newly-integrated Ball High School, today our legends circulate in cyberspace. And being very much one of the folk, I long for a return to when my world was all about optimistic possibilities, not the advent of feared calamity that I see when I read my email. Then again, my longing for a return to a more optimistic time is itself a function of legend, legend of what it would be like to be twenty-five years old and have, as I had in my Ball High days, nothing in my future but optimistic possibilities. It is an attractive legend.

Marissa Gardner

THE TRUTH VERSUS THE LEGEND OF THE INTERSTATE 45 SERIAL KILLER

by Marissa Gardner

⌐⌐

The citizens of Houston know all too well what it is like to live in fear of a serial killer. Between 1971 and 2006, there were thirty-two homicides and six disappearances that occurred on, or in close proximity to, the southeast side of Interstate 45, which runs through Houston. The victims were all females ranging from less than ten years old to over thirty years old, and their bodies were found raped, beaten, and even decapitated. Four of the bodies were discovered close to each other in fields now known as "The Killing Fields," and some bodies were never found. These horrendous crimes were shoved in the faces of Houstonians daily on billboards along Interstate 45 which showed the missing victims' faces. There were also frequent news broadcasts pushing the idea of the murders being the work of a single serial killer, and still today many Houston residents believe that is the case.

However, the idea that one person got away with this criminal activity for over thirty years and is still out there waiting to take more lives is unreasonable. Facts not widely known are that one man was convicted of four of the murders, and another is suspected by police to have committed some of the other murders. In addition, several other suspects are believed to have been involved, and there have been multiple arrests related to the events. Though there is not solid proof that the murders are the work of more than one person, evidence indicates that there were multiple killers, and probably just two serial killers involved.

One of the likely serial killers in the events is a man named Ed Bell. A report tells that "Police are convinced that Bell ended the lives of eight of the victims during the 1970s."[1] The same report shows in very convincing detail that Bell had the murder weapon, the vehicle seen by witnesses to drive away with two of the girls the last time they were seen, a shop that four of the victims frequented, and a residence near the swamp where two of the victims' bodies were dumped. The sadistic killer of these innocent, young female victims was sexually motivated to carry out the crimes. Ed Bell had a record showing his propensity for exposing himself to minor females, which is a sign that he was sadistically and sexually attracted to young females.[2]

Bell was never convicted of the killings, probably because of the lack of technology in the 1970s. By the time technology, such as DNA analysis that could have proved Bell guilty was discovered, most of the witnesses and clues were just not there anymore to contribute to the case against him. An interesting fact which points to multiple killers is that Ed Bell was incarcerated on an unrelated charge in 1978, but the killings continued for almost thirty years after he was locked away.[3] The single-serial killer myth cannot be true if Ed Bell is guilty of the murders he is believed to have committed; however, Ed Bell probably was the only active serial killer in the Southeast Houston area during the 1970s.

One of the five suspects who was arrested for the murders, but never convicted in a court of law of being guilty of committing any of them, is William Reese. A report tells how Reese "was working construction on an early summer night, when he left work and drove by Sandra Sapaugh, a pregnant nineteen-year-old woman, who was fixing a flat on the side of the road."[4] The report goes on to tell how Sapaugh thought Reese had stopped to help her, "but then he pulled a knife on her and forced her into his truck; and as he drove seventy miles per hour north on Interstate forty-five, Reese threatened her with the knife and ordered her to undress."[5] The pregnant woman, seeing no other choice, "opened the passenger door and jumped out of the fast moving truck"; Sapaugh and her unborn child survived the nightmarish ordeal after being rescued by another driver, but she sustained serious injuries.[6]

In his short story "Strawberry Spring," about a serial killer stalking a two-year college campus, Stephen King says that what brought the victim into the hands of the killer was, "Maybe a need for one desperate and passionate romance with the warm night, the warm fog, the smell of the sea, and the cold knife."[7] Was King right about victims in serial killings not being random, but subconsciously craving a fatal meeting with death? Were Sapaugh and the other victims in the Interstate 45 serial killings just victims by chance, or was it fate that brought them into the killers' hands? Maybe the victims were in need of a rendezvous with the angel of death in their fatal last moments.

Another man named as one of the serial killers who contributed to the murders on Interstate 45 is Anthony Allen Shore. It is reported that he was actually convicted for four of the murders and is a suspect in a few of the others. By thoroughly examining Shore's history, one writer uncovered that "Shore had a job that gave him ample opportunity and access to commit the crimes and has a history of child molestation."[8] Shore was in all the vicinities at all the right times to have done the murders, dating back to the very first ones in the 1970s. In the court case against Shore, very important evidence that helped to convict him was the DNA sample gathered from one of the victim's fingernails that matched Shore's DNA.[9]

The report on Shore has extensive details on more than seven other men who are suspects in the case of the murders of Interstate 45. Some of these men were arrested, but none of them were convicted in a court of law because there was not enough solid evidence to convince a jury that these men were guilty beyond reasonable doubt. At least two or three of the suspects were probably guilty of contributing to the killings. One of the suspects actually confessed to many of the murders, but because of the lack of evidence, he was never charged with the murders.[10]

The question remains that if these men really are guilty, then why is there no evidence to convict them of the crimes? The most likely reason is that Interstate 45 is such a busy road that the evidence is lost in the thousands of people who drive on the road every day. Mike Sullivan is a resident of South Houston who pays close attention to all current events, and he believes that the serial killings are the work of at least three independent serial killers. He vividly remembers the facts of many of the cases because he and his young family lived only blocks from Interstate 45 in the 1990s, and he was well aware of the murders that were happening. Sullivan does not believe that the killings were all the work of a single serial killer, and he states, "It is likely that some of the murders were crimes of passion and not related."[11]

Sullivan believes there were so many murders in the same area because, "A main artery in a large city will always be an urban killer's dumping ground."[12] I-45 is an interstate that runs vertically and straight through Houston, which makes it an easy road on which to commit a murder and then to flee at a legal speed of sixty-five miles per hour. One could commit a murder in the center of Houston and be long gone within thirty minutes of dumping the body. It is no wonder that killers choose this spot to murder because it has such a convenient getaway route.

The convenience of committing a crime on this interstate is common knowledge to many criminals; even bank robbers take advantage of the convenience. The Chase Bank located on Interstate 45 is robbed more frequently than any other Chase Bank in Houston. Murder is only one of the many crimes that have a higher rate along Interstate 45.

Many times, people are influenced by the media because they listen to what is said and they automatically believe it without seriously questioning it. The media know this, and also know that the larger the audience they have, the more successful they will be. They try to hype news up as much as they can in order to get the attention they need. Outside influences also can factor into what the media portrays to the public. John E. Conklin, the author of *Criminology,* wrote: "Serial murder is a crime that has commanded great attention in recent years."[13] He goes on to say, "It is a serious crime, but one that has been exaggerated and distorted by various claims makers."[14] Conklin recalls that there was a time when the media was convinced by an outside force to trick the audience. He says, "The Federal Bureau of Investigation's Behavioral Sciences Unit was influential in defining this problem during the 1980's, exaggerating the number of serial murderers active at any given moment."[15] A fact already known, and stated in a report, is that the Federal Bureau of Investigation became involved in the investigation of the Interstate 45 murders as late as 1999.[16] If the FBI exaggerated the number of serial killers in the 1980s, then it is possible that they did the same in the 1990s. Maybe they thought that the public would respond more urgently if people believed there was a serial killer on the loose. This form of lying to the public and playing on their fear through the media causes people to be more vigilant in looking for a killer, resulting in more helpful public tips for law enforcement. In a sick way, portraying separate incidences as the work of one killer could have been beneficial and contributed to the FBI solving the cases.

Adolfo Lopez is another resident of Houston who was very familiar with the homicides that were happening during the 1990s time period. He was so in tune with the news at the time of the murders, and was so eager to help put an end to the serial killings, that he reported his neighbor's suspicious activities to the police. He is convinced that there is one killer who has done all these deeds by himself. His theory of why there is one killer who has gotten away with the murders for all this time is that "the killer most likely made some mistakes in the first murders, but because there was no DNA analysis during that time, he got away with the original few crimes and got better at what he was doing, in order to successfully cover his tracks by the time DNA analysis was discovered."[17]

When asked if he thought Anthony Shore and Ed Bell were guilty of any of the murders, Lopez did not even know who they were. He knew all kinds of little details, such as the color of the truck one of the last victims drove, but he did not have any knowledge of these two likely murderers who are involved in the case.[18] Although some could call Lopez's lack of knowledge a coincidence, it is more likely that these men's suspicious roles in the crimes were not publicized as much as the idea of a serial killer was. If Lopez knew the information about Shore and Bell, he would likely have a different opinion and would believe that there was at least more than one killer. Maybe the reason so many believe that there is one menacing killer who carried out all of the homicides is that they do not know all of the facts, and are unintentionally biased because of the media's exaggerations about the murders.

Another fact that discredits the idea of a single killer is that Houston is such a violent city in general, and the problem of a high murder rate is not exclusive to Interstate 45. Thirty-two murders along one main road in a city seems like a large number; however, the *Houston Chronicle* notes that "Houston is the most violent big city in Texas, and the eighth most violent in the country."[19] Also, in the year 2000, Ellise Pierce wrote for *Texas Monthly*, "In Harris County, which has the third-largest sheriff's department in the country, nearly 450 unsolved murders remain on the books, some dating back to 1972."[20] That number, when averaged out, is equivalent to 150 murders for every ten years, which go unsolved. So, if the rate of unsolved murders stays close to the same, then there are about 600 unsolved murders in Houston right now dating back to 1972. The number of unsolved murders that happened in connection to Interstate 45 actually diminishes when compared to the total number of unsolved murders in Houston.

Killers tend to stick with their own race when choosing victims. According to one study, "twenty-one offenders, viewed as actual serial killers, were selected from fifteen jurisdictions in the Continental United States of America on the basis of the following criterion: two or more sexually motivated homicides perpetrated by the same offender at different times."[21] In this study, "all of the selected murders had sexual gratification as primary objective."[22] The crimes were evaluated, and show a definite correlation between the race of the killer and the race of the victims; "of the chose [sic] serial killers, eighty-four point six percent of the victims of black offenders were black; and eighty-five point three percent of the victims of white perpetrators were white."[23]

All of the victims in the Interstate 45 phenomenon—who were intact enough when found to have their ethnicity identified—were Caucasian, until the late 1980s and early 1990s, when three Hispanic females became victims. It does not seem likely that the killer stuck to his own race for so many years, and then opposing proven statistics suddenly changed his choice of victim, becoming an intraracial killer. It is more statistically likely that the killer who killed the three Hispanics was Hispanic, and the killer, or killers, who committed the other homicides was Caucasian, which is what Anthony Shore and Ed Bell were. This evidence alone points to at least two killers in the Interstate 45 murders, one or more who killed the Caucasians and another who killed the Hispanics.

There is a very minute chance that the serial killer phenomenon in connection to Interstate 45 could have been carried out by a single perpetrator; however, there is too much evidence to not at least doubt the truth to that theory. If we believe everything that we are told, without looking at the facts on our own, we fail to use the most useful ability we possess: our own judgment. Just like many situations that are mysteries to us, the answer to the question in the mystery of the slayings of Interstate 45—which is, "Who did it?"— may never be answered.

Evidence is strong in the cases of Ed Bell and Anthony Shore, and it is almost undeniable that these men are guilty of being serial killers who carried out their heinous acts in a convenient place.

Statistics point to multiple killers in the mysterious happenings of Interstate 45. It is certain, when more than just the publicized information is analyzed, that there were at least two serial killers and probably at least another two killers who are responsible for these events. As with most folklore, publicity and word of mouth have exaggerated the truth behind the legend of the Interstate 45 serial killer.

ENDNOTES

1. "Texas I-45 Corridor Murders!" *Psycho Stalker Ugliness & Serial Killers!* Web. 05 July 2010. <http://psu-sk.tripod.com/frames/contents.html>.
2. Ibid.
3. Ibid.
4. Ibid.
5. Ibid.
6. Ibid.
7. Stephen King. "Strawberry Spring" *Night Shift.* New York: Random House Inc, 1978. 185.
8. "Texas I-45 Corridor Murders!"
9. Ibid
10. Ibid.
11. Mike Sullivan. Personal interview. Monday, June 28, 2010.
12. Ibid.
13. John E Conklin. *Criminology.* Needham Heights: Allyn and Bacon, 1998 Print. 16.
14. Ibid.
15. Ibid. 16–17.
16. Brian Barron. "Police Baffled by Texas I-45 Murders." BBC News. (18 November 1999) Web. 05 July 2010. < http://news.bbc.co.uk/2/hi/americas/525273.stm>.
17. Adolfo Lopez. Personal interview. Thursday, July 1, 2010.
18. Ibid.
19. "Serener Streets." *Economist* 392.8646 (2009). *Academic Search Complete.* EBSCO. Web. 30 June 2010.

20. Ellise Pierce. "Unhappy Trails." *Texas Monthly* 28.2 (2000): *Academic Search Complete*. EBSCO. Web. 29 June 2010. 66.
21. Serge-Moses Pakhomou. "Serial Killers: Offender's Relationship to *the Victim and Selected Demographics.*" *International Journal of Police Science & Management* 6.4 (2004). *Academic Search Complete*. EBSCO. Web. 29 June 2010.
22. Ibid.
23. Ibid.

Francis Edward Abernethy
Photo by Hardy Meredith

GHOST TOWNS OF THE BIG THICKET

by Francis Edward Abernethy

This was back in 1960. Somebody told me that there was going to be a big Josey party on Saturday night at Bleakwood in the high school gymnasium. It sounded like an occasion too special to miss, especially since I was heavy into collecting East Texas folk music at the time. Of course, I had never heard of Bleakwood, even though I had spent the better part of my life in East Texas. I studied a road map but never did find it, which raised a few suspicions, but I returned to my informant and he gave me some pretty good directions—and I took my twelve-old-daughter, who at the time, knew pretty well everything that was worth knowing.

We arrived that Saturday night in the general vicinity. It was June and the evenings were long with sunset, but I drove on through and was a couple of miles beyond Bleakwood before I realized my error. I turned around, and this time carefully retraced my trail until I did finally come to a scattering of houses and off to the right of the road saw a rambling frame building, completely out of place where it happened to be, but looking like a gymnasium with a large number of cars parked on the far side. Sure enough, I had found Bleakwood, or what was left of it.

The Bleakwoodians were having their annual reunion, which consisted of a Josey party on Saturday night, church services and gospel singing on Sunday morning, dinner on the grounds at noon, and graveyard cleaning on Sunday afternoon.

The Josey party was a grand one, and Luanna and I marched (you do not dance at a Josey party) through "Shoot the Buffalo," "Old Joe Clark," and several repetitions of "Weevily Wheat" till late hours.

And we visited with the ghosts that still hovered around Bleakwood, once a thriving railroad and sawmill town on the east side of the Big Thicket. Behind every dance were ghosts of the old ones and the loved ones who had danced to these same songs. The conversations among the guests were about Papa and Aunt Minnie and the sheriff from Kirbyville who had come over when the Bleakwood boys had a "picket pullin'" with some toughs from Bon Wier. They went through the obituaries in their memories to call back the spirits of all those who had lived in Bleakwood, had worked in the mills, played basketball with such spirit and energy, made love in a Model A, married, gave birth, and died in reality—but their presences, their ghosts, still hovered over the place where they had left their memories. The homecomers laughed at the comedy of the past as much as they cried over its loss. Bleakwood had been the center of their world during the intensities of their youth. Then, almost all in the same early-1940s-World War II-breath the timber was gone, and the railroad tracks were pulled. The young men left for the service, the old men—in their thirties and forties!—left for the shipyards, and Bleakwood died a silent death.

The Bleakwood post office was closed in 1943, and by the end of the war, this once small but vibrant, thriving town was just another wide place in the road, and ghosts of the past way outnumbered the citizens of the present. But in 1960 the ghosts were still strong in Bleakwood, strong enough to be visited annually and gently caressed by fading memories.

The area of ghost towns I'll cover is in the Big Thicket, and that is a vague and frequently disputed geographical description. Bleakwood—and Scrappin' Valley and Devil's Pocket—are on the far eastern edge of the Thicket. The old-time, traditional, bear hunters' Thicket is mainly in Hardin County. It is flat, clay-pan, poorly drained soil that includes the Pine Island Bayou. It is about forty-miles long and twenty-miles wide and runs from the foothills of Polk County southeast through Hardin County to the coastal prairie in Jefferson County. That is the heart of the Big Thicket, the land between Village Creek to the north and Pine Island Bayou to the south. My ghost towns come from the heart of the Thicket and its environs.

Ghost towns in the Thicket—in East Texas and elsewhere—
came about quite naturally. In this paper I will consider several
related issues. First, **river ports** ghosted out early in East Texas
Anglo history. **Sawmill towns** sprang up in the big woods, but
died just as quickly when the timber was all gone. **Oil boom
towns** were born when a strike was made, but after the wells were
drilled and the pumps were installed, labor was no longer in
demand, and the towns were deserted. When **railroad tracks** were
pulled or the railroad bypassed a town, towns died from a lack of
business. **World War II** was the beginning of the end of many
small rural towns, because the young men went into the service
and many of the women and the old men (over thirty-five) moved
down to Houston or the Golden Triangle to work in the shipyards—and they never went back. When **farm-to-market roads**
were built, the small rural towns that served the needs of nearby
farms died from lack of business. With roads paved into larger
towns, farmers could afford to live in town with good schools and
WalMarts and picture shows and then drive out to their farms to
work. Small community and country schools died when the roads
were paved to town and schools were consolidated.

Some of the earliest towns to ghost out were the **river ports**.
River ports were built on the Sabine, Angelina, Neches, and Trinity
rivers. Steamboats were plentiful on those waters and regularly at
hand to haul cotton and hides down to Beaumont and the Gulf
markets and bring bolts of cloth and barrels of salt back up river to
the Big Thicket and Deep East Texas. Between 1830 and 1860,
Concord, on the southeast corner of the Thicket, was a bustling
Neches River port. However, competing with the steamboats for
river space after the 1840s were great rafts of logs that sawyers cut
and floated down the East Texas rivers to the sawmills around Beaumont and Port Arthur. Ultimately, when the rivers began to silt up
as a result of washoff from cutover lands and were trashed up with
errant log rafts, steamboat traffic diminished. Then in the 1870s,
when the railroads started reaching into the East Texas forests,
steamboat traffic stopped completely. And Old Concord—and all

the river ports that had been vital to the East Texas transportation, commerce, and economy—moldered back into the woods and are now no more than ghosts sitting on granite historical markers by the riverside.

There is no telling how many **sawmill communities** were born and died during a century in East Texas, say from 1850 to 1950. During the great logging days, between 1870 and 1920, whole towns with churches, general stores, stables, saloons, and whorehouses sprang up around the sawmills. Village Mills was a sawmill town that started in 1881 at a Village Creek crossing in Hardin County. Village Mills flourished for almost fifty years. It had a post office, train depot, a doctor's office, a community hall where the Woodmen of the World met, and a company commissary where everybody bought everything they needed. ("And I owe my soul to the company store!") At their peak of production the sawmills turned out 175,000 board feet of lumber a day, and the residents clocked their lives by the sawmill whistles. In 1889, Village Mills had 600 residents, and by 1903, when John Henry Kirby of Peach Tree Village (another ghost town, this one haunted by both Alabama Indian and Anglo haints) bought the mill, it had a population of 800, 400 of whom worked at the mill. But that was tops. All of the available surrounding timber had been cut by the 1920s and the mill shut down in 1930. The Village Mills post office operated until 1944, when it was moved down Village Creek to the Highway 59 crossing. The woods grew up around another sawmill town, and only the ghosts of John Henry and his sawyers and planers remembered Village Mills when it was an exciting and productive community in the Big Thicket.

Another phenomenon that left villages in a ghostly state in East Texas was the **oil booms** of the early twentieth century. Spindletop was the beginning in 1901, but Batson, Sour Lake, and Saratoga in the Big Thicket came soon after. For ten years wildcatters drilled the holes and pumped the black gold out of the Big Thicket. Then the boom was over, and the wildcatters and the drillers and the roughnecks left. The pumps kept on a'pumping, but the towns shrank back to crossroads post offices and to filling stations that carried groceries.

Batson had been settled by 1840, and most of the settlers raised cattle in the canebrakes and on the prairie to the south. Cattle thieves were bad, so the Batson folks formed a Night Riders vigilante group and made their own laws. When they caught Vailma Raibee stealing a cow, they skinned the cow and sewed up Vailma in the wet hide with his head sticking out and left him to die when varmints ate him or the hide dried and squeezed him to death. There was very little argument about the death penalty at that time.

During the oil boom the population of Batson was reportedly 10,000—all of them rough and rowdy—with four large hotels and ten saloons, always open. Batson was poor in jails and had only a small one. A roughneck named Bolden was a regular prisoner. One day he broke out, bought a can of white paint, and came back and painted the jail. He said that if he was going to spend most of his time there, he wanted it to look nice.

Batson nowadays is a ghost of its former self. It does have a new grocery store-filling station, but the thousands of drillers and roughnecks and whores and speculators who lived there a hundred years ago are spirits whistling at night in the winds that blow up from the coast.

Sour Lake is an oil-and-spa town and is not as ghosty as the rest. The town was founded around a series of mineral springs that were visited in times past by the Indians, who believed in the springs' curative powers. Even before the Civil War folks came from all over Texas to see what the marvelous springs could do for them. Sam Houston came to cure his wounds of war. A huge Springs Hotel was built around 1845, and after The War the baths were presided over by the legendary Dr. Mud, a former slave and medicine man. Dr. Mud created special mud baths and mud beauty packs for ladies. As well as being skilled in his profession, Dr. Mud was diplomatic. One extremely homely lady asked for his special beauty pack, and he told her, "Yes'um, I'll fix you one, but I really don't think you need it."

Sour Lake boomed with oil in 1901, and it had a population of 10,000, pumped 50,000 barrels a day, and boasted fifty-two saloons at one time. The Texaco Oil Company began at Sour Lake. Then the drillers left and the companies pumped the oil until one morning in 1929, when someone noticed that out in a large cow pasture two tall sweet-gum trees were leaning over with their tops nearly touching. Even as he watched he could see the land sinking, and an hour later the sink was fifty feet deep and the sides were giving away. By noon the sink was ninety-feet deep and filling with mud, water, and oil. Twenty-eight years of pumping had created a hollow space that eventually caved in to form a sizeable lake.

The Sour-Lake-sink phenomenon should have been an object lesson in conservation of natural resources, but it wasn't.

Sour Lake nowadays is not your typical ghost town, like Batson or Fuqua or Thicket. It is a thriving community with a modern economy based on lumbering and rice fields and a few wells out near the Thicket woods. But the Sour Lake that was, the watering place of the rich and the famous, then the birthplace of Texaco Oil Company is a ghost town and part of a history that drips from the pine needles on a misty night, when Dr. Mud wanders from spring to spring sampling the mud and the waters to see what he might find that might cure a really bad case of the uglies.

The **route of a railroad track** could determine whether a town prospered or perished. The removal of tracks was an invitation to ghosts. There is not much of a marker at Old Hardin. It's a bronze plaque that hangs loosely on a rusty pipe post. The marker stands near a post oak that was there when grown men played serious marble games on the town's main street and when Warren Collins could whip any man in the Thicket except May Hooks—and that was a draw. That old post oak was there when the Hardin County courthouse stood a hundred feet away with three cedars standing in front. Hardin was founded in 1858, had a population of several hundred, and was at one time the county seat, the political center, and the heart of commerce in Hardin County and the Big Thicket.

Then, in 1884, the Sabine and East Texas Railroad ran a line from Beaumont north toward Woodville, and the tracks left Hardin sitting in the Thicket, all by itself, three miles to the west. Stores opened at the new switch called Kountze, and lawyers and doctors and businessmen began leaving Hardin for the new business center. Some county citizens began agitating for a move of the county seat from Hardin to Kountze. And then something happened to help them make that move. The Hardin County courthouse in Hardin burned down to a fine ash—"under suspicious circumstances," according to the plaque—on the night of March 3, 1886.

Folks say that the culprit who set the fire was Gus Hooks, the fastest man in the Thicket, who outran horses, carried his whiskey around in a soda-pop bottle, had two wives who lived around the bend of the road from each other, and who is immortalized in a bronze bas-relief hanging in the Kountze public library. Whether it was Gus or not, folks saw a man running like a spooked deer from the burning courthouse, and Gus Hooks was the first man that came to mind. Witnesses mounted their horses and headed for Gus's house, six miles away on Village Creek. When they finally got there and rode up to the house, Gus was in bed, sweaty but looking sound asleep, and he seemed to be completely surprised at the news of the courthouse tragedy.

Whoever the culprit was, the citizens of Hardin County built a new courthouse by the railroad tracks in Kountze. The folks who still lived in Hardin, if they wanted to be where the action was, moved to Kountze. Hardin became Old Hardin and now is hardly even a ghost town. It is that bronze plaque and the old post oak tree that still keep the old town's secrets and provide a moonlight roost for the ghosts of Warren Collins, Gus Hooks, and their likes.

Bragg Station also suffered from railroad track withdrawal. Bragg was founded in 1901 on the Santa Fe railroad line, where a spur took off and ran seven miles south as straight as a rifle barrel from the Bragg settlement to Saratoga. The ghosts that haunt the vicinity of Old Bragg Station have wandered down the tram road that carried the tracks of the Santa Fe to Saratoga.

The Old Bragg ghosts now team up with the haunts of the Bragg Road, one of whom was a railroad brakeman who was decapitated in a train wreck. They found his body but never did locate his head. The ghost of that old brakeman now wanders the tram road as a ghostly light looking for his lost head and scaring the bejabbers out of unsuspecting motorists taking a shortcut down Bragg Road. On this Bragg-Ghost Road are also the specters of a Mexican rail gang whom the foreman murdered rather than give them their accumulated pay. Their troubled spirits rise from graves near the old Bragg Road and float like spectral lights or wisps of ectoplasm across the road at night. Young girls scream and the older folk get very still and quiet when the Bragg Light appears.

Honey Island is a ghost town that died, as did Bleakwood, with **World War II**. Back at the turn of the twentieth century, Honey Island was the center of logging and sawmill operations and had a population of around 800 people. The loggers left when the timber was gone, and in the Thirties the Civilian Conservation Corps built a camp there. When the CCC left, Honey Island still had Lloyd's swimming pool, which was fed by hot artesian springs. Also during the Thirties, Honey Island had filling stations and general stores that served much of the rural population of that part of the Big Thicket. The community collapsed when World War II took most of its menfolk to the service and to the shipyards in the Golden Triangle. After that, "How you gonna keep 'em down on the farm, after they've seen Paree—and Houston and Beaumont?"

The main ghosts that haunt Honey Island are the spirits of the old Jayhawkers who hid out north of there in the Thicket during the Civil War and used Honey Island as their supply base. In fact, the settlement got its name from the practice of the Jayhawkers leaving gourd containers of wild honey on this "island" in exchange for salt and coffee and tobacco and other staples necessary for their survival in the wilderness. (An "island" in the Big Thicket, by the way, is a high and dry hummock that rises above the surrounding flat land.) Fifteen or twenty of the Thicket men, under the leadership of Warren Collins—he, the fighter of Old Hardin— were neither political nor partisan. They held no slaves and had no desire to go fight for the glory of the South. So, they hid out in the Thicket. They made camps on what became appropriately named Union Wells Creek and Bad Luck Creek in the north part of the Thicket and stayed out of sight during most of The War, living off the land and what they might get in trade at Honey Island.

Captain Charlie Bullock rounded up several of them, including Warren Collins, in 1864. He put them in jail in Woodville, but Warren whittled them out of jail with his pocket knife, and they headed back to their Union Wells hideout. In early 1865, Captain James Kaiser came up from Galveston with a troop, set on rooting out this nest of Jayhawkers. The soldiers surrounded the hideout at Union Wells and fired the Thicket. They burned two thousand acres of timber and killed two of the Jayhawkers, but the operation was so socially and environmentally traumatic that the Jayhawkers were left alone to the end of the war.

But Honey Island remained their survival center, so if their spirits have at last settled down, they probably picked Honey Island, where they used to come in and trade and visit with their folks. At Kaiser's Burnout one of the Jayhawkers was shot in the back, right where his galluses crossed. His ghost even now is haunting the high ground in Honey Island, looking to swap a gourdful of honey for a new pair of red suspenders.

The final nail in the casket of the old Thicket ghost towns was the **creation of Farm to Market roads**. The idea of paving a road from a rural area to a settled market area had been a part of Texas planning even before WWII. The Farm to Market road system became a legislated road plan after the war in 1949. In Hardin County paved roads reached Kountze and Sour Lake from the surrounding Big Thicket area in the early 1950s. Within a few years the few people left in the rural areas could drive a paved road into Livingston, Woodville, Liberty, Beaumont, and all the surrounding market towns. Farmers and stockmen could live in a town that had large Piggly Wigglies, Western Autos, J. C. Penneys, consolidated schools, and picture shows. They could raise their families with modern conveniences and drive FM roads daily and easily out in the country to take care of their livestock, timber, and planted fields. The little gas station-grocery store towns like Rye and Votaw with their frame school house-community churches that had long served these rural families went out of business. The old ghosts that nowadays remain in the vicinity of Fuqua and Batson are now joined by retirees or folks that make their livings elsewhere. They all have indoor plumbing, telephones, electricity, and enough cars to get them to market on a paved FM road anytime they get ready to go.

It's not hard to have ghost towns in the Big Thicket. In fact, although I never made a count, I would bet that today there are more ghost towns than real towns in the Thicket. That part of the world does not encourage productive farming that might have kept communities alive through and after WWII. Some folks have come back and cleared spots in the Thicket for homes and pastures. Rice fields are reaching up into the Thicket flatlands, looking for more space. Logging still supports some Thicket folk, and a few oil pumps are still pecking away at the clay soil. Hunting clubs abound. And interestingly enough, some people have left the cities and retired back to the Thicket woods, the lands of their ancestors and their families' ghost.

But all of the Big Thicket towns that used to nourish the people of the big woods are ghosts of what they once were— during their prosperity of logging and drilling and being part of an expanding East Texas commercial world. The settlers and their descendants killed out, cut down, and drilled in with no thought that these resources on which they depended for life could be completely destroyed. But with a twist of the kaleidoscope the pattern changed, and that which they most loved and cherished was no more. Treasured ways of life died as quickly as they had been born and left only memories of what they had been in the minds of the old folks. The ghosts of Bragg and Thicket and Nona live now in the reminiscences of the Thicket patriarchs and in the stories that grandmothers tell of an earlier time. Gus Hooks and Captain Bullock and Warren Collins lie mouldering in their graves, but their stories and the histories in which they live are the spirits in which the Old Big Thicket lives.

[This paper was given at the Ghost Towns of East Texas Symposium, April 5, 2003, in conjunction with the East Texas Historical Association and the Texas Folklore Society.]

Stephanie Mateum

THE GHOST LIGHTS OF MARFA

by Stephanie Mateum

They only come out to play at night. They tease—bright lights that dance in the dark, flirting with the spectators that come from all corners of the world to see them perform. They mask themselves briefly in the darkness with their games of hide-and-seek, disappearing for several seconds in the night before popping back into view. They are unidentified lights, the "Ghost Lights" of Marfa, a phenomenon that appears in the Western Texas horizon with no formal announcement, no cause, no explanation. Every year, hundreds of scientists and thrill-seekers trek to Mitchell Flat, the dangerous terrain above which the lights appear, to seek the answer to the question that skeptics and believers have yet to answer: Is there life in the Marfa lights?

The lights have been described to look like many things by many different people, though they are typically described to have the shape of an orb or basketball, and the colors in which they present themselves differ depending on who you talk to. Hallie Stillwell, a former Presidio County teacher who has viewed the Marfa Lights for over seventy-five years, describes her encounters with the lights: "They'd flare up and be kind of red," she says, "then they'd die down, then they'd move elsewhere and flicker a little bit."[1] But Hallie Stillwell's description of "red" lights does not align with the one given by Kirby Warnock, a man whose fascination with the lights is rooted in his childhood. Warnock's late father took him and his brother, Miles Warnock, to see the lights for the first time in 1963; he recalls, "My father shut off the engine, stopped the car, and told my brother and me to watch the desert to our right. After about a two-minute wait, we saw three tiny white lights appear. . . . The lights are of a white color, not orange (like fire)."[2]

Hallie Stillwell first saw the lights in 1916 and has viewed them from afar for more than seven decades;[3] Kirby Warnock, whose family has lived in the Trans-Pecos region close to where the lights have been seen for more than a century, has studied the lights for nearly fifteen years.[4] Though the lights that they see are found in the same place, they are shown to them in different colors: to Stillwell, as red, to Warnock, as white. But Stillwell's and Warnock's lights were singular colors, unlike the lights Katherine Hollingsworth has seen. Hollingsworth claims to first have seen the lights in 1987. There was a group of lights, but within the cluster, one in particular had caught her attention. "One light was the largest," she mentions. She adds, "It seemed to at times have an essence of a soft greenish-blue color quickly changing to a red."[5]

Just as the colors of the lights vary by the individual, so do the unpredictable ways that they behave. Gary Cartwright described his chilling sight of the lights in an issue of *Texas Monthly*: ". . . The first point of light appeared where there had been only darkness . . . a second came dancing above and to the right of the first."[6] He continues, "The points of light appeared one or two or sometimes three at a time, moving diagonally and sometimes horizontally for ten to fifteen seconds. They would vanish and then reappear in some new location. They could have been a mile away, or twenty or thirty."[7] In an interview performed by Judith Brueske for her book *The Marfa Lights*, Cara Lee Ridout describes her experience with the lights differently; unlike Cartwright's description, the lights Ridout had seen were stationary, described in the excerpt to be "holding their ground. . . . I saw three big balls of fire lined up."[8] Jim Sheffield claims to have seen the lights in the same formation in 1984. "The lights started popping up at the base of the mountain. . . . They would enlarge, get very bright. One light got real intense and it split, and then those two split and there were four, in a horizontal line."[9]

What makes the behavior of the lights seem playful, however, is the way that they manage to interact with humans while keeping the secret behind their presence or purpose a mystery. In Hector Escobedo and Marilyn Olson's case, the way that the lights "played" with them was by following them. Escobedo, a former operator of a Marfa gas station, explains his encounter: while he was driving with a delivery en route to Presidio, a "big blue ball of light" had suddenly appeared a few feet ahead on the road in front of him; "I slammed on my brakes," he states "... but it did not move. I decided to keep driving, but it was so bright, I had to shade my eyes to see the road."[10] The light remained in front of Escobedo for miles, only to vanish as suddenly as it had appeared. Marilyn Olson was also driving when she saw the lights for what would be the first and last time; she and her mother were driving back to Marfa, and she says, "Suddenly a huge red and green light appeared right on the back of the car. ... It seemed like it was right on top of the back window," she adds, following her and her mother for a while before parting from them into a field.[11]

One who has never driven down the desert between Marfa and Presidio could assume that the lights were actually from a distant source, and that by driving in a straight line, the lights only appeared to be "following" them from in front or from behind Escobedo's and Olson's cars. The catch is, however, that neither Escobedo nor Olson were driving in a straight line. According to Escobedo, "... the highway never once formed a straight line, as it twisted and turned around the rocks and peaks of the mountain pass."[12] Could Escobedo simply have been following, or Olson have been followed, by another vehicle, and mistook some unusual reflection of car lights on their windows as paranormal lights? The possibility seems unlikely when Ophelia Ward's account is taken into consideration.

In 1973, Ward was driving down the same road, U.S. 90, when she saw one of the lights approaching her from behind, but unlike Olson's light, which stayed at her rear, the light Ward saw pulled up alongside her. The light she described was an orange-red orb that was about two-and-a-half feet in diameter; it moved towards her "from twenty feet away, just on the other side of the fence that parallels the highway."[13] She recalls that ". . . not one other soul, not another car was on the road. . . . And I started stepping on the gas, faster, and it started like it was racing with me."[14]

The second-hand descriptions of the lights' behaviors makes it seem as though they have minds of their own; they've been claimed to approach humans from a distance, but somehow they always manage to evade capture. Pal Keeney describes one of the lights he had seen to even "have possessed intelligence."[15] Keeney, a geologist for the Fort Worth-based Meeker Corporation, has sought to solve the mystery of the lights ever since he had heard of them. On one of his nighttime crusades, he and friend geologist Elwood Wright stalked two of the lights that appeared in the desert; while one of the lights shot off for a nearby airbase hangar, the other remained by the road. Keeney recounts their experience:

> It kept moving around a bush, kind of like it knew we were trying to get near it. . . . It moved around that bush like it was looking for something. Finally, it pulled out in the middle of the road, and twenty yards from us, just hovered there. I had left the engine running, and Elwood said, "Put it in gear and floorboard it." All of a sudden it got real bright and took off like a rocket. It was the damndest thing I have ever seen.[16]

The Marfa Lights are not a phenomenon that has baffled science only recently. According to Hudnall in his book *Spirits of the Border*, "As early as 1840, wagon trains on the Chihuahua Trail reported seeing unexplained lights along the flats."[17] The area, however, was full of hostile Apache Indians, and the risk of death by straying from the trail impeded any investigations into the lights at that time.[18] While no one knows for sure when the Marfa lights were first seen, the first recorded sighting and investigation into the lights took place in 1883.[19] A young cowhand, Robert Reed Ellison, was driving cattle through the Paisano Pass from Alpine to his near-Marfa ranch when he saw the legendary lights in the distance.[20] Camped at the base of the Pass, he and his fellow cowhands mistook the nighttime lights as fires from Apache encampments.[21] The cowboys waited until the morning after to investigate the area where they had seen the lights, but a lengthy combing of the flat revealed no recent traces of human life ever being there.[22] Inquiry by the cowboys about the lights to the other residents of the area revealed that they, too, had seen the lights, but they had no explanation;[23] the cowboys eventually decided that the lights were not created by man, and they began referring to them by the label that still sticks today: "Ghost Lights."[24]

Because of the life-like nature of the Marfa lights, locals seem to have adopted a "live and let be" philosophy about the lights' presence, and are humored by the countless attempts to scientifically explain their origins. Failure to come up with a sound scientific explanation behind the lights' presence has drawn several scientists to Mitchell Flat, all of whom have yet to come up with a theory that cannot be easily discounted by eyewitnesses and local residents. One of the most logical scientific theories about the lights, for example, is that the lights might actually be distant vehicle lights that appear to flicker after passing behind obstructions masked by the darkness; this theory was the conclusion Don Witt, a physics professor at Sul Ross University in Alpine, came to after organizing a student-involved effort to locate the source of the lights.[25] Eyewitness and long-time residents of the area were quick to point out that if the lights were headlights, then the vehicle would have to be headed from Presidio to Marfa in left-to-right traffic, because anyone going in the opposite direction would be showing only tail-lights; the lights, however, did not just move from left-to-right, but from right-to-left as well. This theory meant that if the scientists were correct, then the lights would have been from the vehicles of "crazy" people "backing up on Highway 67 at a high rate of speed on a dark night on a treacherous mountain road in order to make the . . . movements that the mystery orbs have been known to make."[26] Furthermore, sightings of the lights date back to the late 1800s, a time well before automobiles existed.

Locals seem to have given up on the search for a definitive explanation for the lights. Apathy was the response Kirby Warnock received while searching for explanations among the townsfolk; a typical answer he received, he claims, was that "the lights are there, and people have tried to find out what they were before. No one has, and I don't care to waste any more of my time."[27] Instead of science, the townsfolk seem to prefer explaining the lights with lore and legend. In his book *Tales of the Big Bend*, Elton Miles states, "Since the folk mind abhors a missing link in the chain of cause and effect, legend is spawned."[28] In the case of the mysterious Marfa Lights, legends among the townspeople have indeed spawned, most of which are variations of the idea that the lights are human spirits that cross different cultures and generations. A popular American legend is that the lights represent the spirit of a sheriff whose wife was murdered by an outlaw; supposedly, the sheriff remains out in the land with his light, still in vengeful pursuit of the man who murdered his beloved.[29] Several other tales personify the lights as being kind to humans; one such tale is that the lights were guides to early American settlers, and they steered them away from the paths of hostile Indians. Several of the older legends are what Miles terms "pseudo Indian legends," stories that describe the lights as stars that have fallen and chosen the area as their final resting place, or as spirits of deceased Apache warriors that have earned the right to return to the lands they loved with their bravery.[30] Perhaps the most well-known AmerIndian legend is that of Alsate, an Apache chieftain who was captured for thievery and executed by the Spaniards in the mid-1800s; allegedly, the Marfa lights are the fires Alsate's spirit lights as his eternal request for aid from others.[31]

For researchers seeking the truth behind the Marfa Lights, the common pattern seems to be to have more questions born upon investigation than questions answered. With such little uniformity in the descriptions of the lights that eyewitnesses have to offer, one can hardly blame them. The lights seem to present themselves in colors unique to the individual, and behave as if they understand that we humans look upon them with wonder. They have hovered in the night for more than a hundred years, perhaps even for as long as the flats have existed, and have been kept alive to this day with our folktales and uncertainty.

So, to all who venture to Mitchell Flat, the answer to the question "Is there life in these lights?" becomes clear: there is *indeed* life in these lights. It is the life that eyewitnesses breathe into them, personifying them in their stories with human qualities, such as intelligence or playfulness. It is the life of a vengeful sheriff, a helpless Apache chieftain, or one of the hundreds of other spirits that have been kept alive by legends and folktales that have been passed down through the generations. It is the life that the Marfa residents celebrate every year on Labor Day with festivities and dancing,[32] and it is the life that admits every eyewitness into a special community of, as Utley and Beeman put it, "heritage tourists."[33] As one local poet has observed, "They're angels of the desert who radiate this glow, and dance to music of the winds that here forever blow."[34] With the cultural impact that these lights have had on residents of Marfa and Presidio County in the past century, it cannot be doubted that there is life in the lights. One of the greatest unsolved mysteries of the Southwest, these lights are a small part of what makes Texas, simply put, extraordinary.

ENDNOTES

1. Rosemary Williams. "The Marfa Lights—A Mystery." *Texas Highways* 1993. Print.
2. Kirby F. Warnock. "The Marfa Lights." *Big Bend Quarterly* 1988. Print.
3. Williams.
4. Warnock.
5. Judith M. Brueske *The Marfa Lights: Being a Collection of First-hand Accounts by People Who Have Seen the Lights Close-up or in Unusual Circumstances, and Related Material.* Alpine, Tex.: Ocotillo Enterprises, 1989. Print. 157.

6. Gary Cartwright. "Texas Primer: The Marfa Lights." *Texas Monthly*. November, 1984.

7. Ibid

8. Brueske. 159.

9. Ibid

10. Ken Hudnall. *Spirits of the Border*. Vol. 5. El Paso, TX: Omega, 2005. Print. 93.

11. Brueske. 158.

12. Hudnall. 93.

13. Brueske. 158.

14. Ibid.

15. Warnock.

16. Ibid.

17. Hudnall. 88.

18. Ibid.

19. Dan K. Utley and Cynthia J. Beeman. *History Ahead: Stories beyond the Texas Roadside Markers*. College Station: Texas A&M UP, 2010. Print. 363.

20. Hudnall. 88.

21. Utley and Beeman. 363.

22. Hudnall. 88.

23. Utley and Beeman. 364.

24. Hudnall. 88.

25. Ibid. 93.

26. Ibid. 94.

27. Warnock.

28. Elton Miles. *Tales of the Big Bend*. College Station: Texas A & M UP, 1976. Print. 150.

29. Ibid. 160.

30. Ibid. 156.

31. Utley and Beeman. 149.

32. "Marfa Lights." *Marfa, Texas Chamber of Commerce*. n.d. Web. 03 July, 2010.

33. Utley and Beeman. 153.

34. "Marfa-Mystery Lights." 27 March 2007. Youtube.com. Web. 09 July, 2010.

Jennifer Curtis

BEYOND TEXAS FOLKLORE: THE WOMAN IN BLUE

by Jennifer Curtis

Many strange tales lurk in the legends and folklore of the southwest. One of the strangest is one of the earliest: The Woman in Blue. Briefly, in the early 1600s, mission fathers in Texas were asked to investigate a report made by a nun in Spain who said she had visited the area and preached to Indians—while she was in a state of prayer, *in her village in Spain.* In 1629, a group of Indians came to one of the missions and asked to be baptized, stating that a woman in blue had directed them there. The Custodio, Alonso de Benavides, went to Spain the following year, 1630, to meet with the young nun, Marie de Agreda, who had visions of herself speaking to Indians and whose order wore a blue cloak. She knew the Indian sign language, could describe some of the people, and seemed familiar with the country.[1] The mystical idea of bilocation, being in two places at the same time, and the documentation of the accounts at the time, both in Texas and in Spain, have added to the mystery and the endurance of the tale.

In America, we've emphasized the folkloric nature of the account and argued for and against the truth in the tale. However, the woman identified as the mysterious woman in blue, Maria de Agreda, was controversial in life and even more so after her death, when her ideas would divide Europe into two camps, the Agredists and the non-Agredists. She was a woman who influenced people in her own century and through the centuries to the present day. The magnitude of her influence was acknowledged in 1995, when Spain's Radio Televisión Española (RTVE), named her one of the nine "most influential women in Spanish history."[2] Today, she is the topic of scholarly books published by university presses. Her work is studied in courses for women's studies and Spanish Literature, theologians discuss her writings, and Mel Gibson consulted her writings before making his movie *The Passion of the Christ*.[3] So, moving beyond Texas folklore, just who was the Woman in Blue?

She was an unusual child. She was born Maria Coronel in 1602 to devout Catholic parents and, throughout her life, she would have deeply spiritual moments or insights. Her mother counseled Maria to be watchful for such happenings, so that even as a young child she was aware of visions. As an adult Maria would write of a particular vision in childhood: "Suddenly my perception expanded. . . . I saw the extremes of good and evil, of light and darkness, of grace and sin. God etched this awareness into my heart with divine force."[4]

By age four, she had come to the attention of Bishop Ypes, a man who had served as King Felipe II's confessor and who had just completed a biography of Teresa of Avila. Maria was confirmed by him when she was four years old, at a time when it was usual for children to be confirmed when they reached the age seven or more. He must have recognized an unusual bent toward the spiritual in this child, for he urged her parents to give her a special area in the family home where she could pray and study alone. When she was six years old, she attended school for a short time but soon grew sickly and was withdrawn from school, never to return. When she was seven years old, she saw a play by Lope de Vega, *The New World as Discovered by Christopher Columbus*, depicting people in the world without knowledge of God, and it birthed a fierce evangelism in her and a desire to travel to America. Poor health continued through her childhood, and when she was thirteen she was so ill her parents prepared for her burial. At this time, she would write later, she became healed when she accepted her pain. She wrote, "Ever since, I found that when I focused my attention within, I would enter a state of exceedingly quiet prayer."[5] Her focus on prayer was life-long.

In 1615, her mother had a vision for the family. She and her daughter were to create a convent of the family home and enter it while her husband and sons joined the Order of St. Francis. In 1620, this was accomplished.

Although Maria had little formal schooling, she read widely. The year when she wrote her first book, *Face of the Earth*, is debated even now by scholars. Some place it at age fifteen[6] or before her visitation to the Indians, while others place the book at a later date.[7] The book is based largely on other people's writings and her narration is as though she were experiencing being in the place described.[8] She was able to discuss geography and cosmology as though she had been taught, and read Latin with enough understanding to critique a translation. The evidence that she read histories is based on the books in the convent library and the footnotes referencing particular books in her seminal work, *The Mystical City of God*. She was known to have an extraordinary memory and ability for synthesis.[9] Although she attributed her knowledge to "heavenly intervention with an uneducated woman," her writing reveals a well-read woman, which might not have been acceptable at the time.[10]

With illness, prayer, and study dominating her childhood life, she did not have an active life with girls her own age. When she became well as a young teenager, she began to reach out to girls her own age; however, she was aware she was uncomfortable and awkward.[11] By age sixteen, she had again withdrawn.

To sum up, she grew up in isolation, was steeped in a mystical sense of God, read widely and with considerable understanding, and was passionate enough about her thoughts and beliefs to write a book at age fifteen. In today's world, she might have been called a precocious child or a gifted child. Her abilities were recognized by adults, as shown by her early confirmation, and that recognition would continue throughout her life. By special dispensation of the pope, she was appointed the abbess of the convent at age twenty-five—an appointment usually reserved for women over the age of forty. She would be elected to that position for the rest of her life. In addition, Felipe IV, King of Spain, would seek her counsel and establish a correspondence with her that lasted more than twenty years and would include more than six hundred letters.

Her beginning years at the convent, 1620–1623, were difficult—she would refer to them as the "bad years."[12] This was the time of her visions of visiting the Indians more than five hundred times. She confessed her visionary travels to her confessor, who did not keep silent. She would later write of this man that he was enthusiastic about "extravagantly marvelous cases of religious life" and was not a cautious man.[13] She became an "overnight phenomena."[14] She suffered from illness and from bouts of terror, and there were instances when she or her confessor demanded the "hair shirt, the coat of mail worn next to the skin, a girdle of spiked rings, and chains and fetters."[15] It was a difficult time for all the women in the convent. The sisters were tired of this "abnormal creature"; Maria was thought insane, was mocked, beaten, denied communion, punished if she got up to say her prayers at night, and not allowed to see her confessor except for a few minutes a week.[16] At this time, the other nuns would secretly spy on her while she was at prayer to see if her body raised, or levitated, which it was seen to do. During these times, people said they had visions of their futures and healings occurred. Her superiors thought she was drawing attention to herself, but when she prayed for these things to cease at the instruction of a group of priests, her fellow nuns and her mother thought she had fallen from grace because these things did cease.[17] She learned to cope with notoriety, betrayal, and the jealousy of the cloistered women.

She became a competent administrator. When she was made the abbess of the convent, by papal bull in 1627, she was challenged immediately, for when she took over the convent was "in a great state of decay."[18] A building project was initiated. Land had been given to expand, but it needed to be cleared and there was no money for the project. In just five years the land was cleared, and by 1632 the new building had a lavatory with water and a fountain in the garden. In July 1633, seven years after becoming abbess, the convent moved into its new building. In addition to managing the building project, she established a financial future by securing an endowment for the convent.[19] Under her guidance, the convent became prosperous and known as "one of the most fervent in Spain."[20]

She learned from experience. As an abbess, she taught the women in her care with a practical directness that later would be portrayed in her letters to the king. She did not encourage hair shirts and the like, telling her nuns that there were dangers in these things and that a hair shirt was more likely to make you bad tempered than holy.[21] During her early bad years she was tormented with "impure thoughts"—sexual thoughts—and the knowledge of this she shared with her nuns in later years. She would add that this continued for years, saying, "The Devil took advantage of that kind of temptation to give me a very bad time indeed."[22] In addition, as abbess she nursed the nuns and kept the communal privy clean.[23] She did not want the job of abbess and continuously asked to be relieved of the post. She preferred a subordinate position. In 1658, she argued that she couldn't do the convent any more good, that others needed to be trained to replace her, and that it was difficult to rule women.[24]

She was a reluctant authoress. She began writing *The Mystical City of God* in 1637, when she was thirty-five, because her confessor insisted she write it. The book is a biography of Mary, the mother of Christ, and based on the nun's visionary dialogue and experiences. She later burned the book at the insistence of a temporary confessor who believed women should not write. She rewrote the book only under a strict command to obedience and the threat of censure. It was a monumental task, for the "book" consisted of eight large volumes (now condensed to four) and took ten years to rewrite 1655-1665. She worried about how the book would be received, for revelatory literature was not received well in Spain at that time, and wondered if the book was just the result of her active imagination. Her friends urged her to stop writing.[25]

The book was printed in Madrid in 1670, after her death, and condemned by the Inquisition in 1681, put on the church's banned books list because of a faulty translation, but then approved in 1747.[26] According to Pérez-Rioja, the book has been published in more than eighty-nine editions in its entirety, and in more than sixty anthologies and summaries; translations include versions in Spanish, French, Portuguese, German, Latin, Arabic, Polish, and English.[27] Today, this book has been published 250 times and translated into more than a dozen languages and can be ordered through Amazon.com.[28]

The book posed difficult questions for the time: Was the Immaculate Conception of Mary valid, as proposed by the Franciscans? Could man's tradition be deemed equal in authority to the Bible? Europe was inflamed already by the Protestant Reformation's focus on the Bible as the only authority for God. The issue of the Immaculate Conception caused great emotional divisions among Catholics, such that its discussion was forbidden by popes on two occasions, 1616 and 1620. The argument of the Immaculate Conception was finally settled two hundred years later, in 1854, by Pope Pius IX. Until that time, Europe was divided into Agredists and non-Agredist camps.

She learned to cope with opposition. In 1635, she was questioned by a group of six priests appointed by the Inquisition to examine her spiritual experiences. Her confessor was included in the committee and the results were left an open question, but no fault was found with her. Fourteen years later, in 1649, she would again draw the attention of the Spanish Inquisition, and the old 1635 case was brought before the Supreme Council and an interrogation ordered. She had no friend or confessor at the time to help her. She had been ill in the infirmary and was carried into the meeting where she endured ten days of questioning.[29] She would recant a document she signed in 1631 with Benavides, which affirmed her experiences in the New World.

She wrote letters. Phillip IV, King of Spain, passed by the convent, met her, and commanded her to write him. He initiated a system to insure privacy where he wrote on one half of the paper and she answered on the other half while the king's courier waited for her reply. For the next twenty years, they would write more than six hundred letters. Her letters included advice on governing, military concerns, family matters, and her concerns. Her words are forthright from the first letter, asking that the king "forbid the wearing of unchaste clothing which encourages vice."[30] His concerns included the safe arrival of the silver fleet, the silver shipped from the Americas, the Portuguese and Flanders rebels, and the lack of money in the treasury.[31]

She advised the king to begin teaching his son and heir to rule, and later consoled him in his grief at the deaths of his wife, the queen, and his son. She mentioned her concerns: "My dear Lord, I see many people without sufficient to eat and unable to clothe themselves properly; and they are oppressed, disheartened, and indignant, for they and their children cannot survive under the burden of these taxes."[32] In 1661, she wrote:

> Another thing, so many changes in coinage are extremely harmful. A man's savings are the reward of his toil and he preserves them jealously; if the value of them is depreciated, or runs alarming risk of being depreciated, naturally he becomes angry. Your Majesty has many wise and disinterested people who will give you information about this and tell you that what I am saying is true. I am not informed by anyone, but by my inner conviction and my great love for your Majesty have compelled me to say this to you.[33]

In military matters, her writing is clear and practical. In 1643, she noted that "things move slowly with your army and I am sorry that so few come to Your majesty's aid; for the grandees could take an active interest in the army, hearten your soldiers, bring them promptly to the colors, and make the men feel sure they will get their pay."[34] When the king wrote in 1648 that Catalonia will see little fighting and rumors have the French attacking Flanders, she cautioned about misdirection as a military strategy and advised fortifying Catalonia, and in another letter reminded the king that the enemy used spies and weak spots and so warned of methods of recruitment. In another letter, she urged the king to appoint a general, for to delay put the army in a defensive position.[35]

Her letters reveal a confidence to speak her mind with clarity and directness, as well as an understanding of what she had accomplished. In a letter to the king she longed for an ordinary life: "The thing that distresses me the most is that I cannot achieve a buried life. All I have done, and I have done much, to keep secrets to myself seems to be of no avail. . . . I am so worried that I have just burnt some of my writings."[36] "She envied the security of the lives of ordinary nuns, to which her confessor replied that "other nuns do not counsel kings."[37] She asked the king to keep the one copy of *The Mystical City of God* safe: "I am confident that it will not be revealed by Your Majesty in any circumstances, even if the Inquisition asks for the book."[38] In addition, she was known for her charity, supporting a hospital and girls without dowries, and writing letters for people without jobs.[39]

A care for accuracy in writing concerned her. In a letter to her advisor in 1660, she wrote, "I have handed over the manuscript to the Father Guardian with reluctance because I was sure that additions and deletions would be made. They have put questions to me that I answered in writing, and it is easy to make a mistake, especially for me, an ignorant woman." She asked for a "list of the faults with their paragraph-numbers; because now I have the task of reading through and revising my manuscript, and your corrections will come when they are very welcome indeed."[40] Her attention to detail and the breadth of her content belies the reference to herself as an "ignorant woman."

Maria de Agreda died in 1665 at age sixty-three. In 1667, because of cellar dampness and the deterioration of wood, her coffin was opened. Her body was found intact and sweet smelling, and so it was moved to the convent crypt. In 1672, she was declared "venerable" by the Catholic Church, part of the process toward sainthood. A faulty translation of the *Mystical City of God* had put the book on the Church's Forbidden Books list, hindering the beatification process.

Her coffin has been opened fourteen times and her remains viewed by leading figures in France and Spain, as well as doctors, surgeons, and church leaders. In 1989, her body was examined by forty-six people, including the convent nuns and a medical team, and was found "incorrupt and unchanged since 1909"; however, a mask was placed over her face because a bone seen through her skin upset viewers in 1909.[41] The move for her sainthood continues today.

This story represents to me the fascination of folklore. Years ago I was drawn to the tale of the Lady in Blue mainly because of its instance of bilocation and its intriguing documentation. However, moving beyond the folklore, an extraordinary woman emerged—intelligent and widely read, an able administrator, advisor, and author of many books. Named one of one thousand most influential Hispanic Americans by *Grolier Scholastic* in their biography series in 2006, the Woman in Blue continues to be a woman of influence today.

ENDNOTES

1. Clark Colahan. *The Visions of Sor Maria de Agreda: Writing Knowledge and Power*. Tucson, AZ: University of Arizona Press, 1994. 108–109.
2. Marilyn H. Fedewa. *Maria Agreda: Mystical lady in Blue*. Albuquerque, New Mexico: University of New Mexico Press, 2009. 5.
3. Ibid.
4. Ibid. 17.
5. Ibid. 21, 19-24.
6. Ibid. 25-26.
7. Colahan. 29.
8. Fedewa. 25-26.
9. Colahan. 28.
10. Ibid. 30.
11. Fedewa. 21.
12. T. D. Kendrick *Mary of Agreda: The Life and Legend of a Spanish Nun*. London: Routledge & Kegan Paul, 1967. 13.
13. Colahan. 94.
14. Fedewa. 35.

15. Kendrick. 12.
16. Ibid. 12-13.
17. Fedewa. 34-35.
18. "Maria de Agreda." *Catholic Encyclopedia.* 1 Jan 2012.Web.
19. Kendrick. 21, 63.
20. "Maria."
21. Kendrick. 12.
22. Ibid. 13.
23. Ibid. 57.
24. Ibid. 63.
25. Ibid. 72-73.
26. Robert Plocheck. "The Lady in Blue." *Texas Almanac.* 1 Jan 2012. Web.
27. Kendrick. 163.
28. Colahan. 1.
29. Kendrick. 40-41.
30. Fedewa. 129.
31. Ibid. 13-14.
32. Kendrick. 146.
33. Ibid. 147.
34. Ibid. 127.
35. Ibid. 128-129.
36. Ibid. 62, 75.
37. Fedewa. 155.
38. Kendrick. 76.
39. Ibid. 64-65.
40. Ibid. 78-79.
41. Fedewa. 239-248.

The Woman in Blue, María Ágreda

Lee Haile

THERE'S GOLD IN THEM THERE HILLS— OR, SILVER AT LEAST

by Lee Haile

I guess I was bitten by the treasure hunter's bug early in life and it has stayed with me to this day. Luckily, though, I am too lazy to have wasted much time in pursuit of treasure. After growing up digging post holes with just a crowbar and a coffee can to get the dirt out or prying enough rocks out of the way until you had a hole, I would look into these old mine shafts that were dug into solid rock and think, man, that is way too much work!

One of the reasons I do like finding and crawling in caves is the thought of finding treasure hidden there. And to me treasure is just about anything from bones to gold. I heard a few years ago about some people who crawled in a cave over around Georgetown and found a saber-toothed tiger. Now that was a treasure.

When I was going to college in 1980 out at Sul Ross in Alpine, Texas, I ran around some with Hiram Sibley. He told me this story one day while we were out at their ranch in the Glass Mountains.

One time back in the late 1940s or early '50s the cowboys noticed a discoloration at the base of a cliff on a flat topped mountain. Well, there were old mine shafts all over that ranch, and plenty of stories of hidden treasure in that country. The cowboys convinced themselves they were looking at a covered up mine, so one day they rode over and climbed the mountain to the base of the cliff and started digging. After a while, they broke through. Imagine their excitement—it turned out to be a cave. They crawled in and what they found disappointed them, but it would have thrilled me. It was a cache of Indian bows and arrows still in their leather quivers with some other stuff. They thought nothing of it and just gave it all to the ranch kids and none of it survived. Hiram said he wished it would have been given to a museum at least.

We rode over and went into this cave. The entrance was about ten feet wide by twelve feet high. We even discovered a second entrance that had not been covered up and was just big enough to crawl in and out of, that came out under a bush up on top of the mesa. This is what the Indians used for access when they covered up the big entrance in the cliff.

When I was going to college at Texas A&M in 1977, I lived south of College Station down toward Millican, close to the Brazos River. I became good friends with my neighbor, Jim Phillips. He was an older gentleman that was raised over around Madisonville, right on old Highway 21, which is the Camino Real, or "Royal Highway" from early Spanish days. One day when he was young someone showed up asking about certain landmarks along the old highway. The new Highway 21 doesn't follow the old highway perfectly, and sections of the older one are still one-lane paved roads that are sometimes miles from the new one. These people had a map of a section of the old highway with landmarks and an X marked on it. Jim's dad helped them locate the part of the highway that fit the map. After digging around a little they dug up an old chest! But when they broke the lock and opened it, it was filled with old petticoats and clothing. I am sure that was not the first "treasure map" that marked where something was left behind by wagons heading west.

My cousins have a ranch between Sisterdale and Luckenbach, and this story comes from them. I heard it several times growing up. It seems that sometime during the early part of the 1900s (1920–1930), back when people where still just camping out and hunting on the land, someone from the ranch noticed a campfire up on the side of the range of hills over towards Blanco. They figured it was just hunters. This was called the Delaware pasture and those hills were called the Delawares, probably named for the natives who lived there in earlier times. After seeing the fire over several nights, they decided to ride over the next day to check it out. When they got over to the area they figured the camp to be, they started seeing signs of digging. Several of the holes were pretty big, and in one of the big holes they could see in the bottom an imprint of where a square box or chest had been removed. The diggers, however, were gone.

When I was working in the Brazos River bottom in the mid-1980s, I heard this story from Stan Nemec. It seems that sometime in the early 1900s (my guess was before 1940), an old man from Mexico showed up in the area asking about where a certain creek ran into the Brazos from the west. He found out and spent some time in that area. Well, one day the old man showed up at the local hang-out all happy and bought a round of drinks for everyone in there. Stan's dad was there and the old man came over to visit with him. I guess Stan's dad had become friends with him. The old man told him that he was very happy and he was going home the next day, but he wanted to give him something. He handed Stan's dad a pot of about a gallon size that was made out of hammered brass, such as you see made in Mexico. Stan's dad said you could tell it had been in the ground for a long time. Stan remembered seeing the pot on the mantel as he was growing up. Later, it was discovered that that site was of an old Spanish/Mexican fort and there is now a historical marker there. They figured something of value (probably coins) had been buried in it and the old man had come back to find it. All of these stories only inflamed my already vivid imagination and caused my antennae to always be hot for stories of old mines or buried treasure.

Like I said, I was bitten early, and I remember exactly when and where it happened. When I was growing up we had a ranch on the head of the Nueces River. My dad worked in San Antonio and we went up there on weekends and holidays. We would go west on Highway 90 and turn in Uvalde and follow Highway 55 up the Nueces Canyon. One time when I was about ten to twelve years old, we were on our way to the ranch. Somewhere right along where Chalk Bluff is on the river and near what is called Elephant Mountain, Daddy just casually mentioned that there is a vein of silver that stretches across the Hill Country from there to San Saba, waving with his hand in a northeastly direction towards Elephant

Mountain. What was amazing about this is that my dad was not the type to chase treasure or even talk about it. In fact, this was the one and only time I heard him say anything about anything relating to treasures, until later when I was reading J. Frank Dobie's *Apache Gold and Yaqui Silver*. Even then it was just that he remembered his dad, who lived in New Mexico, talking about the "Lost Adams Mine." Well in my young mind, I pictured a vein as thick as a string stretching continuously across 200 miles of the hills. I wondered why we didn't just go find it and start digging it up. I even figured it must pass pretty close to our ranch.

On our ranch there was an old wagon freight trail that came out of the west from the Nueces River drainage and up over the divide and down into the Frio River drainage. Just where it crossed our east property line and started up the grade to the divide, there were signs scattered around. Daddy said it was probably where they camped before they went up the divide. When I was about twelve, I found an Indian mound and campsite there. Nobody believed me until I started bringing back arrowheads and stone axes. I finally took the bulldozer over there and pushed over the cedar trees and cleared out the area. Then I really found a lot of stuff. I knew that Indians did not camp without water. On that whole one thousand acres there was not one spring of water. So, I tried to figure this out.

Just across the wash was a small bluff at the base of the hill that would have been about twelve feet high, except that over the years rocks and dirt had slid down the hill and piled up against it. Just visible at the top of the slide was the top edge of a cave. It was hard to tell how big or deep it was because it had filled in with the slide material. If the arch that was visible continued underground, it would have been eight feet around, big enough to walk into. I figured in Indian days it was open and there was a spring down in it. Then my imagination kicked in. I felt sure that there was either gold or silver bars or coin stacked in there by the Indians or the freighters. That was why they had pulled down the side of the hill—to fill it in! Daddy sold that ranch before I was able to try to

A cave near the Nueces River

bulldoze that cave open. To this day I still have this illogical feeling that there is something in there.

For the last twenty years we have been living in the Hondo Canyon in western Bandera County. Bandera has a rich history going back to the Spanish days. The famous "Bandera Pass" is located a little ways north of Bandera town. I had read J. Frank Dobie's *Tales of Old Time Texas* and knew the story of the silver in Elm Pass. I tell this tale sometimes at some of the local events where I perform. In it the Spaniards are trying to get the silver bars from the San Saba mine back to the safety of the missions in San Antonio. The Comanches have Bandera Pass closed off so they detour east to the next pass, which is about five miles farther on. Olmos or Elm Pass is not as good as Bandera Pass and is much longer, at about four miles through. The short of it is the Spaniards get trapped in the pass by night, hide the silver, and all but one are killed the next morning. I once told my little nephew this tale when he was about fourteen while we were driving through it one day. He got all excited and wanted to stop right then and go look for it. "Where?" I asked, pointing around me. I explained how big an area we were talking about. I bet him that I could bury something on the ten acres where I live and he could never find it. It didn't deter him much.

My ears were always listening for tales of treasure, and I read all I could, including W. C. Jameson's books on buried treasure and lost mines. I had been told by many geologists and others that the Hill Country could not have mines in it because it was geologically not the type, it being sedimentary limestone. Now, the Llano Uplift in the central part of the Hill Country is geologically different, and is well known to have mines. Anything I heard about our area I just figured were misplaced tales from other places.

Then in 2004, I was working on a ranch south of Bandera and while riding one day with Bill Grey, the owner, I asked about something I could see on the ridge that looked like it was made of rocks. He said it was a rock mound built by the Spanish to mark on old mine. Well, the first chance I got I crossed the canyon and climbed up there and found the marker. It was a well-made rock cairn and did not look that old to me. Only half believing that it was Spanish built I started looking for the "mine." I figured I would find a sinkhole cave. There are lots of them in that area, and we had found and crawled in a cave in that same canyon earlier. I found it! It was square and went straight down; I had brought rope so I climbed down in.

I could see the vein in the rock that they seemed to have followed down. It was only about twenty-five to thirty feet deep. I didn't think too much of it, and surely didn't think it was a gold or silver mine. I mean, I had been told and I knew enough about geology to know that the country was all wrong for it. We did find and explore some more caves on that ranch. Then about five years ago an amazing discovery was made in the Hondo Valley just a few miles from my house. Feather Wilson, a retired UT professor, geologist, and member of the Texas Archaeological Society, along with Dr. Tom Hester, professor of anthropology at UT, found a rock shelter way up on a ridge up in a steep canyon that showed signs of smoke and human habitation. That is not unusual, but what was unusual was an inscription carved in the wall. It was written in an old-style Spanish script that translated, "In the year of our lord— 1577." There was also an old Spanish mine shaft nearby that showed traces of silver and lead in its tailings. This is the earliest date recorded of any Spanish in Texas other than Cabeza de Vaca passing through. Now this got my attention.

I started thinking about some of the other mentions of Spanish silver mines I had heard about from people. Sid Chaney over in Utopia had told me about a couple of mines at the mouth of the Sabinal Canyon. Sid mentioned an old book by Duval written years ago that mentions mines on Sugarloaf Mountain. He had not seen them or been up there in over forty years. The old rancher that had it back then found two Spanish bits up on top of the mountain and gave them to Sid. He had them for a long time but didn't know where they were anymore. He also told of an early rancher over on the Seco Creek Canyon that would sell big chunks of pure lead to people for bullets. People would tell him how much they wanted and he would be gone for a while, then show back up with it. Someone when I was living in Hondo in the late '80s told me about one on the west side of the Medina River just a few miles north of Castroville.

So, when I decided to do this paper and started researching, I was surprised how much information there was about them. I called Peggy Tobin and asked what she knew. She has been the president of the Bandera County Historical Association for a long time and publishes the historical newsletter. She said she didn't know much, but she remembered Raymond Hicks tell about people from Bandera County hauling silver ore in wagons over to Uvalde to sell. Her son Tim Tobin was there when I called and I talked to him. He is a landman for the oil companies, which means he finds out who owns the mineral rights of a particular piece of land. He told me that a lot of the original families shared interest in the mine on Bill Grey's place south of town. He thought that if you were to check it out that it would probably be over 2000 that people would have an interest in it now.

Next, I called Lynn Post, who retired from the old SCS (Soil Conservation Service). The first thing he said after I asked was that there were no silver or gold mines around in this part of the hills because it was the wrong kind of rock. He had been all over this country in his years of work and knew it well. We had talked a lot over the years exchanging tales. He told me that it wasn't him that told me about the one on the Medina near Castroville like I had thought because he didn't know about that one. I told him some of what I knew. Then he remembered seeing one in the Seco Canyon. I asked if it was near the mouth of the canyon and he said yes. I asked if it was up on the ridge and he said no, that it was just a little off the creek bed. He said he didn't have any knowledge about it other than it was a square hole down in hard rock. He said nobody knew anything about it other than it had been there as long as anybody knew. He had seen the one on Bill Grey's and the rock cairn marker, and had heard of others but didn't know anything about them. He told me that a number of years ago, he thought it was Steve Gosse that paid a lot of money to have analysis done on the creek crossing trying to see where mineralization was at. They found silver, gold, and lead, but it was in minuscule amounts.

Lora B. Garrison told me that she had seen the one west of the Frio River on Dolph Briscoe's land. This is the one that was supposed to have been associated with Jim Bowie. W. C. Jameson told he had seen this one, too, and heard the Jim Bowie connection. Bowie was also supposed to have worked mines in the San Saba area. When I went to talk to Leann Sharp (Lora B.'s daughter) and her husband Anthony to try to get better directions so I could get a picture of the mine, she told me that the saddle the road went through was called Silver Mine Pass. Anthony then told me this story: "My grandpa was Clive B. Buchanan but everybody just called him B. B. Buchanan. He was a witcher and had witched that well on Lora B. Garrison's." Anthony then pointed to it about half mile away from where they now live on the ranch. He said, "B. was always talking about Billy the Kid and said he was out here in the old days. He had a pair of old binoculars that were solid brass that he kept in the freezer. He said they were Billy the Kid's. He would go get them out of the freezer to show them and start telling stories of Billy the Kid. He had little silver bars about one-and-a-half by three inches. Worth some money nowadays. He was full of tales. He was always trying to get me to go with him to get some gold doubloons in some mines that he knew of. I should have gone with him. He could still ride a horse and could probably have made the trip. This was back in the 1970s. He just wanted to hop the fence and ride in and get them but I was a little leery of crossing people's property. Where they were was if you go west out of Leakey and where you climb up to go to Camp Wood, up on top there used to be a sign 'Lackland Gun and Rod'; you turn left and go down in there. We used to hunt down in there. There was what they call the new mine section and the old mine section. They were both kaolin mines; they mined kaolin. Anyway, you keep on going and back there was a place called 'Bell Springs,' or what he called 'Bell Springs.' That's were those mines were that he was talking about, that had the gold doubloons."

When I went to interview Feather Wilson we talked for over an hour. I knew he knew the most about all this, and I learned a lot. When I first approached him on the phone he was hesitant to talk too much about these mines because they didn't want people to know exactly where they were. I told him I was more interested in the stories around the mines other than the actual location of the mines themselves, and promised not to reveal too much. First, he explained the geology associated with these mines and showed me a map he had developed. Stretched roughly along the Balcones fault line and buried deep is an old mountain range of the Pennsylvania series that used to be 10,000 feet high. There were some secondary movements known as "wrench faults" associated with the leading edge of that range. In Tarpley Pass there was a big one that had a downthrust of 7500 feet and a southward shift of several miles. There are basaltic intrusions associated with these wrench systems. What happened was when these basaltic intrusions came up—post-cretaceous—they brought up hydrothermal solutions that then resulted in contact metamorphosis on the existing rocks, depositing copper, lead, silver, and gold.

Then we began to talk about the rock shelter he had found near Tarpley Pass that had the inscription and date of 1577 carved on the wall in it. They also found an "adit" or mine shaft nearby. There was free silver and free lead, and signs of silver in the analysis of the tailings. Up on top there was an arrow about two feet by three feet, carved out of rock and pointing southwest back towards Mexico. The most significant thing was the date—1577. Nothing earlier of Europeans is known in Texas other than Cabeza de Vaca and three other lost men passing through Texas forty years earlier. This was the earliest physical evidence of Spaniards in Texas.

Feather said that Tom Hester suggested that an individual named Luis de Carabajal y Cueva might have been the one to have carved it. Luis de Carabajal y Cueva was a Portugese Jew pretending to be Catholic, and was the mayor of Tampico in the 1560s. He was sent to chastise hostile Indians at the mouth of the Río Bravo (Rio Grande) and crossed over near what is now Brownsville, becoming the first Spanish subject to do so. He was an entrepreneur and was working silver mines in Mazapil and Zacatecas. He was also a slaver, enslaving the natives and selling them. Even though this was prohibited by the king of Spain it was tolerated by the local authorities. Dr. Hester speculated that Carabajal was making unsanctioned forays into Texas to both mine and capture slaves. Feather told me it may not have been him but he is the most likely suspect.

The first settlement was called Hondo Canyon and was probably set up about this time to both work the mines and work the slave trade. It was three miles up the canyon (north) from present day Tarpley. Feather had found up at UT an old Spanish map from the late 1600s that the Dutch had stolen, which clearly showed Hondo Canyon was well established by this time and was probably started in the early 1600s. This would make it the earliest and longest European settlement in Texas.

I asked about other mines. Feather mentioned the one south of Bandera on Bill Grey's ranch. He said this was the only one so far that had any gold associated with it. He said that there were four adits in the Hondo Valley, including one found just last summer in the southern part of the canyon near the mouth. It just so happens that the carved arrow on top of the hill near the mine near Tarpley Pass points to this other mine six miles away. Tom and Feather have been told by a local rancher about another rock shelter near this new mine with the date 1750 something. That is 175 years later than the first date. They are going up there soon to see and document this one. There is also another rock cairn on top of the hill near the new mine that has the remnants of a small rock hut right next to it.

Looking east from my house, three of the four mines and both shelters, the arrow, and the cairn with the hut next to it can be seen. I have often said that we all have a tendency to think of history happening somewhere else, but I realize more and more that I am living in the middle of it. There are six more adits in the Sabinal Canyon, and four in the Frio Canyon. Feather didn't know of any in the Nueces Canyon, but I had heard of one near Montell associated with the Franciscan mission named "Nuestra Senora de le Candelaria" that was established there in 1762. So, that makes a total of sixteen known mines or adits, with rumors of others in the area.

Both Feather and Tom felt that the rock cairns were trail markers and were probably built in the 1700s. Not all of the cairns are associated with mines, but a lot of the mines have a cairn on top of the hill near them. Most of the cairns are very well built and all have a hole in the top. They felt that the cairns had flagpoles inserted in the holes and the flags marked the old trails, hence the name Bandera (Spanish for flag). They theorize that the hut near the cairn at the mouth of Hondo Canyon housed a caretaker for this flag, since it marked the trail to Spanish settlement of Hondo Canyon and continued on over the hills to the north to another

Spanish settlement called Jappon, on the Guadalupe River where Hunt is now. There is a beautifully built cairn on the Haby place west of Medina lake, three on the Alkek ranch, the nice one on Bill Grey's, two more in the Hondo Valley, and a new one reported but not seen yet near Vanderpool. All eight are on the top of the hills.

Feather mentioned that the settlers had reopened and worked some of the mines, like the one near Tarpley Pass and the one on Bill's place. Then he said that a settler died in the mine on Bill's place. So, more research at the library and then the Frontier Times Museum revealed this. At the museum in the book *A Pioneer History of Bandera County*, published by J. Marvin Hunter in 1922, on page 232 was this: "In the early days F. A. Hicks opened a silver mine the ranch of A. McGill on cow creek about 10 miles west of Bandera. He found some ore that promised good returns but after going some depth it did not pay. A man named Meyer bought the mine and spent a great deal of money on it but without returns. It was finally abandoned. While the mine was being worked a man named Jim Buckaloo lost his life by falling into the shaft."

I asked Feather how he first found out about the first mine at Tarpley and got the classic situation in folklore, the same story attributed to two different events. In Dobie's book *Coronado's Children* in the story "Vicey versy map," I had read about the Robison girl finding a silver bar in Elm Pass and of it being found again later. So, when Feather mentioned that there had been found an old silver bar associated with this mine I mentioned I had heard that it was found in Elm Pass and the San Saba connection. He said that no, this was real and people had seen this bar of silver. Feather told another story about a rancher who lived north of me who told him that there was a rock cairn on the hill just north of my place. I told him I had seen it and thought it was just a surveyor's pile because there was a benchmark near it. Feather said there was another wrench system in that area. That got me to thinking.

About nine years ago Bob Pagett fell and broke both his rotator cuffs in his shoulders and spent most of the summer sitting on his porch healing up. I would see him and stop and visit. One time we got to talking about old mines. He told me that he thought that those people that lived back over in that canyon at the base of that hill (pointing off to the southwest) "must have a gold mine because they always had money but didn't have no way of coming by it that anybody could see." That hill was the one that had that pile of rocks on it. And back when Earl Smith had that place I had access to it. I found a cave on it that we crawled down into some. Well, just before Earl sold the place to the new people his son told me about another cave in the valley on the other side of the mountain near where their ranch cabin was. He told me it went straight down and had an old rotted cedar pole ladder down in it. Feather asked if I had seen it. I told him no, that I never got over to it before he sold it and the new owner was kind of finicky about fence hoppers. Well, if that is a cairn on top of that hill, that could very well be an old Spanish mine, and it is exactly where Bob had said that old family used to live.

One thing's for sure, there are still lost Spanish silver mines and stories of buried treasure out there in the Bandera area waiting to be found, and . . . *there's always tomorrow!*

Winston Sosebee

BEN SUBLETT'S GOLD

by Winston Sosebee

My first fascination with the story of Ben Sublett's lost gold mine began more than twenty years ago. During a bout of telling "war stories" and drinking among some friends of mine, one of my friends told of reading an account of a legend of lost gold in far West Texas. He said the account was in a book by J. Frank Dobie, *Coronado's Children*. After I recovered from being amazed that this friend had actually read a book, I wanted to hear more about this lost gold mine. He was only able to give me the basic facts from the account. I decided then that I would read Dobie's book. That was all it took—I was hooked. I began to search out all information that I could find on Ben Sublett. All of it was kept on reserve for almost twenty years until I had the idea for this presentation.

William C. Sublett, later known as Ben Sublett or crazy old Ben Sublett, was born in 1835 in Alabama. He served during the Civil War in the Confederate Army. Apparently, Ben found time to get married. He then traveled west to Colorado and to Arizona. He spent some time searching for the Lost Dutchman mine and prospecting in Colorado and Arizona. When he moved to Texas, it was with a wife and two daughters and a son. Ben and his family settled first in Monahans in Ward County. Ben made a very meager living for his family hunting buffalo and other game to feed the construction crews of the Texas and Pacific railroads. He also did water-witching to locate water wells for the settlers. He also hauled wood to sell in the Monahans and Odessa areas since trees were sparse there.

Sublett's wife died in 1874, probably soon after they arrived in Texas. Ben was not partial to hard steady work and preferred to spend his time in local bars and saloons. He worked only enough to provide a very simple existence for his children. At some time prior to 1880, he moved his family forty miles to the east to

Odessa. He took out a homestead of 160 acres and built a dugout/tent home on the 160 acre tract. He continued to hunt for the railroad crews and haul wood, but steady physical labor was still avoided. When some settlers began to help him with providing for his three children, Ben took this as a chance to pursue his real interest, prospecting. He made several trips to the Guadalupe Mountains, which are about 150 miles northwest of Odessa. Sublett was repeatedly warned about the dangers of the Apaches in the area, particularly Geronimo. Ben often remarked that if they didn't bother him he wouldn't bother them. His only companion on these trips was his faithful dog, Pete.

Ben Sublett first attracted attention in 1882, when he traded some gold nuggets for supplies. He said someone had directed him to an old Spanish gold mine in the Guadalupes. He was not taken seriously, and many still referred to him as "crazy old Ben." A short time later Ben showed up back in Odessa at a local saloon and announced that he was buying drinks for everyone. He dumped from a leather pouch several gold nuggets, and then he walked out to his wagon and came back with a canvas sack also full of gold nuggets. Ben loudly stated that he had found at last the richest gold mine in the world. He said that he could build a palace of California marble and buy up the whole state of Texas as a backyard for his children to play in.

Ben returned to the Guadalupes a few months later and returned with more gold. He stated that since all the bankers in Odessa were crooks and thieves he was going to deposit his gold in a Midland bank. W. E. Connell was the owner and president of a bank in Midland. He said that the gold that Ben deposited was so pure that all a jeweler had to do was hammer it and shape it. Ben was now getting the serious attention he sought. Whenever his money supply began to run short, Ben would disappear for a couple of weeks and return with more gold.

We now need to explore the Guadalupes, which apparently were the source of Ben's wealth. J. Frank Dobie gives a very good description of these mountains in "The Secret of the Guadalupes" in *Coronado's Children*. Dobie gives an account of some Indians leading a group of Spanish soldiers under the command of a Captain de Gavilan to a rich gold deposit on one of the eastern spurs of the Guadalupes Mountains. In 1680, the great uprising of the Pueblo Indians killed every Spaniard who did not flee; thus, the secret of the lost gold mine of the Guadalupes had begun. The Guadalupes rise to as high as Guadalupe Peak at 9500 feet. They stretch from far West Texas in Culberson County to southeastern New Mexico. The land is very rugged, harsh, and barren. Very little rain falls there, and most moisture comes in the form of winter snow. These mountains have several characteristics of areas that have produced gold. They certainly had during their formation the elements of heat and pressure due to their being formed by volcanic activity. One element that is either missing or is not found in great abundance is quartz. Still, a geologist that I talked with told me that the Guadalupes could very well have gold. The Apaches found their final refuge here in this harsh land. White men generally avoided the Guadalupes, as it was a favorite home for Geronimo and his band. In Dobie's account Geronimo is quoted as saying that "the richest gold mine in the western world lay hidden in the Guadalupes."

Sublett continued to make trips west from Odessa when he needed more money in the bank at Midland. He usually returned with between one to two thousand dollars worth of very pure gold in nugget form. Banker W. E. Connell began to ask about Ben's source of the gold. He never gave a hint about the location, but he told Connell on one occasion that some Apaches had shown him the old Spanish mine. Sublett also stated that "If anybody wants my mine . . . let him go out and hunt for it like I did. People have laughed at me and called me a fool. The plains of the Pecos and the peaks of the Guadalupes have been my only friends. They are my home. When I die, I want to be buried with the Guadalupes in sight of my grave on one side and the Pecos on the other. I am going to carry this secret with me so that for years and years after I am gone people will remember me and talk about 'the rich gold mine that old man Sublett found.' I will leave something behind me to talk about."[1] Banker Connell and rancher George Gray offered Sublett ten thousand dollars if he would show them the source of his cash. Sublett just laughed at them and said, "Why, I could go out and dig up that much in less than a week's time."[2]

Connell and Gray then hired Jim Flannigan to follow Sublett to his mine. Sublett left a few days later in a hack pulled by two burros. Flannigan followed him for about fifty miles until Ben crossed the Pecos River. When Flannigan tried to follow Ben's trail in the soft sand it just played out or quit. How a West Texan could lose the trail of a hack pulled by two burros is hard to understand. When Sublett came back with more gold he had only been gone for four days, hardly time enough to travel the 150 miles to the Guadalupes. This gave rise to the idea that Ben had moved a large amount of gold to the Pecos River area.

On another occasion Sublett took his young son, Ross, with him to the mine. Ross searched for his father's mine until his death in 1954, with no success. Sublett also was said to have given his friend, Mike Wilson, directions to his mine. He also failed to find it. Sublett was also thought to have good friends among the Apaches, and it was speculated that he never actually went to the mine but that the Apaches brought the gold to him and he furnished them with various supplies, maybe including whiskey. Whatever the truth is, Sublett's gold mine has never been found. It is one of the most documented legends of lost gold in America.

Sublett died January 6, 1892 in Barstow, Texas. He had about fifty dollars in gold nuggets in a sack under his pillow when he died. He is buried in an Odessa cemetery, and his funeral, his grave stone, and his burial plot were donated by the Marr family. His grave is not in sight of the Guadalupes and the Pecos is not on the other side. There is a Texas Historical Marker for him on the site of his dugout/tent home at the site of the original Shrimp Boat Restaurant. I have visited both of these sites and plan to travel about 150 miles to the Guadalupes, and maybe then Old Ben Sublett's gold mine will be lost no more.

ENDNOTES

1. J. Frank Dobie. "The Secret of the Guadalupes." *Coronado's Children*. University of Texas Press, Austin. 1930. 232.
2. Ibid.

SOURCES CONSULTED

County Records of Ward County.
County Records of Ector County.
County Records of Midland County.
Journals of the Marr family.
Journals of the Midland Geology Society.

"Just for

Fun" Lore

Garland Petty of Zephyr, in Brown County.
Courtesy, Mrs. James A. Pierce

HERE KITTY, KITTY, KITTY: FISHING WITH BUBBA

by L. Patrick Hughes

＊

Here a hierarchy; there a hierarchy. Everywhere you look, a hierarchy. Folk just seem to want to create pecking orders. In the public and private sectors of business, education, and government, chain-of-command hierarchies proliferate and life seemingly could not long exist without organizational charts graphically separating those with standing and power from those whose lack thereof relegates them to the bottom of the pyramid. In the social arena, patricians addicted to the rarified air of Saks Fifth Avenue and Neiman-Marcus look down their noses at plebeians going elbow to elbow with the great-unwashed masses at Walmarts from sea to shining sea.

The world of sport fishing most certainly reflects this kind of stratification. Those who cast their lines into the ocean blue for sailfish or the legendary silver tarpon of coastal bays occupy the highest rung of the ladder. Your average Joe simply lacks the financial wherewithal to enjoy the challenge of such fishing with its hour-long give-and-take battles between man and the combative creatures of the deep. Trout fishing, however, takes a back seat to no other form of angling when it comes to purism. Essential elements include mastery of the fine art of casting tiny hand-tied flies concealing even tinier hooks, matching wits with browns, speckleds, and rainbows, and attaining Zen-like harmony with a pristine environment of babbling brooks and crisp mountain air. Serious bass fishermen are yet another breed unto themselves. Honest-to-goodness bass fishing in the twenty-first century requires a shallow-draft fiberglass hull boat complete with an array of electronic gizmos propelled by a two hundred horsepower Evinrude capable of propelling one across the water at speeds of forty, fifty, or "Oh my God" miles per hour. Folks, this is serious stuff! Bass anglers in the Lone Star State have enthusiastically embraced both the "Catch and Release" concept and the Parks & Wildlife Department's Lunker program in a concerted effort to grow large bass into monsters.

Down at the bottom of the pyramid, Bubba plies his angling skills in a less ritualized and far more pragmatic manner. Style points matter little in the harvesting of *siluriformes*. That's "catfish" in common parlance. Good ol' boys embrace the practice of "Catch and Consume." Whether served blackened or more commonly, fried, the objective is a good meal.

While a tasty treat, it would be a stretch to argue that catfish are among nature's most handsome creations. Defining characteristics include up to four pair of barbells or "whiskers" utilized in the detection of food, spine-like rays on the dorsal and pectoral fins for defense, and a mucous-covered skin to aid in breathing, in contrast to the more typical scales. Catfish are primarily bottom feeders, sucking up and gulping rather than biting and shredding prey. They range in size from the giant Mekong catfish of Southeast Asia down to the inch-long *candiru* of the Amazon River network in South America.

Texas anglers have to be content with less exotic species. These include channel cats, which prefer large streams of moderate current, and blues that inhabit the clear, swift waters of big rivers and the lower reaches of major tributaries. The grand prize, however, is the flathead, also known as the yellow cat. Distinguished by its flattened head and projecting lower jaw, it's a beast. Unlike channels and blues that are scavengers, flatheads prey only on live fish and prefer the turbid waters of rivers and lakes where currents are slow. According to Texas Parks and Wildlife's Mike Ryan, "they are highly prized by catfishermen. . . . They're secretive and hard to catch and usually the guys who fish for them are not interested in anything else."[1]

Since *homo sapiens* began pulling fish from inland waterways and impoundments to meet their nutritional needs, cane poles, hooks, and floating bobbers have been traditional tools of the trade. Fishing in this fashion is the essence of tranquility. Sit down on the bank and watch the bobber for indications of a strike while trying to resist the natural tendency to nod off to sleep. It's peaceful but not particularly productive. Anglers concerned with numbers are much better served using trotlines with multiple hooks capable of generating a real haul. I remember fondly one particular fishing trip as a child with my father to family property in Webb County. Using a rowboat, we stretched our line across a huge stock tank, baited the hooks, and waited for results. It didn't take long. Within two hours, we'd hauled in nearly four-dozen of the wiggly critters. Luckily, there was a freezer back home in San Antonio to preserve the bounty of our adventure. Jug fishing, utilizing an empty plastic milk or water container, is yet another tactic capable of producing good results at minimum expense.

Bubba may not be the sharpest knife in the drawer intellectually, but even he knows an unbaited hook attracts few fish. Over the years an amazing variety of items have been utilized to lure catfish to their demise. Chunks of homemade lye soap were particularly popular in the Depression years when money was tight and living off the land essential if at all possible. Shaped around a straight shank hook, the soap ball begins to break down once in the water, leaving a scent trail of animal fat for kitty to follow. Today's commercial soaps contain too many complex chemicals to be effective, according to Chad Ferguson, a fishing guide in the Dallas-Fort Worth metroplex. Ferguson, therefore, markets his own brand of the real deal and, understandably, swears to its effectiveness.[2]

Chicken livers were my father's attractant of choice back in the Fifties when I was a youngster. Convenience was more than likely the decisive factor in the selection process. Readily available at any grocery store in town, they seemed to work well enough for his purpose. Dad, however, was not a particularly dedicated angler. He much preferred hunting with a Model 94 Winchester carbine to fishing with an Abu Garcia rod and reel. Fishing was something he did to fill the interminable months between deer seasons.

Those with opposite preferences, however, know from experience that chicken livers aren't sufficiently odiferous for the task at hand. Stench, it seems, is the key to choosing baits for the honest-to-goodness catfisherman. What human nostrils find repulsive, catfish for some reason find irresistible. A Sunday afternoon trip to the neighborhood Academy Sports & Outdoors franchise turned up a bewildering array of commercial products designed to tantalize any catfish's sense of smell. Chum balls of reconstituted animal parts dominated the shelves. Eager anglers had their choice between beef, pork, shrimp, and shad. Blood baits were available in either beef or chicken, along with cheese-flavored globs of God knows what. I found myself with insufficient nerve to put any of it to the smell test. It was, I'm certain, a wise decision.

Do-it-yourselfers in the catfish fraternity prefer to concoct their own bait. They are, by any measure, an imaginative lot. "Jack's Cat Attack," for instance, begins with a blended mixture of one pound of sun-aged chicken livers and a package of hot dogs. The resulting meat pâté is subsequently fortified with two cans of nacho cheese, one can of sweet corn, a quarter bottle of Tabasco sauce, and a dozen diced worms. Poured over bread and kneaded into dough balls, Jack advises curing his stink bait outside in a large plastic container. Another notable recipe labeled "Trinity River Bait" calls for dissolving three beef bouillon cubes in a quarter-cup of boiling water. In sequence the following are then added: three tablespoons of garlic salt and onion powder, five slices of bread, four tablespoons of melted peanut butter, and twenty saltine crackers. Everything is then mixed in a blender and stored in a sealable container until one's fishing excursion.

Not all denizens of Bubbadom, however, possess the patience for hook, line, and sinker fishing or the culinary skills to concoct hybrid baits. Through the ages adventurous albeit foolhardy anglers have utilized a bewildering variety of tools to increase yield. Alfred Nobel's 1867 perfection of a new explosive called dynamite made for an interesting if dangerous addition to the tackle box. In theory, the shock wave caused by the explosion causes the swim bladders of fish to rupture, resulting in a loss of buoyancy—some float to the surface but most sink to the bottom. How long it took adventurous anglers more interested in food than its ethical pursuit to latch on to the technology is undetermined. The earliest mention I've been able to track down involved an exploratory expedition into the Amazon River basin led by Col. Candido Rondon in 1909. The expedition had exhausted all of its foodstuffs and faced the very real prospect of starvation when a Lt. Pyrineus took matters in hand, tossing a stick of dynamite into a pool of water and eagerly began gathering the spoils—piranha temporarily stunned by the concussion. Not the brightest of outdoorsmen, Pyrineus held one in his mouth so as to free up both hands to scoop up more. Unfortunately for the hapless lieutenant, the fish came to and bit off part of his tongue. Luckily, the expedition's doctor was able to stanch the bleeding and Pyrineus survived.[3]

I doubt it took Bubba until 1909 to figure out the utility of the new explosive. One must, however, always exercise great caution when utilizing new technology. Long-time journalist Henry Wolff, Jr. tells the tale of one Bill Lipscomb who, if you'll pardon the pun, nearly blew it. Intending to impress his wife with his fishing prowess, Lipscomb lit and tossed a stick of dynamite out of the boat they occupied into the Guadalupe River down Victoria way. Quoting Henry's Journal, Lipscomb related "somehow it got hung on the side of the boat, [it] took some doing to get away from it and then [it] almost blew us out of the water." Seems Lipscomb's wife was not overly impressed.[4]

While marginally less dangerous to life and limb, "telephoning" catfish is certainly every bit as creative and just as illegal. The tactic first came to the public's attention with a 1954 *Sports Illustrated* article describing an Alabama conservation officer's discovery of two good ol' boys in a river skiff electrocuting their quarry. According to the officer, "they dropped a wire and sinker to the bottom, and trailed a second wire over the side of the boat. Both wires were attached to a little machine with a hand crank. As one man turned the crank, catfish began surfacing around the boat."[5]

Feeling this had to be a violation of Alabama fish and game laws, the officer arrested the anglers. The press picked up the story and almost immediately "telephoning" became a rage that swept the catfish world.

Don't try this with your cell phone; it won't work. The vital equipment required is the magneto from older hand-cranked wall-mounted models. Turning the magneto handle rapidly produced the electricity required to ring the bell elsewhere down the telephone line and to carry the audible message from caller to recipient. Adapted to angling, the mechanism sends an electrical charge through the water, stunning catfish and causing them to float to the surface. Just scoop 'em up and fire up the deep fryer. Realizing the scarcity of such magnetos in the twenty-first century, entrepreneurs have sprung forth to fill the market niche. You can pick up a modern catfish stunner over the Internet from Donald W. Kendrick, Jr. of Pineville, Louisiana for a mere $55. Kendrick's CATFISHSTUNNER web site does contain a warning that use of the product is not legal in all areas of the country. Nonetheless, there seems to be a market for his wares.

If supposed "reality shows" such as Animal Planet's *Hillbilly Handfishing* and the History Channel's *Mudcats* are to be believed, the current rage in the catfish world is the technique of "noodling." Frankly, I have serious doubts as to how widespread the phenomenon is; it's simply too physically demanding for most folk. "Noodling," known to some as "grabbling," involves fishing by hand. After finding a nesting male flathead holed up in a crevice underneath the shoreline or in a decaying submerged log, the angler probes the hole or brush pile in hopes of either grabbing the fish by the jaw or having the animal grab onto him or her. This method of fishing by hand in all likelihood dates to Native Americans in prehistoric times, but it's certainly nothing new. Garland Petty of Zephyr in Brown County was adept at it in the 1930s. A natural outdoorsmen and hunting guide, Petty, according to relatives, always wore long sleeved shirts regardless of weather because of the ever-present "river rash" up and down his arms—abrasions from wrestling flatheads from creeks throughout that region of the state.

Such scabs and scars are the least of a noodler's worries. Those interested in hand fishing are advised to ply their craft in waters no more than four or five feet deep. Large flatheads weighing fifty pounds or more have the agility and strength to drag noodlers underwater. A number have drowned trying to escape the vise-like grip of their prey in an aquatic environment where the giant fish may very well enjoy the advantage. Furthermore, there's no guarantee that the critter you grab (or that grabs you) is going to be a catfish. Noodlers have lost digits to gars and snapping turtles. Water moccasins have caused many an angler involved in such mano-a-mano combat an emergency trip to the hospital. Such encounters would perhaps be better than finding oneself down in the muddy water with a critter such as the 880 pound, thirteen-foot-long alligator harvested from the Trinity River in Leon County this past summer. You never know for sure what you'll come up with once you get down in the water fishing by hand.

Bubba exhibits no less ingenuity when it comes to displaying his piscatory prize once the harvest is complete and the fillets are carved away from the carcass. Get off the interstate highways and drive the back roads of Texas and sooner or later you'll see some unique sights. My "what the heck" moment came in the early 1990s whizzing down Hunter Road between Hays and Comal counties. So out of the ordinary was the sight to my life experience that I had to turn around and photograph two alligator gar heads strung up with pride on some property owner's fence line. Now, catfish are a whole lot more prevalent than gars in this area of the world. Therefore, you're more likely to see a display of giant flatheads, such as the one Dan Utley, employed at the time with the Texas Historical Commission, witnessed and documented. Like ornamental balls hung from a Christmas tree, it shows genuine inventiveness on Bubba's part.

One less decorative but far more utilitarian form of catfish tree was located in the Trinity River bottoms. The process for it is simple. Impale your catch on a tree or post using a 10-penny nail through the skull. Once properly secured for stability, make an incision behind the gills and peel the skin from the body, exposing the valued fillets. Hacking the rest of the remaining skeleton from the head when finished is optional. Either way, over time Bubba builds a putrefying totem to his fishing prowess.

Display possibilities seem unlimited. One Llano County property owner chose to adorn the gate to his property with his monster cats. If vertigo or acrophobia makes climbing ladders problematic, just smash your flathead skull down on any convenient fence post. Bragging rights are, after all, bragging rights.

Now, I know the question is on your mind. Why not just take your trophy to the local taxidermist and have it mounted permanently and professionally? The answer is two-fold. Remember that the catfish's skin is different than most fish—mucous-covered and lacking scales. According to Jared Lawrence, owner of On Target Taxidermy in Bangs, Texas, catfish really can't be mounted because the skin continually dries out and breaks. Such a mount requires constant repair and alienates customers. Therefore, he and other practitioners of taxidermy will only make reproductions—what you get back is absolutely artificial, containing not one iota of the actual animal portrayed. It does, however, look and smell a lot better on the coffee table over time. Then there's the matter of price. Lawrence quoted me a price between $600 and $700 for a reproduction of a fifty-pound flathead. Your typical Bubba may not be Mensa material but, given a choice between a spray-painted plastic reproduction of what at one time was a catfish and $600–$700 of new fishing equipment, he usually makes the right decision.

The only thing better than a big old flathead—either mounted on the wall or frying in a pan—is an even bigger and even older flathead that's just waiting out there somewhere to be harvested.

Endnotes

1. Mike Leggett. "Nothing Says Texas Like Flatheads on a Fence." *Austin-American Statesman*, July 11, 2004.
2. http://www.chadferguson.com/what/, and http://www.catfish baitsoap.com/about-catfish-bait.html.
3. Theodore Roosevelt. Through the Brazilian Wilderness. Available online at Project Gutenberg as EBook #111746. Accessed at http://www.gutenberg.org/files/111746/111746-8.txt. 22–23.
4. Henry Woolf, Jr. "Dynamite Fisherman." *Victoria Advocate*, March 11, 1983.
5. Emmett Gowen. "Phone for Your Fish: The Guts of Obsolete Telephones Are Raising Havoc Among Catfish." *Sports Illustrated*, September 27, 1954. Accessed online at http://si.com/vault/article,MAG1128948/indext.htm.

Pat Parsons in front of the Bethel Primitive Baptist Church, built in 1901 in McMahan, Texas, where Pat's great-grandfather was pastor

TEXAS COUNTRY CHURCHES

by Pat Parsons

Don't you just love to read church signs? One of my favorites is, "The Fasting and Prayer Conference includes meals."

Texas country churches are special places. At eleven o'clock on Sunday morning you'll hear the preacher shout out the door, "Y'all come on in now." This past summer in our little church in Prairie Lea we took up a Special Offering . . . a new septic tank. When we had that one little ole rain fall last summer, we opened the door so we could hear it, over the preaching. Country preachers all have their own way of dressing. Some wear a three-piece suit and tie, others wear jeans and a plaid shirt . . . but both will be wearing their boots! How do you know when you are loved in a country church? Miss a Sunday morning service and before 2:00 you'll have a dozen phone calls asking, "Who's sick at your house?"

Church in Texas has always been unique. The first organized Baptist church to come in under the radar of the Mexican Government was Elder John Parker's Predestinarian Baptist in 1833. These early Baptists built Fort Parker and tried to live quiet, Godly lives in a country still filled with Indians and Mexicans. . . until the capture of Cynthia Ann and the others. In 1835, William B. Travis appealed for Methodist preachers to be sent to Texas claiming that, ". . . they could produce much good in this benighted land."[1]

Texas attracted men who gambled, raced horses, and loved to fight. One of those men, who was known for his wild ways, happened to attend a brush arbor camp meeting in Bastrop in 1856, and, much like Saul on the Road to Damascus, had an about face. Andrew Jackson Potter went home that night and told his wife he was a changed man and was going to be following The Lord from now on. By 1860, they were living on a farm just outside of Lockhart and Rev. Potter was preaching every Sunday, although the

Methodist Church Conference would move him every two years as the Bishop saw fit.

Now, Potter was truly a man of God, but he also had lots of common sense. When traveling in Kimble County he kept his Winchester nearby and didn't hesitate to use it when confronted by Indians. The Bishop did not like it when the story got back to him and he said to Potter, "Our weapons are not carnal," meaning . . . "Our weapons are of the Spiritual Nature." Potter replied, "There were no Indians there when that was written." Many a time Rev. Potter had to get the attention of men when he arrived in a new town. His first sermon in San Angelo was given in an empty saloon with his .45 lying beside his Bible. He told the men gathered that he had heard there might be some trouble and he promised if there was, there would be a bunch of mighty sick roosters.

Potter remained in San Angelo for twenty years, a much unusual length of time for a Methodist preacher to stay in one place. Rev. Andrew Jackson Potter was known as "the fighting parson" and made his mark on Texas Country Churches . . . even in the way he went out. It was in 1895 at Tilmon Chapel in Caldwell County when, at the close of the sermon, Potter said, "I think I have heard my last sermon. I am going home I believe." And with those words, he fell dead in the pulpit.[2]

We often turn to old preachers for their words of wisdom gained from living a long life in the church. Back in 1888, Texas was experiencing a terrible drought. Some of the local farmers were discussing having a special service down at the church to pray for rain. They went to the old pastor and asked his opinion. He listened to them intently and answered, "As long as this wind keeps steady from the west it won't do any good to pray." Besides comforting their flock in times of natural disaster, preachers also had to contend with man-made dangers.

Two Polish priests had arrived in Texas shortly after the Civil War and discovered they had two kinds of snakes to deal with.

There were those that crawled and those that walked on two legs. During Reconstruction in South Texas the good God-fearing people struggled against the lawlessness that was rampant. Church services were often disrupted by men coming into the service and terrifying the worshipers. The priests had to carry revolvers in one hand and their rosaries in the other, and were known to fire over the heads of the unruly men. At our Genealogy Library we are transcribing old Church records, and in one we actually found it recorded in the minutes that, "All guns must be checked at the door."[3] As far as the other type of snakes . . . after finding one wrapped around the water bowl at their first baptism the priests learned to keep an eye out for those slithery creatures and dispatch them quickly.

One circuit riding preacher was gone a lot, leaving his family on their own much of the time. Rev. William Biggs had five boys at home. They knew the rules that Papa had set out for them: Sunday was a day of rest and reflection, whether there was church services or not . . . but boys sometimes don't follow the rules. It was a hot Texas summer Sunday and Papa was gone over to the next town to preach. The boys just couldn't resist heading down to the nearby creek. By nightfall their backs were sunburned. On Monday Rev. Biggs returned home and was made aware of his son's activity on The Lord's Day. Now, Rev. Biggs was a great outdoorsman himself and often would take his boys to enjoy God's nature with camping and fishing trips. On this day he instructed the boys to prepare their backpacks and he led them on an all-day hike. Years later the boys, then grown into men, told how they endured the day without complaint because otherwise they would have had to confess their sin of swimming on the Lord's Day to their Papa.

Getting married used to be easier than it is today. In December of 1887, just as evening services closed at the Luling Methodist Church, a young couple, bent on matrimony, drove up in a buggy to the front of the church. The preacher was called out and they asked him to tie the knot. He invited them into the church for a proper ceremony, but they declined—so he performed one while they were seated in the buggy, and they drove off happy.

Debating theology was regarded as a form of entertainment in those days long before TV. It was noted in the Seguin newspaper that the Methodist preacher was delivering a sermon on infant baptism and the Baptist preacher attended—and took notes (perhaps preparing for a debate?).

It was also in Seguin that a young lady was sneaking peeks across the church at the young man who had won her heart. It was difficult to listen to the words of the minister when all she could think about was the marriage proposal she was sure was coming soon. When her handsome young man's eyes met hers she began to feel terribly strange. Her skin began to tingle. Could this be love? But then she noticed a tension in the room and the eyes of the congregation all seemed to be glassy and transfixed with strained expressions. And she had the terrible urge to scratch. From beneath the floor the contented grunt of pigs was heard. Soon, the minister ended his sermon and dismissed church. The next day the church was scrubbed down with lye and a fence was built to keep the pigs *and their fleas* from nesting under the church.

As towns became more settled in the late 1800s the womenfolk wanted two things: a school for their children's learning and a church for their spiritual growth. A group of ladies were determined to have a church in their town. They had very few roads, no mail service, no telephones, and no automobiles, but these faithful women would spread the news about a fundraising dinner and have as many as 200 tickets sold. They also had lemonade festivals, sold quilts, and had pie suppers. When the ladies wanted a church they got a church!

One community got their church but had a big debt owed to the bank. The pastor was inspired one Sunday morning and encouraged everyone to buy the chair they were sitting in. After services as he walked to his home he heard a male member calling out his name. The man had a chair in his arms and asked the preacher, "Brother Carter, could I also buy a chair to take home to my wife?"

Did you know that the religious standing of a congregation could often be understood by the seating? There would be men on the north side, married couples in the center, and ladies on the south side, with saints in the front and sinners to the rear. Cowboys understand this. Once up in the Panhandle a preacher was expounding to a bunch of cowboys on how to live like a Christian. He warned them, "Some of your freshly branded calves don't suck the right cows."

Over in East Texas a Baptist Church was greatly concerned about a saloon that was going to be built across the street from the church. As construction began the church members organized petitions and prayer rallies. The night before the saloon was to open it was struck by lightning and burnt to the ground. The church members bragged on the "power of prayer." Then the saloon owner sued, claiming the church was either "directly or indirectly responsible" for his loss. In court the church denied that they had any involvement in the fire, leading the judge to state he didn't know how to rule since it appeared he had a saloon owner that believed in the power of prayer and an entire church that didn't.[4]

The BIG event every year for some denominations is the Camp Meeting. They have been going on in Texas since the 1890s, according to historical records. These meetings usually last for three or four days today, but in the early days they sometimes went on for up to two weeks. Today, people bring in their RVs or stay in the closest Motel 6, but when I was growing up we pitched a tent for four days out under the mesquite trees. During that time there would be three church services a day with singing, praying, and preaching. Breakfast, lunch, and supper were cooked, usually by the men, and served on the grounds. You know how some people take their dogs everywhere they go? Well, one year the Baker family took Bonnie the Duck to Camp Meeting . . . and what a stir she created!

Bonnie came into our life as a wee little duckling. My sister Martha was in the 3rd grade and had a friend named Bonnie. One day Bonnie showed up at school with this duckling in a paper cup. Mrs. Cage, the teacher, was a kind-hearted woman and understood about friends sharing their treasures. She filled the sink in the girl's restroom with water and all day long a steady stream of kids came by to see the little yellow duckling swimming in the basin. Ducks like water, you know. At the end of the school day Bonnie was put into a box (that's the duck not the girl) for Martha to take home on the school bus. Mother got out her small wash tub, filled it with water, and put Bonnie in it and set her out in the back yard. But Bonnie kept trying to get out. Repeated attempts to make her stay in the water were useless. Daddy decided Bonnie was worn out from trying to stay afloat all day, and he put her out on the grass to run around. Bonnie *never* in her life swam *ever* again.

But this is supposed to be a "church story," so let's get back to it. Summer came and soon the family packed up to go to South Texas for the annual Camp Meeting. We knew we couldn't leave Bonnie on her own with cats and dogs and coyotes, so Daddy built her a traveling box and she rode in the back seat of the old Ford with Martha and me. At daybreak the first morning we heard Momma ask, "Where's Bonnie? She's not in her box!" Daddy examined the cage and declared that our duck was so extraordinarily smart she had figured out how to raise the latch. He wasn't too worried that she would get too far away from "her family." Sure enough, he found her over at the cooking tent where biscuits were baking and eggs being scrambled. Bonnie *loved* biscuits and scrambled eggs and she *loved* the men tossing her bites to eat. There are people today who remember the Nixon Camp Meeting not so much because of the great preaching and singing, but because that was the year of Bonnie the Duck.

In 2003, a professional journalist from Colorado was sent to the small community of McMahan, Texas, to cover the Southwest

Texas Sacred Harp Singing Convention held at the Bethel Primitive Baptist Church, a little country Church constituted in 1852. McMahan had been holding organized Sacred Harp Singings since 1900, when folks from Alabama and Georgia brought the unique shaped note gospel music with them. Kathryn Eastburn did her research before she came to Texas and knew the "facts"—what she didn't know was the "Spirit" of what she would see and hear. She was thrilled and moved by the sound of the a cappella singing done by the two hundred voices in that little country church. The words of the songs praised God and thanked Him for His mercies. Many of the songs were the same old church songs that brought back memories of Kathryn's granddaddy and his church in Kentucky where she visited as a child.

Mid-morning a young man took his turn at leading and called out his selection number 484, "My Country 'Tis of Thee," and said he wanted the group to sing it in honor of the Texas soldiers recently deployed to the war in Iraq. Of course, Kathryn knew the words to the song, but it tugged too much at her heart. Her son, an Army reservist, would soon be sent into the war—a war she did not believe in, a war that she knew this country was divided over. But as she looked across the faces singing those words, she saw not flags waving, not salutes, not hands across hearts, not arguments against the president's actions . . . but faces filled with love for country and thankfulness to God for the ability and freedom to sing about that. And her heart softened.

Kathryn had found a place where love of God and love of Country were celebrated. In her own words she tells what that meant for her, and I pray that we each find this place: "Just a few years ago, my hardened heart cracked open and let in the sound of unadorned voices raised in praise. Restored to me was many treasured parts of a life past and gave me hope for a spiritual future, for grace, amazing grace."[5] And she had found it in a little Texas Country Church.

ENDNOTES

1. Rev. Olin W. Nail, General Editor. *Texas Methodist Centennial Year-book*. Elgin, Texas: Nail Publications, n.d. Travis letter reproduced on p. 36.
2. "Minutes of the Thirty-Seventh Session of the West Texas Annual Conference Methodist Episcopal Church, South." November 20–25, 1895. Excerpts archived in the Genealogical & Historical Society Library, Luling, Texas.
3. Interview with Gwen Waldrop in Genealogical & Historical Society Library, Luling, Texas. February 2012.
4. Ibid.
5. Kathryn Eastburn. *A Sacred Feast: Reflection on Sacred Harp Singing and Dinner on the Ground*. Lincoln, Nebr.: University of Nebraska Press, 2008. 158.

Rev. W. H. H. Biggs, minister of the Methodist Episcopal Church, South.
Courtesy, Pat Parsons

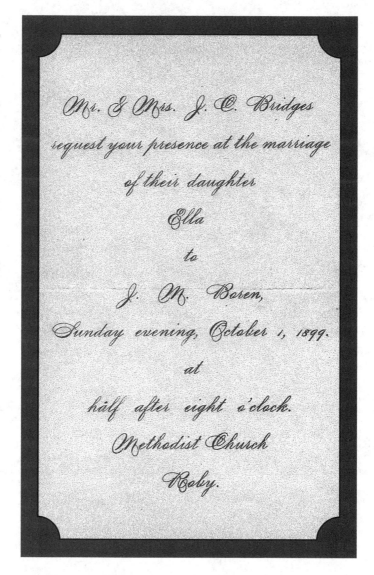

Mr. & Mrs. J. C. Bridges
request your presence at the marriage
of their daughter
Ella
to
J. M. Boren,
Sunday evening, October 1, 1899.
at
half after eight o'clock.
Methodist Church
Roby.

Invitation to a "town" wedding at the turn of the century

TEXAS WEDDINGS: RATTLES ON THE GARTER AND "BARBWIRE" IN THE FLOWERS

by Mildred B. Sentell

An important precursor to a Texas wedding is the engagement announcement. It is important to establish the family, family connections, grandparents and, in a town in which the family is well established and has been for generations, the occupations of the previous ancestors, as well as such issues as the pioneer experiences of the same and such information as would ensure the interest of readers who scan the hometown paper. Recently, in the *Snyder Daily News*, the announcement of a regional couple's engagement included the information that the future groom's father had been a World Champion Bull Rider and the mother of the bride to be had been a very good barrel racer. The announcement also told how the couple met and shared the information that the bride wasn't eager to meet the intended, being a friend of the incumbent wife, but that when she did meet him, she was "smitten." The wedding write-up was equally instructive, giving the detailed description of the bride's wedding dress and the provenance of the groom's Levis. (More on this later.)

Yet another announcement, though much more brief, in the *Post Dispatch*, detailed the high schools, colleges, and jobs of the couple, as well as the occupations of the parents (all seven) and the information that the bride's sons were announcing the engagement. And still another example to be noted is one that appeared in the *San Angelo Standard Times* of a ten-month-old baby announcing his parents' engagement and upcoming marriage.

Due to the isolation of ranching families in the late 19th and early 20th centuries, weddings were often held on Christmas Day or within a day or two of that holiday. Families were visiting, ranchers were able to get away for a few days (if they had hands to stay on the ranch and feed), and the bride and groom could stay on for a spell until such a time as they were able to establish themselves with a job in town or on a ranch. It was a custom in Kent County for rancher families to come to the town of Spur and stay for a week at Christmas time at a well known hotel of great comfort. That presented an excellent opportunity for a wedding, with the guest list including all the hotel guests. Also, some weddings were held during the spring roundup or on the Fourth of July.

A bride then would, if living in town, often have a formal church wedding. Texas, having been largely settled by Southerners after the War, saw many brides given a lavish wedding and some education, while her brothers inherited the parents' property, according to Southern custom.

Depression weddings were often simple, sometimes in the bride's home with, on one occasion, the bride's father conducting the ceremony, he being a judge. As frequent were the marriages in the manse or parsonage of the presiding minister, with his wife as witness. The wedding dress would be appropriate for long wear to church or other dress-up affairs, and the groom's suit was certain to see years of service.

A whole new concept of what was demanded by a prospective bride changed with the start of WWII, when the couple involved might have at times only a weekend or short leave earned by the groom, and the marriage was, of necessity, hasty. One case in Crane, Texas, presented an example of extreme haste when the bride, a school teacher, took off her lunch hour, met the fiancé at the bus station, accompanied him to the justice of the peace, married him before seeing him off on the bus for Ft. Bliss, and then went back to finish the school day. The dress was also simpler in war times: the bride in a suit, a corsage and at times a spectacular hat, and the groom in uniform. The bride's suit would certainly be something that could be worn later and, of course, the groom would get a lot of wear from his uniform.

The end of WWII brought about the Great Barbie Doll Weddings. Conventions were observed: the engagement would be announced six weeks before the wedding, often at a "tea" given by the mother of the bride (henceforth referred to as the MOB) and usually a day or two before the newspaper published the picture and short announcement. The picture, depending on the family's place in the community, could be almost life-sized; certainly, the formal bridal portrait might be. The tea signaled the start of "courtesies," among them a giant tea hosted by friends of the MOB, kitchen showers by the bridesmaids, and finally a bridesmaids' brunch the morning of the wedding. Wedding dresses came into play very often, with a tight bodice and full skirt over hoops and with miles of lace. "Tea length" was popular, such being just above ankle length. And the costume was completed with a short veil. The groom? Ah yes, the groom, resplendent in a white "dinner jacket" and black pants, both almost certainly being already in the closet from the demands of his college parties. If the groom possessed no dinner jacket, he simply wore his good suit: he did not rent something. All this was followed by a reception in the church fellowship hall or a large home and was the occasion for a wedding cake, nuts, and punch.

The rather rigid habits of the soon-to-be-married underwent something of a sea of change in the sixties when the "hippie" culture began. Young couples who had decided against "free love" and wanted to marry, still contrived to splash out. There came the Rock-in-a-Stream phase. Couples in East Texas had a somewhat easier time marrying in a stream than those in West Texas, the West being replete with dry creek beds but rather short on streams. Variations could be met, however, by choosing a pasture (with a plan B available in case of inclement weather, usually a sandstorm), a country Cowboy Church (usually neither air-conditioned nor heated), or the courthouse gazebo. Dress might be informal in the extreme: the groom in jeans and the bride in anything besides a white lace dress. One such wedding presented the groom, his attendants, and his father in jeans and western shirts. The bride, notwithstanding the time of year, that being August, held the wedding in a cowboy church—rustic and charming, but hot. The females were still hotter, dressed as they were in genuine suede divided skirts and vests and long sleeved silk shirts. For various reasons, probably the wedding itself, the marriage was remarkably short-lived.

The Great Rubber Tree Wedding was a prime example of cowboy-country out of control. One bride had seven attendants, stair-stepped in size from age sixteen to about four years old. All were in "prairie" style dresses. The groom, with his seven groomsmen of about the same ages as the bride's friends, wore black jeans, white shirts, and black cowboy hats, which remained on the males' heads throughout the ceremony. Taped Country Western songs were chosen for all the music, those songs being between two-and-a-half to three minutes long each. The bridesmaids followed by the bride and her brother (her father was the minister) marched down the aisle in about fifty seconds. The song was only just started; the females were obliged to wait a full two minutes for the song to finish. The smallest of the bridesmaids and groomsmen became restless and began to whine. Finally, the ceremony began; the Unity Candle was unfortunately lit to yet another Country Western song. The lighting took fifteen seconds. The song lasted another three minutes. All of the attendants became restless, not to mention the bride's efforts to look at the groom in a loving manner for that length of time. At last the ceremony ended. The professional photographer was constantly hampered by the aunts, cousins, and grandmothers of the marrying couple who were devoted to taking pictures from any perceived advantageous location. They popped up, cameras flashing, all during the service, crossed the room in front of the altar, wriggled up behind the palms to get shots of the couple's faces, and in general marked the occasion thoroughly. The wedding adjourned for the reception to another church of the same denomination, a lovely church with a vestibule suitable for a bridal portrait. The bride's feet were killing her, so she took off the extremely high heeled boots and sat for her portrait rather than stand in those boots. As the couple started to leave, they, in their

Western clothes, went out the side door to leave in the back of a pickup, sitting on a bale of hay, and rode around the church, then exited the pickup and got in a car and left. At the back of the hall was a table of gifts, including a small metal tree with clips intended to be used for gifts of cash for the couple. There was no money in the clips; there was only, in every clip, a small foil packet.

While the couple of the famous bull riding father and barrel racing mother were married in a simple ceremony, the bride wore a noteworthy creation made from fifteen yards of white satin and sported a six-foot train: the groom wore his "lucky" jeans, those being ones he had worn in three of his previous weddings. Recently, that bride, in order to honor her grandfather, and in an extreme sense of nostalgia, started a business of street paving. Her grandfather had owned a paving company and taught her to love and long for the smell of hot tar and asphalt, she said.

As time marched on, the grooms began to assert themselves in matters of dress. Often seen in the 1970s and '80s, was the pastel colored tuxedo: one might observe all the males in the wedding party in baby blue, maroon (actually quite attractive), brown, or even pink, not to mention the occasional white, usually chosen to go with the bridesmaids' frocks. The father of the bride (FOB) is usually thought of as a nonentity, sitting in the background, writing checks and contemplating bankruptcy. One FOB in recent years, always one to assert his individuality, joined the groom and groomsmen in choosing black tuxes, but while theirs were conservative, conventional, and tasteful, the FOB tricked himself out in tails, striped pants, and a top hat. The man was very tall anyway, and with the added inches of high heeled patent leather boots and the hat, caused some nervous giggles among the congregation, who feared that he would fall off his stilts or drop his sign.

The Motif or Theme Wedding continues to advance. One couple, the groom of which was an air traffic controller, married in the control tower in which he worked, having obtained permission, one supposes, from the Amarillo Airport Board. Another happy couple, owners of a skating rink, tied the knot by wearing roller skates and marrying at the rink. Luckily, the bride's 71-year-old father was able to skate to the altar also, with his daughter on his arm.

If one's fiancé is a radio newsman, it is sometimes possible to cram bride, groom, friends, and family into a radio control booth, with a disc jockey broadcasting a morning show and pausing to put the ceremony on the air. The groom in this case noted that the employees of the station were like a big family, and since they couldn't take off work for the wedding, the couple just had it there. In yet another instance a judge, being impatient with delays in a trial, ordered a bride and groom to appear in court, married them, and seated the groom as juror, rather than delay the trial once again for the groom's wedding plans. That joining took ten minutes.

Sentiment, never amiss at a wedding, sometimes takes peculiar forms. The most popular, besides the rose for the mothers of the bride and groom as the bride proceeds, seems to involve favorite pets as ring bearer. In gratitude to one woman's racing armadillo for winning a race, she decided to appoint the racer as ring bearer. Armadillos, not noted for being biddable or indeed trainable, raced off predictably with the rings, occasioning a busyness among the attendants of the sort seldom seen at a ceremony. Yet another bride wishing to have a "happy and joyful wedding" set the lighthearted tone to the ceremony by having her Labrador carry the rings in a "beautifully decorated basket." The dog dropped the basket and roamed about the church. A truly touching occasion occurred when a bride, being blind, was led to the altar by her guide dog, which behaved beautifully.

Attitudes and actions of the MOBs vary from delight to reluctance to obdurate objections. If the daughter has made what is termed a "good" match, the MOB will tend to flutter and remark with great frequency to all and sundry on the "dear boy's" assets and sterling qualities. One such MOB exaggerated the matter so that the father of the groom (FOG), embarrassed, began to speak incessantly to all about the drought, the high price of feed, the low price of cattle and oil, and the difficulty of making a living on a small ranch.

A reluctant MOB, though going along with the determined daughter and considering the mechanics of hosting a wedding, might, in the presence of the daughter, ask her favorite clerk in a department store to show her a dress appropriate for the bride's mother to wear to the funeral.

The drama queen MOB has been known to declare in response to the couple's intentions that the girl will not marry and, if she does, there will be no wedding, and that the MOB will not come if there is a wedding. Then, having declared herself to have a headache, she will gear up, plan the most elaborate affair of the season, engage five bridesmaids, order 500 invitations (printed rather than engraved because of the time factor), arrange to use the church, see to the wedding cake, send the invitations, and find her own costume all in a week's time.

One obdurate MOB, the zaniest of all, actually became hysterical in the vestibule of the church as the wedding was set to begin. The groom's parents, already seated, saw the groom and the best man emerge, along with the priest, who signaled to the organist. The MOB had not been seated. The priest welcomed the congregation; still the MOB was not seated. He heard a commotion in the vestibule and, smiling in hopeful fashion, went back out of the nave. The MOB was not seated. The groom and best man went back out to the vestibule and witnessed the MOB crying that her daughter "can't marry. She is too young [at age twenty-six]; she has never spent the night away from home; the couple will have to live with me for at least three months before my daughter can survive away from Mother." The groom's mother told the father that they must pray. The father said that he had already prayed and God told him to go out front and belt the MOB. The groom and best man discussed seriously going to the Bar & Grill less than a block down the street. The groomsmen considered joining the groom and best man in the walk down the street. The priest took control, told the MOB to wipe her face and get herself to the front of the church: the wedding was about to begin. And so it did, thirty minutes late. The groom and best man re-entered; the bridesmaids marched in; the FOB, still sane somehow, escorted his daughter to the front and the wedding did indeed occur.

The reception themes or motifs reach ever more startling heights. There was the Western theme of a reception in San Antonio, which was complete with chocolates (reportedly delicious) shaped as cow patties. There was the turtle theme with candies shaped like turtles. A ranch theme dictated copies of the couples' brands on the cakes, the groom having his spurs on the table before the cake, deer antlers under the cake stand, and a mason jar of flowers and small jars full of jelly beans as favors. There was the groom's table with wood-stained mesquite rounds as base for a marbled pottery container with wildflowers and barbed wire ribbons.

There was one with toy earth-moving equipment. In the same wedding, the couple lighted a kerosene lantern instead of a unity candle. The couple, being understandably unfamiliar with such lanterns, didn't know to turn it down. Fortunately, the ceiling did not catch fire and a hefty breeze blew the black smoke away after the bride's grandmother hastened forward to lower the wick. The bride in this affair wore a satin and lace strapless gown with sequins sewn from the waist to the hem. With this garment she wore brown, square-toed cowboy boots.

Sometimes the passions and fascination with certain entities approaches the creepy. Probably the best unusual, even odd wedding occurred in Houston and was related to me by Henry Wolff, who not only guaranteed its authenticity, but gave me permission to use the incident herein.

One couple with an enthusiasm, indeed an obsessive interest, for rattlesnakes and guns were married in Houston among the displays for an annual weapons collectors' meeting in the civic center. When the ushers spotted the bride coming down the aisle, a few minutes late, they left the stage, fully, indeed excessively, armed to encircle her and make room for her son-in-law who was to give her away. The son-in-law, rather underdressed and under armed, wore lizard boots and a black hat. He and the bride proceeded through lines of men dressed in army fatigues, Foreign Legion berets, army MP regalia, and carrying everything from shotguns to M-16s. The groom, however, showed no such restraint in dress. He wore a rattlesnake-covered top hat with a plume of twenty rattlers gracing the back and coat, along with boots, belt, holster, pistol handle, and buckles all covered with rattlesnake skin. The bride, entering into the spirit of the thing, reportedly wore rattles on her garter. The daughter of the bride apparently decided on an attitude of sanity: no snake skins. The cake, reportedly delicious, was decorated with rattlesnakes.

Who knows why certain marriages last for fifty years or more? Practice? Doesn't the fourth or fifth marriage guarantee better results than the first time for both? Does a rattlesnake wedding, besides demonstrating tolerance and ice-cold nerves, increase the chance for longevity of the marriage? Can a thirty-minute ceremony between bus stops and classes make the relationship more precarious? In Texas, couples have tried venturing into the unknown in every conceivable vehicle. And amazingly, many are still married. In fact, most are still married years later. We are now reading daily of the Barbie Bride celebrating her Golden Wedding Anniversary with the very husband whom she married in the church so many years ago.

Sheila Morris

SALLY AND CHANCE:
AN UNUSUAL LOVE STORY

by Sheila Morris

If you spend time in a small town in Texas, you can be pretty sure you'll meet a storyteller or two and be thoroughly entertained with gossipy tales about town politics and politicians, or a hurricane that blew through a few years ago, or the high school football team that won state, or the best game the Aggies and Longhorns ever played, or what happened to the Cowboys when an Arkansas boy named Jerry Jones bought them, or why in the world the Houston Oilers had to move to Tennessee. Most likely you'll find out who has the best chicken fried steak and hamburgers in town, and the name of the newest Mexican food restaurant that's run by authentic Hispanics and not one of those dagnabit chains. For sure, the number-one topic in every small town in southcast Texas in the summer of 2011, however, was the drought, as in no rain. Not a drop for weeks. Record triple-digit temperatures for days and no rain to cool off anything or anybody. And so on. My listening ear was almost on autopilot and I could nod my head at appropriate intervals and tsk! tsk! about the weather with the best of them.

And then I met Sally, and no, my name isn't Harry. Sally woke me up with a real Texas love story. Good storytellers can appear in the strangest places and at the most unexpected times, and this one was no exception.

My friend Carol and I drove over to Tomball, a small town between our home town of Montgomery and Houston, the giant behemoth of a city forty miles southeast of us. We both took items to be framed because Carol said she knew the best frame shop in the county and it was in Tomball. She knew the woman and her husband who ran the shop and vowed they were the best framers in the business. Well, that was good enough for me.

Carol was a reliable resource for all things artsy craftsy antiquey and anything in between.

When we entered the little shop, I saw it was an art gallery as well as a frame shop, but I wasn't surprised because many retail stores combine the two, particularly in a town the size of Tomball with its population of 9,089. I could also see right away I would love the unpretentious shop, because much of the art displayed on the walls and scattered about on easels was Texana. You know what I mean: cowboys and cows, boots and spurs, horses, Indian chiefs—all the nostalgic western images that made Texans, both native and transplanted, believe they remembered who they were. You either got it and liked it or didn't get it and made fun of it. I got it.

The shop was empty except for Sally and her husband Bill. The first thing I noticed about this woman was her hair. She had big hair, as we used to say when we described my Aunt Thelma's signature beehive hairdo or the coiffures of the women who attended the Pentecostal Holiness Church. Sally's suspiciously colored reddish blonde white hair was swept up and back and appeared to be longer than it probably was. Regardless, it was big and suited the woman who greeted us with a smile the same size as her hair. She exchanged pleasantries with Carol, who introduced me to Sally and Bill and explained our mission. We had brought our assortment of pictures and posters and prints in with us, and Sally escorted us to the back of the shop where we could lay them out to be measured and matched with mats and frames. Bill disappeared into his work room.

Carol told me to go first with my things and I began to put a few pictures on the counter top in front of Sally, who sat down and reached for her measuring tape. But then, she seemed to lose interest in the job ahead of her and launched into a monologue about the heat that summer. And could we believe it? Lightning struck her air conditioning unit at her house earlier that week and she and Bill had been without cool air for two days and nights. The first night they turned on all the fans they could find and toughed it out, but the last night she had looked at Bill around 8:30 and told him they had to go spend the night in a motel because she couldn't stand the heat. Now, Sally wasn't a small woman and I could empathize with her need for cool air, and I found myself caught up in the drama of spending the night in the Comfort Inn to flee the hot, humid, natural air of a house struck by lightning.

Sally embellished the story with disclosures of her being a member of the Tomball Volunteer Fire Department and some ancillary marshall's role with the Montgomery County Sheriff's Department that allowed her and Bill to drive a county vehicle. I settled in for the long haul when I recognized Sally was the genuine article: a good ol' gal, Texas storyteller. I noticed Carol slipped away to browse through the shop. She evidently had heard some of these stories before.

Sally interspersed her stories with getting down to the framing business at hand and periodically produced a frame for me to consider, along with mats of various colors and textures. I remarked that I thought the pictures in her shop were great and that I loved Texana. She stopped measuring and her eyes lit up with the excitement of discovering a kindred spirit. She asked me if I had noticed the pictures at the front near the cash register. I hadn't.

"Well, I want you to go take a look at them right now," Sally said. "They're pictures of me and Chance, the love of my life. Go on. Have a look."

I obediently followed her instructions and walked over to see the two 8×10 glossy photos hanging on the wall next to the check-out counter. One was a black-and-white photo of a younger Sally in a western outfit with three not unattractive cowboys posing with her. They stood next to a large Brahman bull. I tried to pick out the one who was Chance. The other photo was in color. Again, it was a younger version of Sally in a rodeo outfit with her arm around the same bull. I walked back to Sally and told her I thought the pictures were great and wondered which one was Chance.

"Chance is the Brahman bull," she said and pronounced it bray-man. I had always called it brah-man. "Wasn't he beautiful?"

Sally asked in a reverent tone. I'm sure I looked surprised, and she chuckled as if she and I now shared a wonderful secret. Chance the Bull was the love of her life. I waited for the whole story.

"I got him at an auction when he was ten years old," she said. "My husband at the time, not Bill, said I ought not to take a chance on him, but I looked right into that bull's eyes and we had a connection. A real connection. It was love at first sight. So we got him, and I named him Chance. I had him for more than eleven years, and that bull was the sweetest and gentlest animal I ever knew. I've had dogs meaner than him. I used to ride him in rodeos and the parades for the rodeos, and he never minded the noise and fuss people made over him as long as I was with him. He was oblivious to everyone but me. It was love at first sight all right, and he loved me as much as I loved him for as long as he lived. I've never felt the pure love I felt from that bull from any person in my life, including my husbands and children and grandchildren."

She took a breath and continued. I didn't dare interrupt her.

"He got to be so popular in Texas that Letterman's people called and asked us to come to New York to be on the *Late Night* show. So, we put Chance in his trailer and off we went to New York City to be on TV. The deal was supposed to be David Letterman was going to climb up and sit on Chance in front of his live audience and, of course, I would be standing right there with him. Well, honey, you should've seen those New York City folks' faces when I walked Chance through the TV studio; and I was never prouder of my big guy. He didn't pay them any mind at all."

"Really?" I exclaimed. "Did David Letterman climb up on your bull?"

"I'm just getting to that," Sally replied as she warmed to the storytelling. "I was waiting in the little room before we were to go on and watching the commercials at the break when I felt someone standing behind me. You know how you can tell when somebody's behind you."

I nodded, and she pressed on.

"Well, it was David Letterman in the flesh," Sally said. "I must have looked kinda funny at him because he said, 'Listen, lady, are you going to make sure nothing happens to me with that bull of yours?' So I said, 'Mr. Letterman, as long as I'm with Chance, you're as safe as if you were in your own mother's arms.' He smiled and said that was good enough for him. But the funniest thing was when we went on the air, he chickened out at the last minute and wouldn't get close to Chance. But then, the audience took over and made such a production that he ended up getting on him for about a second. He couldn't believe how gentle my Chance was—but he wasn't interested in pushing his luck, let me tell you." Sally laughed and stopped talking. She began to fidget with the mats for my pictures.

"Wow," I said. "That was some story. You and Chance were TV stars. Amazing. Whatever happened to him?"

"Oh, he died an old man's death," Sally said. "Peaceful as he could be, but it nearly broke my heart. I cried for days when I lost that bull. But, I'll tell you something about Chance. Some of those professors at A&M—Texas A&M University—took skin cells from my big fellow and they cloned him. Yessiree, they cloned him and called him Chance II. First successful cloning of a Brahman anywhere."

"You're kidding," I exclaimed. "Did you ever go see him? Was he just like your Chance?"

"I didn't go for a long time," Sally said. "But my husband finally convinced me to go and yes, he looked exactly like my beloved Chance. Exactly like him. But you know what was different? The eyes. They were the same color as my Chance's eyes, but we had no bond. No connection. He let me pet him but I wouldn't trust much more than that. He didn't have Chance's soul." She took off her glasses and wiped a few tears from her eyes. I was mesmerized by the story and pictured her trying in vain to recapture her lost love in an experimental lab at A&M. So close—and yet so far away.

Sally told me other stories that afternoon while I made my selections for frames and mats from her suggestions. She had started riding wild bulls in rodeos when she was forty-one years old and had ridden for a year, but she retired when the broken bones and bruises became too much for her battered body. I tried to figure out how old Sally was and guessed she was in her early seventies, and I wondered how many stories she could tell to her customers who were good listeners. She finished with my items and gave me a total that was reasonable for the work she and Bill were going to do. And it was especially a bargain when you consider the storytelling was free. I looked at the clock and realized we'd fiddled with my pictures for forty-five minutes. Carol must be ready to kill me, I thought.

Luckily, she wasn't and I waited for her to pick out her mats and frames. Sally stuck to her business, and Carol and I left a little while later. On the way home I asked Carol if she'd heard Sally's stories about Chance and she said she'd heard them before today, but they were good ones so she didn't mind overhearing them again. I smiled and said I was already looking forward to my next trip to Tomball. I was a sucker for a good love story, and Sally knew how to tell one.

Tomball welcome sign. Courtsey, Sheila Morris

Charles Williams

THEY'RE STILL SINGIN' AND SAYIN' ON THE RANGE: COWBOY CULTURE ENTERS THE 21ST CENTURY

by Charles Williams

~

Virtues, Values and Dreams
by Charles Williams and Tater Paschal

The small café bravely lights the evening sky,
Boarded up windows stare with an empty eye,
The tank at the gas station's long since run dry,
Small town America's barely gettin' by.

Farmers an' ranchers an' a small business man or two,
Left behind by the youth as to the cities they flew,
Complainin', "There's nothin' here to do"
An', "What did all this hard work ever get you?"

"We want the things TV says life means,"
"An' havin' 'em now is important, it seems."
They've traded small-town virtues, values and dreams,
For the big cities' greed and appearances and schemes.

But in the end, it don't matter where you live, but how,
There's no special virtue in chasin' a cow,
And dreams can even live in a city somehow.
What's important is to what God do you bow?

There's more to life than fancy shoes an' designer jeans,
An' those farmers an' ranchers are richer than it seems,
No country can survive on greed and appearances and
    schemes.
America needs her small-town virtues and values and
    dreams.

We all have the picture firmly in our minds. The herd of long-horn cows has bedded down for the night. Most of the cowboys have gathered by the chuckwagon and eaten their nightly meal of steak, baked potatoes, salad and beans, with biscuits on the side and followed by apple cobbler a la mode. Now they lounge around the fire while some pull out guitars and the sound of tightly har-monized Cowboy songs drifts skyward, echoed by the night riders as they slowly circle the peacefully sleeping herd.

Of course, we all know that that's just a romantic vision of a life that probably never existed, and even if it did, both it and cowboys are long gone. After all, cowboys have gone the way of Western movies, a fond memory recalled by brief flashes of TV movies and commercials and an occasional "real" big screen drama set in the West.

Like most things we "know," both extremes contain a grain of truth surrounded by rocks and boulders of myth, exaggeration, and romanticism. Certainly there were herds of longhorns driven north by cowboys during the late 1860s and early 1870s. If they were two or three year old steers, they would generally tame down and drive easily—it was mostly the herds of mixed stock that gave trouble. The nightriders did make noise as they rode around, although singing might have been a tad strong word for it. The rest is pure Hollywood, especially the part about singing around the old campfire (and the food, which in real life was mostly bis-cuits and beans and pork, unless someone else's cow could be killed.) Guitars were unknown on the trail; the best you could hope for was a harmonica or maybe a fiddle. Most nights, the hands ate quickly and turned in early to get what sleep they could. There were occasional pauses long enough to make a camp, but more stories than songs were likely to flow around the campfire.

The picture of the chuck wagon evening, complete with singing, is not myth, however. It takes place today routinely all over the West, and has for at least the last ten years. Ironically, there was probably more singing to guitar music (tightly harmo-nized or not, and mostly not) by a wagon this past month [March

2006] than there ever was during the days of the trail drives. Chuck wagon cooking and cowboy camps are alive and thriving in the 21st Century. There may very well be more "authentic" chuck wagons in operation in 2006 then there were in 1876. The American Chuck Wagon Association has been formed in response to the need for uniformity of rules in chuck wagon cook-offs. While cookoffs are still largely a rich man's hobby, catering off a wagon (with a meal closer to the first one described above than the standard trail fare) is profitable enough to support many wagons.

For an extra nickel, most of these wagons will throw in a cowboy entertainer. Usually a singer, and often a member of the cooking crew, he will strum a guitar and sing the old trail classics—you know, "Tumbling Tumbleweeds," "Cool Water," "Colorado Trail," "My Adobe Hacienda," "Back in the Saddle Again," and so forth. Seriously, most Cowboy and Western singers have a number of the old Hollywood Western classics in their repertoire, as well as some that were actually are old trail classics: "Chisholm Trail," "Old Paint," "Lorena," and others of that time. However, he (or she) is likely to have modern classics in there as well, such as "Night Herder's Lament," "Man Walks Among Us," "Double Diamond," or "Sonora's Death Row," among an ever-growing list.

Which brings us to our second mythical picture, that of the vanishing cowboy. In the first place, as long as there are cows, there will be cowboys. Moreover, the cowboy life still remains close to the same as it always was, with periods of intense boredom, hard work and loneliness, interspersed with wrecks and encounters with thousand-pound animals intent on doing you bodily harm. However, as the saying goes, they just can't be seen from the highway.

What is very visible, and becoming more so, are the manifestations of growth of the cowboy culture in the 2000s. I have been very privileged to be in a position to observe this phenomenon at close range. I have been a member since its inception in 1996 of the Academy of Western Artists, which is the umbrella organization for the various aspects of the contemporary Western heritage movement. The AWA was founded by Bobby Newton, editor and publisher of "Rope Burns," which is the unofficial newsletter of the entire Western Heritage movement. Shows, ranch rodeos, chuck wagon cook-offs, Western Swing events, and reviews are printed in it. The AWA honors outstanding achievement in contemporary Western skills through the Will Rogers Awards. For the remainder of this paper, I would like to address the current state of the Western Heritage and cowboy culture from the Academy's traditional three areas—representational, practical, and performing arts.

The representational arts include fine art and cartooning. There are over thirty current cowboy cartoonists busily at work chronicling life through their unique point of view. While the dean of cowboy cartoonists, Ace Reid, passed away several years ago, such highly talented artists as A-10 Echiverry, Daryl Talbot, Boots Reynolds, Wendy Liddle, Bonnie Shields, A. W. Erwin, Mad Jack Hanks, Robert Miller, M.C. Tin Star, Bob Rohan, Jonathan Rankin, and a slew of others carry on the work of illustrating the foibles of cowboy life. They are good, and there does not seem to be any end of fresh, new material for them to draw on.

Western fine art has always been the most popular art in America, and why not? The combination of spectacular scenery, dramatic colors, and epic action make it a natural for bold and unforgettable images. I have no idea how many artists are working in the western genre today—it may be literally countless. Those honored by the Academy include Bill Owens, Tim Cox, Janet Hurley, Chuck DeHaan, Mike Andrews, and Red Allen. There are many, many more.

The following was written by the author and first used in the 1998 Will Rogers Award Show Program; it has been used in all the programs published since then:

> The tools of the cowboy's trade are also the cowboy's trademark. His ropes, belts, spurs, saddles and various pieces of horse gear are more than just functional articles he can hold up his pants with or

hangs on his fancy boots or throws in the back of his pickup so you can tell him from the truck drivers and drugstore cowboys. They are designed to do specific jobs, but that does not mean they are strictly utilitarian. His gear is a blank page upon which the personality of the owner can be stamped, carved, tooled, sewn, engraved and permanently recorded. Everything with a flat surface and most with a curved surface as well can be used in this expression of pride and expertise. These deceptively humble items continue to achieve great popularity with collectors, who appreciate the high standards of craftsmanship, the purity of design and the link to the rich heritage of the cowboy.

We have already discussed the boom in chuck wagons, but a similar story can be told for the other practical arts as well. Collectors, who started with spurs and are now investing in all the handcraft arts of the Western lifestyle, have driven much of this. Ironically, many cowboys can no longer afford some of these tools of their trade, and they often have to make do with imports. The craftsmen, on the other hand, are doing just fine, and well they should, for they are extraordinary artists in many mediums. The latest fields to attract attention appear to be hitching and braiding, which are two different skills. (Hitching is done with a series of knots, while braiding is—well, braiding.) Multi-colored braided objects are both very beautiful and scarce, because there are not that many good braiders. The engravers have always been a special group of artists, and waiting times for buckles and jewelry from the top artists can be up to eighteen months. A special mention should be made of presentation saddles, which are works of art never meant to be used. The current trend is to tool them and restrain the use of metal and jewels. Some hand-tooled saddles have almost fine art painting detail, and are amazing in the depth they achieve. Almost all of these saddles are produced on order, and very few are ever offered for sale.

Most of the current surge of interest in the contemporary cowboy culture, however, rests in the performing arts—Cowboy poetry, Cowboy and Western music, and Western Swing. Western Swing has begun to move beyond Bob Wills with large numbers of new bands and talented songwriters. While many of the traditional musicians who performed with the Wills brothers or other early Western Swing bands are still going strong, there is an exciting group of newcomers now playing. Western Swing is also helped by the current popularity of big band swing. Bandleaders such as Jackie Green, Dave Alexander, Billy Mata, and Craig Chambers are taking swing to new heights.

One measure of the popularity of both Western Swing and Western/Cowboy music is that there is now a Top Ten in *Billboard* for single play records and albums. When the AWA started over fourteen years ago, there was no category for radio stations or disk jockeys, because there were not enough of them out there to register. Now, well over 300 stations feature western music as a significant part of their programming. Many are even east of the Mississippi.

Western and cowboy songs have had an interesting history. The night riding cowboys of the trail driving days did indeed make a noise somewhat resembling singing as they rode around the cattle at night. They sang tunes familiar to them: Civil War songs, gospel hymns, folk tunes, and sometimes just words to a simple tune, such as "Polly Wolly Doodle." The words were generally traditional folk song words changed to suit their own circumstances, a true example of the folk process at work. Around the turn of the century, the classic cowboy poets started writing, and some of these poems were set to music—again, for the most part with simple tunes. These are the songs Jack Thorp and others collected.

Then came the golden age of the Hollywood Western, and the wonderful singing cowboys most of us grew up with. Starting with John Wayne (yes, he was the first one hired specifically to sing, although Ken Maynard was apparently the first to actually sing in a film) down through Rex Allen, they moved the cowboy song to the top of the charts. Even real cowboys sang them. It's sort of interesting to note how many of the Hollywood Singing Cowboys were actually cowboys, or least familiar with farm and ranch life (as opposed to Hollywood cowboys in general, many of whom had to be more or less tied to the saddle.) Those who knew the Singing Cowboys rated Rex Allen as the best all-around cowboy, and he earned great respect among real cowboys with his abilities working stock.

As the golden age faded away, Western morphed into Country and Western, and then into Rock and Roll. People still sang the old standards, but it took the revival of the poetry movement to jump start the music as well. All of a sudden, people stopped singing "Little Joe the Wrangler" and "The Zebra Dun" and started singing "Roundup Time on the Pitchfork" and "I'll Be Back in the Fall." New names popped up, including Royal Wade Kines, Brenn Hill, Joni Harns, Jean Prescott, Jill Jones, R. W. Hampton, Jeff Gore, Lorraine Rawls, the Gillette Brothers, and a host of others. Dan Roberts and Belinda Gail, among others, quit the pop scene and started singing Cowboy full-time. It is only a matter of time before one of these highly talented and entertaining artists "crosses over" and becomes a popular hit.

Which brings us to a subject near and dear to my heart—cowboy poetry. The current revival in the serious Western performing arts got kick-started over twenty years ago in Elko, Nevada, when a folklorist originally from Utah named Hal Cannon got together with cowboy poets and decided to hold a Cowboy Poetry Gathering. In the words of Waddie Mitchell, one of the better known poets, they "expected tens, hoped for hundreds, and got thousands." With the success of Elko, other communities jumped in, and today on almost any weekend of the year there is a Cowboy Poetry Gathering somewhere. They are a combination of performances, theater, family reunion, and revival meeting. They work best in smaller cities and towns, because they are a rural phenomena. Performers typically include poets, singers, perhaps a storyteller or two, and a dance featuring Western Swing music. Most singers do a couple of poems, and many poems are still being set to music, following in the tradition of the early cattle drives. The performers form an extended family, and there is a strong sense of community throughout the movement.

The poetry itself still mostly rhymes, and follows the rhyme schemes laid down by the spiritual father of cowboy poetry, Robert Service. While Service was neither, strictly speaking, a cowboy poet nor the first to write cowboy poetry, his popularity and the accessibility of his poetry made him the perfect role model. While there is cowboy poetry written in all sorts of meter and even free verse, the best of it follows one unwritten but strong guideline: keep it cowboy, and keep it understandable by the boys around the fire. Cowboy poetry is about expressing strong feelings, convictions and values, not intellectual exercises in arcane symbols and subtle nuances. It is still driven by the rhythm of the horse's hooves on long, lonely rides. There are three questions which are guaranteed to start a hot discussion at a Cowboy Poetry Gathering: Is free verse real cowboy poetry? What is cowboy poetry? Do you have to be a cowboy to do cowboy poetry? These are, of course, trick questions, as there are no definitive answers, only a wide variety of strongly held opinions.

A significant portion of Cowboy poetry is humorous. Humor is ingrained in the cowboy view of life, and most of them believe you can't laugh at others until you can laugh at yourself, especially after you've just completely messed up and gotten yourself and perhaps several dumb animals around you into some sort of perilous physical predicament—what the cowboy calls a "wreck." If they're not carrying you away on a stretcher (or even if they are), the only acceptable response is a humorous comment. Therefore, all sorts of things end up in poems. They love the twist and the surprise ending. If Service is the spiritual father, O. Henry is the favorite uncle.

Another factor in the popularity of cowboy poetry is the increased availability of it. There are CDs of course, but more important is the widespread access to the written form in both books and on the Internet. Each year, The AWA presents the Will Rogers Medallion Award for Outstanding Achievement in Publishing, and the quality and quantity of cowboy poetry books on the market has risen sharply. Such books as *Born To This Land,* by Texas' Official Cowboy Poet Red Steagall, are impressive works by any measure in any field. Cowboy Miner Productions has released books by many of the classic poets as well as present day poets, and their books are outstanding for publishing as well as literary quality. On the Internet, www.cowboypoetry.com has become the site for poetry and news. The official Will Rogers Medallion Award site, www.willrogersmedallionaward.org, has updates on the Will Rogers Award and the applicable entry forms. There are Wrangler and Spur Awards now given to Cowboy poetry books as well.

There are many very outstanding poets performing and writing today, both male and female. I could go on at great length with names, but I will only mention a few to give you a taste and hopefully give you a place to start. Besides Red and Waddie, most people have heard of Baxter Black, who was the first cowboy poet to make it big on TV. Equally as funny, if not more so, are Pat Richardson and Dennis Gaines. Chris Isaacs and Andy Nelson, as well as Doc Stovall and Clay Lindley (both now deceased) are always good for belly laughs. On the slightly more serious side, Joel Nelson, Jessie Smith, Mike Dunn, Rod Nichols (also deceased), Daren Brookman, D. W. Groethe, and Larry Maurice are among, but by no means all, of the best writing today. On the female side, Yvonne Hollenbeck is as funny as anyone male or female, and Doris Daley, "Buckshot Dot" Dee Strickland Johnson, Virginia Bennett, Ann Sochat, Debra C. Hill and Elizabeth Ebert are among the galaxy of outstanding female poets. These lists are not even scratching the surface, and several trips to cowboypoetry.com are prescribed for cowboy poetry deprivation.

As long as there are cows, there will be cowboys, and as long as there are cowboys, there will be singin' and sayin' on the range.

A SELECTED ANNOTATED BIBLIOGRAPHY
(COWBOY POETRY ONLY)

Basics
These three anthologies are must-haves:

> *The Big Roundup.* Margo Metegrano, ed. San Francisco: New West Library, 2002.
>
> This is the ultimate cowboy poetry source. Both the classic poets and almost all of the contemporary poets are represented with a poem. Another valuable section (even if slightly dated) in the book is the extensive reference section. Poet biographies, publications, museums and Western heritage sites, annual events, organizations and associations are listed. If you only have one book of cowboy poetry, *this is the one to have.*

> *Cowboy Poetry: A Gathering.* Hal Cannon, ed. Salt Lake City: Gibbs-Smith, 1985.
>
> Hal Cannon is the folklorist who helped get Elko and thus the whole Cowboy Poetry movement started. This small volume (it's pocket sized) has poetry by both classic and contemporary poets. Hal has a very valuable and extensive bibliography in his book.

> *Humorous Cowboy Poetry: A Knee-Slapping Gathering.* Salt Lake City: Gibbs-Smith, 1995.
>
> Fifth in a series of anthologies published by Gibbs-Smith, this is the best of what cowboy poets do best, humor. Almost all contemporary, it is a very, very funny book. Men and women poets are almost equally represented.

The Classic Poets
Robert Service

There are several complete works of Robert Service around, most of which are out-of-print but readily available in used book stores or libraries. Service wrote of the three stages of his life: his years in the Yukon, his experiences during WWI, and his later years in France. His Yukon poems are of most interest to Cowboy poets and are really his best poems, although some of his WWI poems are extremely powerful. My personal choice of the several volumes I own is:

Robert Service. *Dan McGrew, Sam McGee and other Great Service.* Dallas: The Stonesong Press, 1987.

Published by Taylor Publishing Company and illustrated by Mark Summers, it has the best of Services' Yukon and WWI poems. Besides the title poems (and "Dan McGrew" (p. 57–61) is the single most recited poem in the English language), " The Ballad of Blasphemous Bill" (p. 20–23), "The Pines" (p. 53–54), "The Baldness of Chewed Ear" (p.35–39), "The Ballad of Pious Pete" (p. 113–118), and "The Haggis of Private McPhee" (p. 154–157) are among the best.

Cowboy Miner Productions

Many of the classic cowboy poets are out of print or otherwise difficult to find. Mason Coggin, and after his death, his wife Janice, have gathered, edited and published the works of several of these classic poets. While I will list them under the poet's names, the collecting and the editing were done by the Cowboy Miner Productions team. They are all uniformly well produced and published.

S. Omar Barker. *Cowboy Poetry: Classic Rhymes by S. Omar Barker*. Phoenix: Cowboy Miner Productions, 1998.

S. Omar Barker was an amazing prolific writer, with over 2000 poems as well as 1500 short stories and novelettes. "Tall Men Riding" (p. 15) is my personal favorite, but "Code of the Cow Country" (p. 26), "Pert Near" (p. 55–57), "Jack Potter's Courtin'" (p. 70–72), and "The Last Lone Trail" (p. 202) are right up there.

B. Kiskaddon *Cowboy Poetry: Classic Rhymes by Bruce Kiskaddon*. Phoenix: Cowboy Miner Productions, 1998.

Kiskaddon was a cowboy during the last years of the 1800s and the early 1900s, and his poetry is gritty and authentic. His two most performed are "When They've Finished Shipping Cattle In The Fall" (p. 203–206) and "The Broncho Twister's Prayer" (p. 26–28).

Knibbs, H.H. *Cowboy Poetry: Classic Rhymes by Herbert Henry Knibbs*. Phoenix: Cowboy Miner Productions, 1999.

Knibbs was a Canadian who traveled extensively in the West and became an expert in Western history and people. Many of his poems are sung, most notably the lovely "Where the Pones Come To Drink" (p. 79–80). He wrote many poems of law and order, such as "Charlie

Lee" (p. 143–145) and "The Shallows of the Ford" (p. 21–22). He also penned the immortal "Boomer Johnson" (p. 156–158).

D. J. O'Malley. *Cowboy Poetry: Classic Rhymes by D. J. O'Malley.* Phoenix: Cowboy Miner Productions, 2000.

O'Malley, the N Bar N Kid, was a Montana cowboy who wrote such classics as "When The Work's All Done This Fall."

B. Clark *Cowboy Poetry: Classic Rhymes by Badger Clark.* Phoenix: Cowboy Miner Productions, 2005.

Badger Clark (1883 1957) parlayed four years of cowboy life on an Arizona ranch into a forty-year career as America's most successful cowboy poet.

Other Classics

S. Omar Barker. *Rawhide Rhymes.* Garden City: Doubleday & Co., 1968.

Out of print now, but still available, this collection of S. Omar Barker's poems is still one of the most enjoyable to be found. Barker is one of the few Cowboy poets that critics mention.

Katie Lee. *Ten Thousand Goddam Cattle: A history of the American Cowboy In Song, Story and Verse.* Jerome, AZ: Katydid Books and Records, 1976.

Very personal and totally delightful, Katie still does the most thorough job of tracing the evolution of cowboy culture I have ever seen.

Best Loved Poems of the American West. John T. and
   Barbara T. Gregg, eds. Garden City: Doubleday & Co., 1980.
      This is another nice anthology, with several
   types of poems besides Cowboy poetry in it.
   There is even some very nice free verse in there.

The Buck Ramsey Award Winners

Each year if there are enough nominees, the Academy of Western
Artists members vote on Cowboy Poetry books for the Buck Ramsey Award. The award is named after Buck Ramsey, a much-loved
singer and poet who died in 1998. These are the books then their
peers feel are the best of the year.

1996

Wallace McRae. *Cowboy Curmudgeon & Other
   Poems.* Salt Lake City: Gibbs-Smith, 1992.
      This is a well-produced paperback with all
   of Wally's classics in it, including "Reincarna-
   tion" (p. 49).

1997

Ann Sochat. *Cowhide'n Calico.* El Paso: 1996
      These are very personal poems about grow-
   ing up Hispanic on a ranch in West Texas. Ann
   is a very dynamic performer.

1998

B. Kiskaddon. *Cowboy Poetry: Classic Rhymes by
   Bruce Kiskaddon.* Phoenix: Cowboy Miner
   Productions, 1998.
      There was some discussion when this was
   awarded the Buck Ramsey, as Bruce Kiskaddon
   had been dead for a long time, but in the end,
   it got the most votes.

1999

Andy Wilkinson. *My Cowboy's Gift*. Lubbock: Gray Horse Press, 1998.

Andy is also better known as a singer and for his Charlie Goodnight; His Life in Poetry and Song, but this is a nice collection of Andy's poetry that is non- Goodnight. Much of it is modern-day, and not all is range-related.

2000 — No Award

2001

Leon Flick. *A Cow's Tail For a Compass*. Plush, OR: Juniper Press, 2000.

Leon Flick is the only Cowboy poet I ever saw come on stage wearing a pair of bull slippers (see "Bull Slippers," p. 177) and get away with it (besides, mine were mooses). This is a delightful volume of poems and short stories by an Oregon cowboy.

2002

The Big Roundup. Margo Metegrano, ed. San Francisco: New West Library, 2002.

Margo is probably the most knowledgeable person in the world on Cowboy poetry.

2003

Sonny Hancock and Jessie Smith. *Cowboy Poetry: Horse Tracks Through the Sage*. Phoenix: Cowboy Miner Productions, 2002.

Sonny Hancock (now deceased) and Jessie Smith are two of the most respected Cowboy poets performing today. Sonny's "The Bear Tale" (p. 26–31) is a true classic, as is "The Horse

Trade" (p. 84–89). Jessie wrote "The Bet" (p. 193–196), which is often performed, and "The Silence" (p. 200–201), which should be.

2004

Red Steagall and Skeeter Hagler. *Born To This Land.* Lubbock: Texas Tech University Press, 2003.

The poems are by Red Steagall, the photos are by Skeeter Hagler, and this is as close to perfection as you are likely to get with any poetry book. Everything works, and it is an outstanding book of any genre.

2005

Rolf Flake. *Cowboy Poetry: Cloud Watchers.* Phoenix: Cowboy Miner Productions, 2005.

Rolf's book is as good as his CD, which is very good, indeed.

The Will Rogers Medallion Award winners
Because the quality of published Cowboy poetry books has taken such a giant step forward, which we in the AWA believe is at least partially due to the Buck Ramsey Award, and because there is only one Buck Ramsey Award, we decided to honor other outstanding books with the Will Rogers Medallion Award. It is a judged competition, and quality of publication counts as well as quality of poetry. These books are listed in alphabetical order with no breakout by year. The Buck Ramsey Award winners were also Medallion Award winners, so they will not be listed again.

Mike Dunn. *Somewhere Between Earth and Heaven.* Mesa, AZ: Linda's Letters & Publications, 2002.

This is an example of the high quality of Cowboy poetry books even when self-published. Mike is a real cowboy, and his poetry reflects that life.

Yvonne Hollenbeck. *Where Prairie Flowers Bloom.* Clearfield, SD: Hollenbeck, 2002.

Yvonne is a ranch wife and mother, a quilter, a Cowgirl poet, a comedian, an organizer and a founding member of the First Church of Everybody's Business. These poems are full of humor, insight and warmth—like Yvonne.

Carole Jarvis. *Time Not Measured By A Clock.* Phoenix: Cowboy Miner Press, 2003.

Carole has been a rancher's wife for 40+ years, and her poems reflect both that life and her love for it. Larry Bute's illustrations are a real plus.

Dee Strickland Johnson. *Arizona Herstory: Tales From Her Storied Past.* Phoenix: Cowboy Miner Productions, 2003.

This is one of the most incredible books I have ever read. It's the history of Arizona written in poetry, mostly from a woman's point of view (although a lot of it is pretty genderless, and just good history in verse).

Lyn Messersmith. *Ground Tied.* Sioux Falls, S.D.: Pine Hill Press, 2003.

Lyn writes both rhyming and free verse (see "Burnout" (p. 94)) with sensitivity and deep feeling. This is really an extraordinary book.

Jane Ambrose Morton. *Cowboy Poetry: Turning to Face The Wind.* Phoenix: Cowboy Miner Press, 2004.

This is a history of the West, as seen and written by one western woman. Poems, stories, pictures and memories blend in a very personal story.

Rod Nichols. *A Little Bit of Texas*. Boise, ID: Passage Publishing, 2002.

Rod is a very prolific poet whose poetry is of uniform high quality.

Pat Richardson. *Pat Richardson Unhobbled*. Sioux Falls, SD: Pine Hill Press, 2003.

The quote on page 33 says it all: "Pat has a viewpoint that provides a nice contrast to the real world. . . ." There are a couple of serious poems in here, but most of them aren't.

Virginia Bennett. *Cowboy Poetry: The Reunion*. Layton, UT: Gibbs-Smith, Publisher, 2005.

Virginia Bennett has edited a fine collection of contemporary cowboy poetry.

Jesse Colt and Val Moker. *Short Poems & Tall Cowboys*. Manitoba, Canada: Friesen's Business Machines, 2005.

Jesse Colt (poet) and Val Moker (artist) put together an unusual but very well done book celebrating the life of a rodeo cowboy.

Daren Brookman. *Where Sagebrush Grows*. Hollis, OK: Pair'a Spurs Press, 2005.

Daren is genuine working cowboy, and his poetry reflects a deep love of his occupation, his heritage, and his land.

Discography

A lot of Cowboy poetry is recorded and seldom published. Here is a short list:

Dakota Cowboy Poets. *Where the Buffalo Rhyme*. CD. Lemmon, SD: 2003.

Rodney Nelson, Elizabeth Ebert, Yvonne Hollenbeck, and Jess Howard recorded live, giving the feeling of a typical poetry gathering.

Rolf Flake. *Cowboy Heritage.* Tape. Gilbert, AZ: 1999.
   Six generations of Arizona cowboying are distilled on this tape. Rolf has been a rancher all his life, and he is one of the most authentic voices around today.

Dennis Flynn, *Life's Choices.* Tape. Azle, TX: 1999.
   Dennis does the classics as well as anyone, along with his own poetry. This tape also uses music practically and effectively (with some great musicians).

Dennis Gaines. *Son-of-a-Gun Stew: A Texas Cowboy's Gather.* CD. Kerrville, TX: TeePee Productions, 2003.
   Dennis is one of the funniest Cowboy poets performing.

Yvonne Hollenbeck and Jim Thompson. *The Verse and the Voice: Reflections of the West.* CD. Spearfish, SD: Creative Broadcast Services, 2003.
   This features Jim Thompson reading Yvonne Hollenbeck's poetry. Jim is a DJ, and he has a wonderful, interpretive voice for Yvonne's poems.

Chris Isaacs. *Both Sides.* Tape. Edgar, AZ: 1996.
   Chris makes excellent use of music on this tape, including a great version of Kiskaddon's "When We've Finished Shipping Cattle in The Fall."

Tater Paschal. *Cowboy Livin'.* Tape. Weatherford, TX: 1999.

Tater is a great poet, a good friend, and a co-author of poetry with me. He's got a great voice for cowboy poetry (he is a working cowboy), and this is an excellent tape.

Pat Richardson. *B.Y.O.S.—Cowboy Poetry by Pat Richardson.* CD. Merced, CA: Pat Richardson, 2002.

This may be one of the funniest CDs ever recorded.

Jay Snider. *Cowboyin', Horses & Friends.* Tape. Cyril, OK: 2000.

Jay is the real deal—a working cowboy—and this tape is a reflection of his life and experiences. It's not as slickly produced, but it is comfortable listening to a good poet.

Internet

The only current site for cowboy poetry on the Internet is:

www.cowboypoetry.com

Newspapers

The trade newspaper, with reviews, schedules, reviews of music and poetry, and general information on cowboy culture events is:

Rope Burns. Bobby Newton, ed. Gene Autry, OK. Now online at: www.ropeburns.org.

Francis Edward Abernethy, Distinguished Regents Professor Emeritus of English at Stephen F. Austin State University, was Secretary-Editor of the Texas Folklore Society from 1971 to 2004, editing or co-editing over twenty volumes of TFS publications in his thirty-three years of leading the organization.

Len Ainsworth deals in rare and collectible books on Texas through his Adobe Book Collection. This allows him to read some, buy some, sell some, trade some, and keep some back for later. An emeritus professor and vice-provost of Texas Tech University, he continues to follow the trials and occasional triumphs of Red Raider and Lady Raider sports teams.

Scott Hill Bumgardner is a real estate consultant, retired Houston cop, grandpa, rancher, writer, and professional storyteller. He has served several terms as president of the Houston Storytellers Guild, and has been a member of the Houston Rodeo Speakers Committee since 1991. His foundation in historical tales and cowboy poetry has taken a turn for the outlandish. Funny, far-fetched tales keep falling out of his head. The lighter side of his nature keeps the audience on the edge of their seats as his fun, action-packed tales come roaring by.

Jennifer Oakes Curtis is an author, a storyteller, and a life-writing consultant. Although she lived in Houston for more than twenty-five years, she currently resides in Pennsylvania, but is still frequently in Texas visiting her children and grandchildren.

Robert J. (Jack) Duncan has taught at Collin College and Grayson County College and has worked in staff positions at Collin College and Richland College. He was President of the Texas Folklore Society in 1980, and is a life member of the Texas

State Historical Association. Jack is a widely published freelance writer, in both scholarly and popular periodicals, including *Reader's Digest*. For the past dozen years he has worked as a writer/editor/researcher for Retractable Technologies, Inc., a manufacturer of safety needle medical devices in Little Elm. A life-long learner, Jack continues to frequently take graduate courses at UNT in a variety of disciplines. He has lived in McKinney most of his life, and he is married to his high school sweetheart, the former Elizabeth Ann Harris; they have two sons and five grandsons. Jack and Elizabeth have been active members of the Texas Folklore Society for more than forty years.

Courtney Elliott is from Alvin, Texas, and is a junior Agricultural Leadership and Development major at Texas A&M in College Station. She became a member of the TFS as a freshman at San Jacinto College South Campus. Her personal involvement in rodeo competition and serving as Miss Jasper Lions Club Rodeo, Miss Texas High School Rodeo Region 7, Miss Rodeo Austin, and Miss Rodeo Texas Teen inspired the topic of her paper entitled "The Legacy of Bill Pickett, The Dusky Demon," which was presented at the 2012 TFS meeting in Abilene.

Jenson Erapuram received his associate's degree in business administration from San Jacinto College, where he was a member of the honors program and the Walter Prescott Webb History Society. He is currently .pursuing a bachelor's degree in healthcare administration at the University of Houston-Clear Lake, where he serves as the community service chair of the National Society of Leadership and Success, the largest student organization on campus. He enjoys spending extra time serving the community through volunteering with organizations such as Healthcare for the Homeless—Houston and Crossroads: Community Partnership for Youth.

Lee Haile has been a member of the TFS since 1981, when he gave a paper on folk toys while still in college. He graduated from Texas A&M in 1982 with a degree in entomology (bugs). He lives with his wife Karen in the hills of western Bandera County, where he is building his home using all native stone and wood that he has sawed in his sawmill. He is a woodworker, musician/singer/song-writer, writer, folklorist, and nature guide in the Hill Country. He has been the Folk toy maker at the Texas Folklife Festival for the last twenty-six years. He is still enjoying life!

L. Patrick Hughes is currently trying to figure out the vagaries of retirement after thirty-six years as a professor of History at Austin Community College. He is a past-President of both the Texas Folklore Society and the Texas Oral History Association, and former board member of the East Texas Historical Association.

Sue M. Friday's "Hemphill: Revisiting Small Town Texas" is her fourth article for the Texas Folklore Society. She is a native of Houston, but currently lives and writes on a farm outside Charlotte, North Carolina. In 2001, she and her late husband Tom rescued her grandparents' dogtrot house outside Hemphill, and she still visits twice a year. When beer and wine sales were approved for Hemphill in the last election, she felt five generations of Sabine County ancestors turn over in their graves.

Marissa Gardner, a twenty-five-year-old native of Kerrville, Texas, moved to Houston with her six-year-old son four years ago to attend college. She is currently in the Bachelor of Science and Nursing program at the University of Texas Medical Branch in Galveston, Texas. Her graduation will be in December of 2013, and she plans to eventually pursue her master's degree in nursing. When she has free time, she likes to read, write, exercise, and spend time with family.

Jerry B. Lincecum, a sixth-generation Texan, is Emeritus Professor of English at Austin College. He holds the B.A. in English from Texas A&M University and M.A. and Ph.D. degrees from Duke University. A past-President of the Texas Folklore Society, he has presented many papers at annual meetings of the Society and co-edited *The Family Saga: A Collection of Texas Family Legends* for the TFS in 2003. Since 1990, he and Dr. Peggy Redshaw have directed "Telling Our Stories," a humanities project at Austin College that aids older adults in writing their autobiographies and family histories. He also serves as a trainer and editor for the Legacy program at Home Hospice of Grayson County, which collects the life stories of Hospice patients and publishes them in booklet form.

Alex LaRotta is a first-generation Colombian-Texan with a strong respect and affection for both of his cultural heritages. Alex graduated from Stephen F. Austin State University in 2006 with a B.A. in Political Science. Following graduation, Alex moved to Bogota, Colombia, for six months, where he lived with his lovable, though often-fussy grandmother, tutored English, and perfected his Spanish. Upon his return, Alex received a wonderful job as a sound engineer for KLRU-TV's Austin City Limits. Yearning to return to higher education, Alex enrolled at Texas State University in 2011, and he is happily pursuing his M.A. with a focus on American popular music and twentieth-century American history, and working part-time as a Teaching Assistant.

Gretchen Kay Lutz, a native of Bowie, Texas, has been an educator for over thirty years. Her college teaching experience includes positions at San Jacinto College, the University of Houston-Clear Lake, Houston Community College, and West Texas A&M University. Gretchen's public school experience includes positions at Galveston Ball High School, Chavez High School, and Houston ISD. Her degrees, all in English literature, include a B.A. from Texas Christian University, an M.A. from the University of Houston, and a Ph.D. from Rice University. She has published sixteen articles in professional journals, and has made over thirty presentations at professional meetings. This fall and winter Gretchen will present at the South Central Modern Language Association meeting in San Antonio and the American Name Society in Boston.

Stephanie Mateum grew up in the small, sunny town of Tujunga, California. She moved to Texas in 2010 to study psychology at the University of Texas at Austin, and spent a year working as a research assistant for a laboratory on alcohol-related risk-taking behaviors. She currently lives in Houston, and enjoys reading books by the lake with her dog.

Sheila Morris was born in Navasota, Texas in 1946, and was raised in Richards in the midst of family members who were consummate storytellers. Her grandmother, Betha Robinson Morris, was the best of the best storytellers and entertained her husband and their children and grandchildren at her kitchen table for more than sixty-five years. Betha's great-grandfather was Benjamin W. Robinson, who was one of the soldiers in Sam Houston's Army for the Republic of Texas, so Sheila is a sixth-generation Texan. She is a graduate of the University of Texas at Austin and has a master's degree from the University of South Carolina in Columbia, where she lived for forty years before returning to Texas in 2010. She is the author of three nonfiction books, two of which have won awards, and the most recent published work is a collection of essays entitled *I'll Call It Like I See It: A Lesbian Speaks Out.* Sheila blogs as her alter ego Red, a rescued Welsh terrier, at www.redsrantsandraves.com. and her author's website is www.writersheilamorris.com. A longtime social justice activist, her favorite times today are observing life from the front porch of her house on Worsham Street in Montgomery, Texas, or traveling the back roads of Grimes and Montgomery and Walker Counties in an old Dodge Dakota pickup. She is pleased to be a member of the Texas Folklore Society and to be included in this publication. Somewhere her grandmother is telling somebody about it.

Chuck Parsons was born in Iowa on a farm and, until attending the University of Minnesota, had hardly ever been off the farm. However, during those growing-up years he experienced adventure a-plenty watching black and white cowboy movies on Saturday afternoons. His love and appreciation of the Wild West that began in those years has never stopped. During the near thirty years as a teacher and later as a high school administrator he found the time to research and write, his favorite "bad man" being John Wesley Hardin and his favorite "good guys" always being the Texas Rangers. He has been fortunate to find publishers who believe that his work is worth preserving. His first Ranger biography was of John B. Armstrong, published by Texas A&M, followed by a study of the Sutton-Taylor Feud and then a biography of Ranger John R. Hughes, the latter both published by the University of North Texas Press. His biography of John Wesley Hardin, with co-author Norman Wayne Brown, was published by UNT in 2013, and the letters of Ranger T.E. "Pidge" Robinson (with annotations) was published by Texas A&M, also in 2013. Chuck has also had numerous articles and book reviews published in a variety of publications. Although retired, he feels busier now than when he had a full-time job.

Pat Parsons, a fourth-generation resident of Caldwell County, Texas, resides in Luling, only a few miles from where her ancestors settled when they moved from Alabama in 1853. Her time is devoted to her passions, historical research and four little grandsons. She served as a past- President of the Caldwell County Genealogical and Historical Society and is a contributor to its publication the *Plum Creek Almanac.* She is a past co-chair of the Caldwell County Historical Commission and continues as an active member. One of the highlights of each year is when she gets to be an actor in the annual *Speaking of the Dead: Night Ramblings in a Texas Graveyard.* She has served on the Luling Main Street Board, working to preserve and revitalize downtown Luling. She is President of the Friends of the J. B. Nickells Library, supporting their local library. She writes book reviews for the *Luling Newsboy and Signal* and also the *Journal* of the Wild West History Association. *Bringing the Gospel to Texas: The Life of William Henry Harrison Biggs, 1840–1932* was her first book. It is the story of her great-grandfather, a

Methodist Circuit-riding preacher. She is currently working on a second book, the story of a 1903 shooting in Sanderson, Texas.

Veronica Pozo was born in Houston to Fred and Lucy Bishop, and she currently lives in Pearland, Texas. Veronica earned her high school diploma from Brookside Christian Academy. She is now a student at San Jacinto College, where she is a member of the Honors program and the National Society of Collegiate Scholars. She was also selected as the first-place winner of an essay contest at San Jacinto. Since then, her career goals include becoming a published author. She has recently completed her Associate's degree, and she plans to transfer to the University of Houston, where she will major in English. She currently works as a reading/writing tutor, so she is deeply considering entering the field of education as well. Veronica and her husband, Mauricio, got married in June of 2012; they have three boys: Izaiah, Jeremiah, and Eliahs.

Mildred Boren Sentell was born in Post, Texas, and brought up in Post and in Crane County. She graduated from Post High School, attended North Texas University and Texas Tech University (both four-year colleges then) before marrying B. J. Boren (who had the same last name) and having three children: Mary, David, and Jane. After B. J.'s death, she and the children moved to San Angelo, Texas, where she finished her B.A. and M.A. at Angelo State University. She was offered a place in the English Department upon graduation, and she taught there her entire teaching career, doing post-graduate work at Tech. After she married Joe Sentell of Snyder, she retired and moved to Snyder. After Joe's death she moved back to Post, where two of her children and many other family members live.

Winston Sosebee was born September 13, 1940, at Noodle, Texas, in Jones County, and he has never lived more than 150 miles from his place of birth. Winston graduated from Abilene High School in 1959. He attended San Angelo College from

1959–1960, and he took creative writing courses at Midland College from 1981–1983. Winston married Mary Klinger in June 1960, and they have three sons: Scott of Nacogdoches, Jeff of College Station, and Shannon of Geneoa, Florida. Winston is a member of the East Texas Historical Association, the West Texas Historical Association, and the Texas Folklore Society. He enjoys writing poetry, giving historical presentations, and is currently working on an historical novel on the Lincoln County War.

Lucy Fischer-West grew up in El Paso, the daughter of a Mexican mother and a German father. Her memoir, *Child of Many Rivers: Journeys to and from the Rio Grande*, was published in 2005 by Texas Tech University Press; it received a Border Regional Library Association Southwest Book Award, a WILLA Literary Finalist Award from Women Writing the West, and a Violet Crown Special Citation from the Writer's League of Texas. Her essays have appeared in *BorderSenses, Password*, and three Texas Folklore Society publications: *The Family Saga, Both Sides of the Border, and Celebrating 100 Years of the Texas Folklore Society*. She is featured in *The Best of Texas Folklore —Volume 2* from the Writer's AudioShop, *Literary El Paso*, and *Grace and Gumption: The Women of El Paso*. A career educator, she was a finalist for the Mary Jon and J. P. Bryan Leadership in Education Award, and she currently teaches world history at Cathedral High School. She is past-President of the Texas Folklore Society.

Charles Williams attended his first Cowboy Poetry Gathering fifteen years ago, in Oklahoma City at the Cowboy Hall of Fame. He had already been a professional storyteller for about thirty years, and this new art form entranced and enticed him. Since then, he has attended somewhere close to eighty Gatherings, including the Granddaddy of them all, Elko. He has written close to seventy Cowboy poems, has a tape and a CD out, and is published in an anthology. He retired as the Executive Vice President of the Academy of Western Artists and the head of the Poetry Section, and now is the Executive Director of the Will Rogers Medallion Award organization. He produced "Campfire Tales" at the Ft. Worth Stock Show and, up until recently, the Cowboy Poetry Gathering at the Texas State Fair. Recently, he combined his love of reading and history along with his presentation skills into a new (for him) art form—book reviews. He comes by it naturally, as his mother was a librarian most of her life, and he has now written book reviews for several newspapers. In his day job as an engineer, most recently with TI (from which he retired), he developed analytical and report writing skills—along with a storehouse of stories about the strange, wonderful, and occasionally weird things that happen in science. He has also spent some time in the classroom, as an Associate Professor at Richland Community College, and as a substitute teacher in DISD. He followed a lifetime of interest in folklore by joining the Texas Folklore Society, and he has served on the Board in a Councilor position. Charles has presented several papers and taken part in Hoots since joining (even though he says he's been told he sings in the key of "L"—or, at least it sounds like "L"). To sum him up he says you can just quote the late L. B. Allen: "He ain't a cowboy, but he's a real interesting person to talk to."

Jerry Young taught high school speech and theatre for twenty years, and spent ten years as a district administrator. He taught speech communications as an adjunct instructor for fifteen years at El Centro College, Dallas. Jerry has been a professional storyteller since 1992, and he is recognized by audiences in Oklahoma and Texas. He was a featured teller at the Spirit of Oklahoma Storytelling Festival and at the Squatty Pines Storytelling Festival. He also told at the George West Storyfest, the Texas Storytelling Festival, and the Voices in the Wind Storytelling Festival. Jerry served as President (2005) and Treasurer (2009) of the Tejas Storytelling Association. In 2009, the Association recognized Jerry for his contribution to storytelling with the John Henry Faulk Award, the organization's most prestigious award. Jerry's eclectic writing resume spans four decades. He has written for professional periodicals, assignments for church periodicals, and a variety of adapted and original stories. He wrote fifteen stories for the Texas University Interscholastic League 2nd and 3rd grades Storytelling Contest. His tall tale "A Thanksgiving Catfish" was published in the Texas Folklore Society's 2011 annual (PTFS #67) *Hide, Horn, Fish, and Fowl: Texas Hunting and Fishing Lore*. He holds a B.A. from Oklahoma Baptist University (Shawnee, Oklahoma) and an M.A. from University of North Texas (Denton Texas).

INDEX